Kiss & Make Up

Katie D. Anderson

AMAZON CHILDREN'S PUBLISHING

Amazon Publishing
Attn: Amazon Children's Publishing
P.O. Box 400818
Las Vegas, NV 89149
www.amazon.com/amazonchildrenspublishing

ISBN: 9780761463160

Book design by Virginia Pope
Editor: Marilyn Brigham

Printed in the United States of America (R)
First edition
10 9 8 7 6 5 4 3 2 1

For my mother—who always believed

IT'S IMPORTANT THAT YOU KNOW:

My obsession with lip gloss has officially ruined my life.

If I hadn't been so absorbed in the pale-blue UPS box delivered to my house today, I would have heard my phone chirp earlier. And if I had heard the cricket-sounding chirp, I would have seen my best friend Trina's text. And if I had seen her text, I would have read the following life-changing announcement:

Gt 2 the pool ASAP. spin the bottle!!!

Admission: I am fourteen and have never been kissed. But in my defense, neither has Trina.

Until about an hour ago, apparently.

"Can you go any faster?" I ask my aunt Arch as we drive down Lexington Avenue. The WELCOME TO HAYGOOD, MISSISSIPPI sign passes in a watery blur as thousands of tiny raindrops pummel the windshield like frustrated, angry tears—the kind I feel like shedding over missing my first and only chance at a real, male-to-me kiss. Ugh.

"I'm going as fast as I can, Emerson. What on earth is so important?" She is turning onto Elderberry Street, which I know for a fact will delay our journey by at least two minutes; but we both love seeing the old homes and their incredible landscaping. So I suck it up and try to enjoy the view.

It's not working.

"Emerson?" she repeats, pulling her eyes away from the new brick house on the left. "What's so important?"

"It's nothing," I lie, rereading the stream of messages that followed Trina's first spin the bottle alert. "Trina just wants to show me something."

I don't tell her that "something" is a boy.

A boy Trina kissed.

A boy who is currently sitting in her house like a zoo exhibit just waiting for me to admire him.

And I don't tell her that I want a "something," too. Instead, I look at my watch and pray the boys are still there. Trina texted me thirty gut-wrenchingly-long minutes ago to say that she had left the pool with Luke, her neighbor Trey, and some guy named Silas and that they were headed to her house. Arch was busy at the time, so I'd bitten my nails and paced the house while waiting for her to drive me over. Since then I've been picturing Trina and the boys laughing.

And talking.

And kissing.

Without me . . .

But then, about seven minutes ago, I got this text: **Guess who's here?**

Me: **Who?**

Trina: **Vance!!!!!!!**

Translation: My beloved: Vance *His Royal Hotness* Butcher. VANCE BUTCHER!

Oh, why did I leave my phone upstairs to look in that stupid blue box? Why!

"There's the McNeelys'," Arch says cheerfully. "I just love that house." She slows down, and I glance over at the giant white house on the corner—a two-story, southern plantation-style home with porches on both the first and second floors.

"Isn't it beautiful?" Arch says dreamily. "Let's stop. I told Cheryl I'd drop the new catalog by." She reaches her right arm over the backseat and fumbles around blindly while driving with her left hand.

"But it's raining," I say, looking at the time on my cell phone and wondering how long it takes for regular boys to get bored of kissing.

Arch weaves into the left-hand lane, still trying to get a catalog out of the box on the backseat.

"Stop," I tell her. "This is as bad as texting. I'll get it." I lean over the seat and grab the new catalog. "Seriously, Arch. Trina needs me *now*. So please don't talk forever. Okay?" My aunt Arch is the top-selling Stellar Cosmetics rep in our region, so dropping off a catalog is no more a quick-and-easy mission than flying to the moon. She can talk about products for *hours*.

"It won't take two secs," Arch says. "You can even do it for me."

"Really?" I ask, suddenly relieved.

"Sure. Just run the catalog up to the door." She pulls into the McNeelys' driveway and lets out a satisfied "Mmm-mmm." The object of her affection: a plump row of hydrangeas bursting with periwinkle blooms sitting proudly at the top of the driveway. "I'll bet those are as old as Mr. Wilson."

"I hope her son doesn't answer the door," I say, uninterested in the bushes.

"Who? Edwin?" Arch pulls her eyes away from the bushes and pats my leg with one hand while she collects a handful of samples from yet another box on the floor at my feet. Then she stuffs the samples into my lap. "Don't be silly. That boy is adorable. And such a gentleman. I saw him just last week at The Pig—The Piggly Wiggly on Brunson Street—and he asked about you." She cocks her left eyebrow as if this bit of news will interest me.

"Ew," I say. "He's a band geek. What'd he say?"

"I guess it doesn't matter what he said," Arch replies, grinning. She's waiting for me to beg her. She always wants to know what's going on with me and my friends. But I don't have time today. I need to get to Trina's STAT. So I curl the catalog around the samples and reach for the door.

Aunt Arch can't resist. "He asked if you were ready for the new school year," she blurts out.

"Is that all?" I chuckle. "Arch. He was obviously just being polite to a grown-up." Parents can be so dense sometimes.

"Mark my words." She wags her finger at me. "That boy is going to be handsome someday. Have you seen his pores?"

I laugh, then open the door and step out onto the rain-soaked sidewalk. But I turn back to say, "Well, he might have good pores, but he hangs out with weirdos."

The McNeelys' house sits at the end of an antique brick sidewalk that winds across the yard like a curl of ribbon. The porches on both the upstairs and downstairs give the house that vintage southern charm, making it a must-see on the Garden Club's annual holiday house tour.

I run through the rain to the end of the brick path and step onto the porch, where two very tall wooden doors face me. They're flanked on both sides by iron urns the color of coffee, each supporting a tremendous fern with feathered leaves that spread out in all directions. The overall effect is stately and, yes, beautiful. The doors, however, have these vertical glass panes in them, so I can't help but look inside the foyer, which is totally awkward. Instead, I take a step back and scan right and left for the doorbell.

No doorbell, just one of those fancy box things with a small red button. Nice. I'm going to have to announce myself. Pressing the button, I practice what I'll say. *This is Emerson Taylor?* No. Wait. I'm not coming over for tea. *Stellar delivery?* No. Too much like the UPS man. Um . . .

"Can I help you?"

I turn to the right and see Edwin McNeely at the far end of the porch reclining on a hanging swing. He has a guitar in his lap and has rolled over to face me. How weird is that? I mean, he could have said something as I was searching for the doorbell. Maybe he was asleep. He *is* wearing sweats and looks a bit disheveled.

"I, uh . . . I have makeup?" I ask, then answer my own question. "Yes. I have makeup." I lift my hands. "And a catalog."

"That you do," he says, standing up and walking toward me. "Are those for my mom?" He waves at Arch, who is sporting a Walmart-sized grin in the car. She's shameless—she's got the window down and everything.

"Yep."

He runs his hand through his brown hair, sweeping a chunk of bangs across his forehead from left to right. "*Love Struck*, huh?"

"*WHAT?*" I gasp.

"*Love Struck*," he repeats slowly, pointing at the title of the new Stellar catalog—the one I am currently holding.

"Oh. Yeah," I say, suddenly analyzing his pores.

"It's for your mom. From my aunt." I nod back at Arch again, who is staring at us like she's at a drive-in movie. "It's makeup," I add, as if the royal-blue PT Cruiser with Arch's face on the side and the word *Stellar* isn't clear enough.

"I think we've covered that." He smiles and reaches for the samples, but there are so many tiny tubes and vials that I have to sort of dump them into his now-cupped hands.

"Oops." One of the samples falls onto the wooden porch—a tiny plastic jar of face cream. I lean down to pick it up at the same time he does, and we end up grasping each other's fingers. An electric charge shoots through me as I pull my hand away and stare at him. "Uh, sorry."

He smiles and we stand there for a second, his face so close I can almost smell his breath. It strikes me as strange that I've never been this close to a boy before and yet I'm about to go to Trina's in order to kiss one (hopefully).

Edwin barely flinches—just chuckles with his perfect pores and noticeably straight teeth. "No biggie."

"Welp, I gotta go." I turn and run through the rain toward Arch's blueberry monstrosity.

"See ya at school," he says so softly that I wonder if he whispered—or if I completely made it up.

"Let's get out of here," I say, rapidly pulling the car door shut and throwing my coat over the backseat.

Arch is trying to suppress a giggle, but I will not let Edwin McNerdy and our awkward run-in disarm me. I'm about to experience my first kiss!

After taking a right at the next corner, we turn down Trina's street. I inhale and narrow my eyes, trying to see bionically through our rainy windshield all the way *into* Trina's house. Honestly, we can't get there fast enough. But at the same time, my heart is starting to move north into choking territory, and I am wildly trying to remember the How to Kiss steps I read in my sister Piper's magazine last month.

Step One: Make sure your breath is minty fresh.

Check. I just brushed my teeth.

Step Two: Loosen lips and make eye contact with your partner.

Or was that tighten your lips? I turn away from Arch and press my lips together and then loosen them, trying to figure it out. I think it was loosen them.

Step Three: Lean in and gently let your lips touch.

"How do you feel about fried catfish for dinner?" Arch asks me, interrupting the more pressing matters in my mind.

I want to say, "FRIED CATFISH? FRIED CATFISH! WHO CARES ABOUT CATFISH AT A TIME LIKE THIS?" But instead I say, "Mmmm. Sounds really good."

What step was I on?

Oh yeah. Four. Step four is easy: *Pucker slightly and slowly press your lips to his.*

Good. I got it.

Shifting my attention to the blue box beside me, I look through Arch's newest shipment. There's nothing like a little cosmetic distraction to slow a beating heart. My aunt's name, Mary Ellen Archer, is written in black cursive across the frosted-blue label. As usual, a lip gloss catches my eye, and I pick it up and read the tiny circular sticker on the bottom of the tube. "Can I have one of these Kiss Me Kates?"

"Yes," she says. "I ordered a few extra. But don't tell your sister. I forgot to get that mascara she wants."

Unscrewing the top, I slowly pull the wand through the peachy-colored gel while a Stellar-induced calm overtakes me. There's just something magical about makeup.

I repeat the kissing steps in my mind one more time while expertly wiping the excess gloss on the rim of the tube. Then, in professional form, I flip down the mirror and smear it across my virgin lips.

Mwah.

The car stops. "I'll be back in an hour to pick you up. Audrey and George are coming over for dinner," Arch says.

"An hour? But that's so soon." I groan.

"Oh, come on. The Wilsons just want to spend time with you, Emerson. You and your sister never see them anymore."

"Yes, I do," I complain. "I pull their trash cans to the curb almost every week."

"Shoo! That's not the same, and you know it. They do so much for us. This is the least we can do. They love you, baby—like their own grandchild."

I am distracted by a boy running across the street up ahead. *Could he be going to Trina's?* My breath catches in my chest. I'll be there in less than thirty seconds.

"What's really going on with you, honey? You always loved to visit the Wilsons. Remember when you used to do those funny little tap dances for them?"

Twenty-seven seconds.

"And Piper was always wanting to wear Audrey's jewelry around the house."

Twenty-four seconds.

"Emerson? Are you even listening to me?"

"Hmm?"

"Is this about Trina? I don't want to pry, but why does she need *a friend* so badly today?" Arch narrows her eyes like a CIA agent trying to decode a mystery.

Fifteen seconds.

Confession Time: After Trina's first few texts, I went all-out Code Red, telling Arch my bestie was in dire need of a "friend" and we had to leave the house PRONTO. I was hoping that since they operate on the same radio frequency—both being hopelessly addicted to *Oprah* reruns, *Dr. Phil, Dr. Oz,* and any TV show related to self-help—she'd get the idea and rush me over. But here we are almost forty-five minutes later. I've probably missed all the fun.

"Nah. I'm fine," I say. "I mean, *she's* fine. I'm sure it's just boy stuff."

Three seconds.

"Ahhh . . ." A knowing smile crosses my aunt's lips, and she slowly rocks her head forward and backward. Mystery solved.

I quietly rub my sweaty palms on the sides of my shorts.

"I'll pick you up after I make these deliveries. Okay?"

"Gotcha." Turning away from her eagle eye (known to detect all kinds of flaws), I pop out the door and run up to Trina's back porch. Sadly, as fate would have it, in those three seconds my shoulder-length brown hair plasters down onto my head into what must surely resemble a wet helmet.

Nice.

I let myself inside as fast as I can. The hallway mirror in the back foyer reveals lips are good, cheeks are fine, but hair is *horrible.* And now that I'm looking, I notice my eyes are red, too. Stupid contacts.

"Trina?" I yell, frantically working my fingers through my hair to install some pouf. "Where are y'all?"

"Down here!" she shouts from the basement. I grin. *It's showtime.*

Trina's father is a supersuccessful game table manufacturer, so her basement is ginormous and full of things like pinball machines, a large poker table (Luke's favorite spot), and a giant green pool table.

On the way down the steps, I can hear the boys' voices, and I'm suddenly nervous. *Is it possible to fail a kiss? What if I fail?*

What if IT happens? Maybe kissing is a pool-only kind of thing? Or what if they are playing spin the bottle again right now, and I walk down to find Trina and Vance making out? Oh, stop it. Chill, Emerson, chill!

I turn the corner at the bottom of the steps, and there they all are.

Doing nothing but hanging out.

No lip-lockage in sight.

I deflate a little.

Luke and Trey are playing poker, and Vance and some other guy are talking on the sofa with Trina.

"Emerson, this is Silas," Trina says, casually pointing to the new guy. He is lounging with both arms spread out along the back of the sofa, pride oozing from every pore. He has on a long bathing suit and a T-shirt, like everyone else; but with his gold sunglasses perched up in his dark-brown hair, this Silas character looks like some kind of sexy Italian movie star. I bet he has one of those washboard stomachs under that shirt, too. It's no surprise that Trina's boy-crazy eyes are twinkling. Heck, they're so bright, her toothy smile is glowing from the reflection.

"Come with me," she says, tilting her head toward the bathroom.

"Sure." I glance back at Silas. "Nice to meet you."

He nods to the TV, barely acknowledging my presence.

"Ace!" Luke says from behind a perfect spread of cards, toothpick stuck in his mouth. "Glad you could make it."

I half glare at him. It's hard to stay mad at Luke for long, but he totally knows about my crush on Vance. He's my next-door neighbor and as close to a brother as one can get. I can't believe he didn't text me when spin the bottle was suggested.

I would have so texted him if I had been the one at the pool and *he* was the one frozen in front of a baby-blue box . . . or, you know, a deadly computer game or something.

Trina grabs my arm, now violently jerking her head toward the bathroom. So I say, "I'll be back in a minute," and follow her around the corner.

"Where were you?" she asks after closing the door.

"Arch took forever. Who's the new guy?"

"Silas Martin," she says. "He goes to Saint Joseph's. Is he hot pizza or what?"

"Did you kiss him?" I ask, feeling part excited and part jealous.

"Well, duh."

"Dammit," I say. "I am *never* going to kiss a guy. This is as bad as that old movie *Love Affair*, where the beautiful girl misses her chance to get together with the man of her dreams at the top of the tower because she gets hit by a car."

"You're so drama," Trina says. "Don't worry. I'm sure we'll play again."

"Easy for you to say. You're on a smooch-induced high. You've been kissing all afternoon."

"I know!" she squeals. "It's easier than we thought, by the way."

Ugh.

"And I hate to say it, but Luke is an incredible kisser."

"Gross!" I say. "He's like my brother." I'm suddenly glad I wasn't there. Talk about awkward. Actually, the idea of kissing all the boys sounds a little icky, now that I think about it. But I don't tell Trina that.

Trina reaches into her pocket and retrieves a small metal box of mints and pops one into her mouth. "It was fun!"

"You're killing me. You know that, right?" I look in the mirror over the sink and stare at my lips, feeling completely inexperienced. "Give me one of those."

She hands me a mint, then stares me square in the eyes. "Don't worry. I have a plan. Did you see that bottle I placed on top of the pinball machine?"

"No."

She fans out her fingers in excitement. "You'll see. I'm just waiting for one of them to notice it. It'll start a new game for sure, and then they'll think *they* came up with the idea: but really, *I* am controlling their subconscious. Cool, huh?"

"Okay, Doc," I say. "We'll see if *that* works."

She rubs her hands together like a mad scientist and smiles excitedly.

Good grief.

I reach for the knob to go back into the room when she says, "Fix your hair."

Sigh. More scrunching, frantic fingering, and unintentional knotting.

Three ringtones and two whopping minutes later, the whole plan falls apart. Luke, Trey, and HRH Vance suddenly have to leave for various reasons, leaving me, my still-virgin lips, and my squirrel's-nest hairdo alone with Trina and Silas.

"Do y'all want a Coke or anything?" Trina asks. Silas and I are sitting on opposite ends of the sofa.

Raising his hand, Silas smiles.

She looks at him and grins, making me feel like a total Third Wheel.

"I'm fine," I say, wondering if I should excuse myself to go to the bathroom again. But I don't want him to think I'm sick or anything.

The door shuts at the top of the steps, and even with the TV on, the silence is deafening.

I look over at Silas and smile nervously. How did Trina hang out with him all day? I barely know what to say for the length of time it takes to pour a drink.

He turns to me, holding my gaze like a professional flirt, then slides over next to me on the couch. He's so slick I half expect him to roll off something Italian, or maybe French.

A pinball machine dings behind our heads, and my mind races to think of something clever to say—in English.

Nothing comes.

So I look at his eyes, trying to imagine what color eye shadow might complement them, but even that doesn't work because he's beaming them at me like laser guns. They are intensely focused, but soft—freezing me in their peculiar stare. I am so flattered and confused by his attention that I am powerless to move or even to speak. He's way out of my league, and yet he's looking at me as if he thinks I'm pretty or something. This is some kind of superhero power that I am totally unprepared for.

"I don't think we've kissed," he says, leaning toward me.

I thought I wanted a kiss. But not now. Not with Silas!

I feel my face flush and get steamy. "Silas . . . ," I whisper.

"Shhh," he says before pressing his full lips against my mouth. He tilts his head slightly and brings his hand up to touch my face. It feels nice. Scary nice. This is the real thing—hands and all—but how can I kiss him when my heart belongs to Vance?

"Stop!" I say, pushing him back.

"Relax." He nudges me backward with a force that startles me momentarily and kisses me again, moving his fingers into my hair. The kiss isn't as wet and slobbery as I imagined it might be, and I find myself analyzing it instead of fighting it like I want to. Trina was right. It's not that hard to do.

But almost immediately I start feeling feverish, and my right ear starts to buzz and hurt.

No! I think. *Not when I kiss boys, too!*

"Silas, get off me," I say.

But he isn't stopping, and it starts happening like it always does—except different. Because I've never read the mind of a boy. And suddenly I'm too curious to stop.

Now I can see them: various pieces of his past float through my mind like a film. As his lips smash hungrily against mine, I see a vision of him kissing this girl I know from another school. And I can taste his memories, too. He's excited, so his memories taste strongish, like those blood oranges Arch served at Christmas last year. But with all this movie-style making out, the painful buzzing in my ear intensifies, distracting me from both the kiss and the vision.

I've never experienced this for as long or with as much energy as I am right now. But as I attempt to pull away, his grip tightens and he pins my body down, pressing his lips harder onto mine. The pain gets epic. I inhale deeply through my nose and focus on the vision.

The girl is fading, and now I see him lighting a match. I can taste his intense anger and excitement like cinnamon. For some reason, though, I'm not scared. I feel it, but I know it has nothing to do with me—it's the emotions he had as this event took place. Then I see him set fire to the Longs' shed. Whoa! I remember when that happened. It was the talk of the town. The police knew it was arson, but they never figured out who did it. I feel my skin crawl at the realization that it was Silas—the boy whose lips are currently wrapped around mine.

"Em, your aunt's here!" I hear Trina shout from the top of the steps.

Gasping for air, I yank my head back and wipe my lips while the disturbing visions rise in my throat like bad Indian food. I feel like a peeping Tom, ashamed of what I saw and equally horrified that I let him control me like this. Who is this guy?

"See ya later," he says. A wicked grin eases across his face as he slides to the other end of the sofa and resumes watching TV.

I stumble off the sofa and mumble something unintelligible, then fly up the steps to safety.

Trina is standing on the landing, two Cokes in hand. "So?" she asks. "What's the verdict?"

"About what?" I ask, confused.

"Silas," she says. "I'm *totally* crushing. We'd make a perfect couple, don't you think?"

"No!" I say. "He's . . . he's . . ." I stand there, trying not to implode from a combination of guilt over kissing her new crush and horror, but what am I supposed to say?

"Emerson?" Her head tilts to the side, and a deep crease forms in the center of her forehead.

Luckily Arch starts honking the horn, so I push past Trina and head for the back door. "I have dinner with the Wilsons!" I say. And as I walk outside, I get this awful feeling. As if my entire body is being squeezed by a serpent—constricted by a gift that no one can see or will ever understand. *I am not like other girls. I will never be able to kiss a boy again.*

Ever . . .

TWO YEARS LATER

CHAPTER ONE

Mandarin Dream

My Spanish teacher, Mrs. Gonzalez, needs a makeover.

Pale pink isn't bright enough for her olive skin tone. I may not know the answers to the test, but I know this: she'd look great in that new coral lip tint Arch got last week. *What was it called?* I chew on the end of my pen, trying to remember the name, then find myself looking around the room. Luke is feverishly writing, probably acing this stupid thing; and Trina is, too.

Turning my head to the left, I check out Vance. Unlike Luke and Trina, Vance is leaning back in his chair, his legs stretched out long underneath his desk. They're crossed at the ankle, and his top foot is wiggling back and forth inside his shoe. *Cute.* Unaware of my stare, he reaches up and laces his fingers behind his head like he's lying out by the pool or something. I study the slight curve of his lips, wishing I wasn't cursed and hoping this boy—this blond-haired dream machine—will someday ask me out.

All of a sudden he looks up at me and smiles.

"Emerson?" Mrs. Gonzalez calls from her desk in the front of the room.

Uh-oh. My face flushes red, feeling twenty-four pairs of eyes all zeroed in on me.

Mrs. Gonzalez makes a peace sign with her fingers, then points them at her own eyes before forcefully pointing down at her stack of papers. "Eyes on your work!" she whisper-shouts.

I nod apologetically and drop my head to look at my test. Mandarin Dream! I think. Yes, *that's* the lip tint: Mandarin Dream. If only I could remember these answers as easily.

Flipping back to the front of my six-page nightmare, I recheck my answers. I'm pretty sure I got the section on vocabulary right, but I've screwed up these verb tenses for sure. And now that I'm thinking about it, I probably bombed the history quiz this morning, too. Ugh. All together with yesterday's chemistry monstrosity, I'm doomed.

Trying not to daydream the rest of my time away, I close my eyes and bring my thoughts back to the task at hand: Spanish. But then Mrs Gonzalez shouts, "Ten more minutes!" and I realize it's all over. I'm out of time. It's the last day of January, and this is my last challenge of the week. Oh, well. Ten more minutes and I'm home free.

Thank. Goodness.

Three days is all it takes for Arch to check my grades. One measly weekend without even a party to enjoy before she calls to me in her I-mean-business voice from downstairs.

"I'll have to catch you later," I tell Trina before hanging up the phone. "Arch has seen my test." Ever since Arch discovered how to check my grades online, she's been reviewing them on a weekly basis.

When I get downstairs, I find my aunt sitting at her desk in the small office area of her bedroom. She's wearing her old blue robe and her glasses. Stellar invoices litter the floor, and there's a stack of bills to the right of her desk. She has her auburn hair pulled back in a short, chunky ponytail, and her eyes are glued to her computer screen and my school's website.

"Before you get mad," I say, "I can explain." I have no idea what I'll "explain," but I'll try to think of something.

However, instead of reprimanding me like she usually does, she slowly turns to face me. For the first time in a while, I see that she isn't wearing her full face of makeup. Instead she looks pale and sickly.

"Are you okay?" I ask.

"No." She takes off her little black glasses and sets them on the side of her desk, then rubs the top of her nose with her thumb and forefinger. "I'm tired, Emerson. Tired of breaking my neck so you can go to the best private school in town, only to have you get these kinds of grades." She waves her hand absentmindedly at the computer.

"Yes, ma'am." I know when to disagree with her, and this is *not* one of those times.

"I'm not sure you can stay at Haygood next year," she says.

My breath catches in my throat. "What?"

"I just can't justify it anymore. It's obviously not paying off. Your first semester average was a low C. How are you going to get into those colleges we discussed with these grades?"

I lean my hand on the edge of her desk. "Did you say you were pulling me out of school?" I might collapse. *Is she crazy?* "You can't, Arch! Haygood is the only school I've ever been to! My friends . . ." A knot forms in my stomach. "I'll study! I promise!"

"Don't argue with me, Emerson. I don't know what else to do. It costs too much for you to get Cs all the time."

"I'm sorry, Arch. Just give me a chance!" I shout. "One more chance. Please!"

"What's going on?" Piper asks, rounding the corner.

"Nothing," Arch says. "Nothing is going on. Certainly not any studying."

CHAPTER TWO

Tantastic

I am a Jelly-filled Cookie.

According to the personality quiz in Trina's latest magazine, I project a straight-laced, innocent vibe on the outside. But on the inside I'm complex, exotic, and full of flavor.

I can't decide which is worse: the secret exoticism that no one can see or the boring innocence I apparently wear like a dress. I mean, do I really seem "straight-laced"? I guess I am, but can other people see it as easily as what I'm wearing? Am I clothed in the inexperienced innocence of one who has (almost) never been kissed?

Oh, who am I kidding? Of course I am.

Trina, on the other hand, is a Fortune Cookie: "a rather normal person, except extraordinarily lucky in life. People gravitate toward you in the hopes of being lucky, too!"

Figures.

"Is this supposed to cheer me up?" I ask Trina, who insisted I come over after I called her back in tears.

I should have known the study preparations she had in mind would involve quizzes of the magazine variety. Before almost every one—be it Compatibility, Personality, or even those awful Love-and-Sex ones—Trina says in her perky, we're-about-to-get-the-keys-to-the-universe voice, "Remember, Emerson, knowledge is power." But seriously . . . *since when is a jelly-filled cookie powerful?*

"At least Arch is letting you finish out the year," Trina replies. "My parents would have yanked me straight out if my grades were as low as yours."

"Thanks. That makes me feel *much better*."

"I'm just kidding," she teases.

Trina's next suggestion to get my mind off things is to "help someone in need." The disadvantaged recipient? Trina herself, of course, who's apparently in dire need of a little color. Before I know it, I'm sitting on the lid of her toilet and shaking up a can of Arch's miracle Tantastic tanning spray. As usual, I have one of the last cans in circulation due to end-of-the-year sales, so tanning seems like a brilliant afternoon event. According to Trina, "A little sun makes everything better." I have to give her props. She's right—even though the "sun" is being applied to her, not me.

"Hold still," I instruct her from my position in front of the bathtub. "And brace yourself. I think it's cold."

She giggles. "Bring it on, sister!" She's standing in her bathtub, wearing an old towel. Her long blond hair is swept up into a shower cap, but even like that she still looks pretty. It's her eyes, I decide. They're blue, but not your basic blue—more like gray-blue steel. A truly original shade. It doesn't even matter that she's fairly short and kinda curvy. It all just works.

I turn and look at myself in the mirror over the sink,

subconsciously comparing my long, brown, barely there waves and pale, white skin to hers. *Meh.* I run my hand through my hair, but it gets stuck in a tangle of dry split ends. Total Hair Fail. So I make a mental note to hit up Arch for some conditioning repair serum.

Trina insists that "tanning" is numero uno on the list of Things That Make a Girl Gorgeous; and even with frost on the grass outside, who am I to argue? This list changes as frequently as the objects of her affection, but since I am forever boyfriendless—and in possession of more makeup than Cleopatra—I tend to be available to listen. Not to mention that I come armed with everything one needs to beautify.

Trina's tactics are no doubt taken from the article I saw thumbtacked to her bulletin board entitled "Tanned Fat IS as Good as Muscle." While it's not about love, I ignore these kinds of articles for one main reason: I am scared/fearful/ignorant/intimidated and/or nervous around real, flesh-and-blood boys. And all of Trina's articles are meant to help her secure a boyfriend in some way or another. As for me, I prefer to lust after them on-screen or from afar—like across the cafeteria—or in fantasies. For example, I want to make out with Vance Butcher while leaning up against the side of my locker, or maybe on the back of a sleek, white stallion. I want to feel his hands gently resting on my face, and I want him to have my number on speed dial. But I want him to do this only *after* taking me out a few times and romancing me like that sexy Leopold guy in one of Arch's old movies, *Kate and Leopold*.

Like I said, it's pure fantasy. Because in reality, after the Day of Doom in the basement that summer, I swore I'd never suck-face/kiss/makeout/smooch again. But swearing off boys for so long makes it easy to forget how to talk to them, much less flirt. And I'm getting tired of being a single, shriveled-up prune while Trina morphs into a glistening goddess of love.

I'm thinking about this very dilemma in a "What would Harry Potter do?" kind of way when Trina says "I'm hungry" and moves out of the way of my spray can. "You think it worked?"

Pushing Vance and Harry back into the attic of my mind, I decide to help out Trina by reaching my chalk-white arm toward her tan one and innocently saying, "I dunno. Let's compare."

She quickly aligns her damp, bronze arm next to mine and emits a helium balloon squeal of delight, then steps out of the bathtub and rubs herself with the dark-green towel from the bar on the wall. "Oooh! It's glittery, too!"

I look her over, and sure enough, it is. She's as sparkly as Edward Cullen. "Vampish," I say with a smile.

"It's time for popcorn. Wait for me in my room."

So now, here I sit on the small "psycho-sofa" in her room— the hugely thrilling (and way too pale) Jelly-filled Cookie.

When Trina comes back, she begins eating popcorn by the handfuls and I lie back and pretend to be her "patient." I'm tired anyway, so I close my eyes and try to relax.

"I've been thinking," she begins. "Do you remember when my mom had that breast cancer scare, and she had to get mammograms every three months?"

"Yeah."

"Well, there was this woman who asked Mom what she was going to do to improve the state of her body during the ninety days *before* the mammogram. Ya know—to boost her immune system."

I laugh, remembering well. "She made you drink beets with her!"

"Yes! She juiced all that stuff. I'll never eat a red vegetable again."

"You mean *drink* a reggie—that's a red veggie, if you missed it. Ha!"

"See? You're feeling better already. But it gives me an idea: in order to keep you in school, we should do something to boost the state of your *mind*!"

"You want me to drink superfoods?"

"No." She walks over to her bookcase in the corner and pulls out a bright-red book with a large, yellow smiley face on the front, then holds it up and strokes its cover as if it's Today's Special Value at QVC. "This book says happy people are successful people."

"And . . ." I sit up, having no idea where this is going.

"And there's nothing that will make you happier and more successful than having a boyfriend!" Trina's eyes are bugging out. I've never seen her more excited about a project in my life.

"I don't get it."

"Listen. I could help you study, but it would be a lot more fun with a guy, right? And boy*friend* is a natural side effect of study partners! Not only will you have someone to help you improve your grades, but in your sheer state of love-induced bliss, serotonin and dopamine will start swimming in your bloodstream! They're the superfoods you need to make you calm, cool, collected, and . . . drumroll, please . . . *focused*!" She exhales. "Having a *boyfriend* will solve all of your problems."

"Hmmm . . ." I purse my lips in thought. "Sounds dope."

She laughs. "You're clearly not good at making connections. See if Vance will study with you! He gets good grades."

Her brilliant idea is trickier for me than she realizes. *Should I finally tell her about the kissing thing?*

Nope. She'll think I'm a freak show. She'll want to study me and call people from her magazines to profile me.

She continues, "I know it's early February and all, but let's make it official. Let's set New Year's resolutions!"

I slide my tongue into the gap in my bottom side teeth and try to think of an alternative.

"Seriously," she begins, "this year we're going to have boyfriends. No more silly crushes. We're going to have real boys who call us and take us out and stuff."

I quickly lie back down, feeling dizzy. A black smudge on the ceiling catches my attention.

"Emerson," she continues, annoyed, "are you even listening to me?"

"Yes," I say. "That sounds great, but I'm not sure this will work. I can't *make* a boy ask me out."

She thinks for a minute, chewing on her bottom lip.

"Shouldn't we pick something more practical?" I offer. "Like reading more." But even as I say it, I feel the pathetic boredom of my answer. I want a boyfriend just like she does. Only I don't want to say it.

"Reading more?" she asks in disbelief. "Are you kidding? I mean, I know that's obviously necessary for general grade improvement, but I'm talking about changing the chemistry of our brains, Emerson! Our resolutions need to be *big*. As big as that frickin' fruit-and-veggie pile Mom was always juicing. Instead of beets and kale, we're going to juice up with something *fun*. Something made of snips and snails and puppy dog tails."

"Yeah. Yeah." I finish the rhyme. "That's what boys are made of."

"Exactly," she says. "*Boys* . . . I am declaring this year the Year of the Boy."

I want to laugh with her—to be excited and giddy at the prospect of having a boyfriend. But having boyfriends leads to kissing, and kissing leads to reading minds; and I know where *that* leads.

She adds, "And don't tell me we can't do it, because we can. I, for one, am adopting the 'act as if' principle."

Propping myself up on my elbows, I look at her again. "The what?"

Her eyes flash like neon Frisbees. "I read about it in that self-help magazine Arch gave me last month. It's all about being positive. You act *as if* what you want is already true."

"So, what? You're going to act *as if* you already have a boyfriend?" I lie back down. "That'll be sure to make someone ask you out."

"No, Miss Negative. I'm going to act *as if* I'm date-worthy. I'm going to seduce a hottie with unprecedented psychic positivity."

I flinch at her mention of the word *psychic*, but maybe she has a point. Maybe I *can* finally get rid of this kissing problem. Or at least brainwash myself to believe I'm over it. Maybe there's even a way for me to *block* the visions during a smooch. Heck, if Snape can teach Harry to block Voldemort's memories, why can't I do it, too?

"Can I act *as if* I'm a straight-A student?" I ask, changing the subject.

"Sadly, no"—I hear her flipping pages—"but how about another quiz?"

"No. No more quizzes. I'm still upset about being a Jelly-filled Cookie."

"Why?" She pops another handful of popcorn into her

mouth. "It said you were exotic." She makes a moaning sound that I think is supposed to be sexy and animal-like, but in all honesty, it makes me feel worse. I've lost any ability I had to flirt, much less purr or growl. I need some mojo STAT. This no-kissing-boys thing is getting old.

"All righty then," she says. "You wanna talk about your mom?"

"No thanks." I so *don't.*

"You sure? Because, personally, I think she might be the reason you can't concentrate on school."

"She took her life, like, ten years ago. I'm okay," I say, although I know it's not true. I'll never be okay about that. Trina likes to ask me about Mama from time to time; and while I appreciate Trina's interest, I just don't know what to say about it anymore. I miss my mother. . . .

"Are you?"

I don't look at Trina, but I envision her leaning over her magazine and narrowing her eyes, looking for answers to all of my issues. "Yes," I say forcefully. "No more psycho-babble!"

She offers me some popcorn, then says, "Moving on. Let's choose a potential crush for you in the Year of the Boy. Who should it be?"

"I dunno," I say as I watch the black ceiling smudge magically morph into Vance's adorable face.

"Are you one of those girls who is afraid of boys?" Trina wildly flips more pages. "Wait. I read something about this. Yes! Here it is." Her voice gets soft, and she begins to speak as if I won't understand unless she reads at the speed of sludge. "It's called fear of intimacy, and it makes perfect sense because you never really had a father. That's it! You simply have a healthy fear of intimacy."

First my mom and now *this*? I turn my head to glare at

her. I've had it with this head shrinking, and I'll never be able to explain to her what my problem with boys *really* is. "Trinnaaaa . . ."

"Emersonnnn." She leans forward over her magazine. "You can relax. It's no big deal. All you need to do is to face your fears." She stands up and walks to the bulletin board, where the tanning article is pinned. She taps a new yellow bumper sticker with a perfectly manicured finger. "This. Read this."

I squint to read it without getting up. "'To conquer your fears, face them. At full speed!'"

It's not as if I've never heard that before, but she has a point.

"Or . . ." She pauses. "And don't take this the wrong way, because I am totally cool with it, but maybe you're gay? Maybe you need a *female* study partner? It's very chic, you know."

I sit up, laughing for the first time all day. "Please, Trina. Be serious."

She walks back to her bed and sits down. "My magazine says it's sometimes really hard to come out." She makes quote marks in the air when she says "come out."

"I'm not gay," I say, lying down. "And if I were, I'd tell you. It's just . . ." I look again at the ceiling and stare at the Vance-shaped smudge.

"It's the parent thing," I say, hoping I've covered all of my issues. "Fear of intimacy. I think you're right. You're gonna be a great doctor one day." I grin and lift my eyebrows for extra effect.

She closes her magazine and exhales a peaceful "Mmm." I wait for a "Namaste" to float out of her mouth. "That settles it. In order to improve your grades and become a happy and successful person, you *have* to secure a hot study partner. Let's get you in the tub. You've got some tanning to do."

Swinging my legs over the side of the sofa, I stand up and make my way to the bathroom with a renewed spring in my step. I'm gonna do this. I'm going to be a newer (tanner), more courageous me. But how can I fall in love with Prince Charming when his every thought will dive-bomb my brain? It's as distracting as trying to learn chemistry while sitting in Vance's lap!

Oh, let's face it. I'm not sure I'm ready for all this.

CHAPTER THREE

Sunrise, Sunset

My mother left me like Moses in a basket.

At least that's the way I like to think about it. In reality, rather than a basket on the Nile, it was in the front yard of my aunt's bungalow when I was six years old. And she left my sister, too—a bit too big for a basket, I'd say.

Piper and I had been playing outside—she with her Barbies and me with my chalk. We visited Arch a lot—especially after my daddy left us, which was almost as soon as I was born.

That day Mama had asked us to go outside and play "Right now!" which usually meant loud, angry, grown-up talk was about to happen inside with Aunt Arch. We knew better than to argue with her. Those two fought a lot.

After a while Barbie boredom set in, so we lay down on the pavement and outlined each other in fat white chalk. Piper, being the fashion-minded one, drew a beautiful pink line across my chalk-body middle that jutted out both sides of my chalk-girl hips.

"What's that?" I asked, admiring her work.

"A skirt, silly." She began coloring it in with short, scratchy strokes.

I smiled, then followed her lead and drew a pair of green circles across her chalk-body head where the eyes should be.

"What are you doing?" she barked.

I looked up from my masterpiece and beamed. "Making you glasses. Like mine."

"They make me look ugly!" she said while trying to brush away the green lines with her foot. "I like to be pretty."

I tilted my head sideways and stared at the green lines, not understanding what was wrong. Was she saying I looked horrible? Or not pretty?

She corrected herself. "What I *meant* was that glasses look good on *you*." She glanced down at the drawing. "Just not on me."

I crinkled my forehead trying to figure out if she was lying. But just then we heard something loud inside. "Shhh!" I said.

Piper grabbed my hand, and we ran up to the door. We could hear someone crying.

The door opened, and Mama came out. She knelt down on the porch and held us by the shoulders. She was wearing her serious eyes, and I was scared that I was in trouble again. *Does she know I made Piper's drawing ugly?*

"You girls be good," Mama said. Her face was splotchy red. Clearly she was the one who had been crying.

We nodded our heads.

"And do well in school." Narrowing her eyes, she looked at me, and I felt my heart sink. (Even back then I had school issues.) Maybe my teacher had called her, I worried. But I wasn't the *only* one who'd failed that spelling test. I'd have bet my allowance that Jimmy Eason did, too.

"Your studies are important," she said sternly.

I swallowed, clenching my jaw, and pushed my glasses farther up my nose.

Piper nodded and smiled at Mama's advice. Her straight teeth gleamed as she blinked her non-vision-impaired eyes.

I sat perfectly still, waiting for the rest of Mama's instructions; but she said nothing—just stared out into the trees and then past them clear on into the next county.

Not sure what was happening at that point, I reached over and grabbed one of Piper's Barbies and began to twirl her hair.

Mama turned her head abruptly, so I put down the doll quietly in my lap.

"Barbie should be with Ken," she said quietly, her eyes looking fevered and tired.

I nodded, desperately wanting to please her. But I didn't have Ken, so I grabbed my old Ernie doll from the stoop.

"Not Ernie!" Mama said with frustration. "He's a loser." Then she paused and looked out into the distance again. "Just like your father was."

"Yes, ma'am," I said, not sure if I should agree that Daddy was a loser—but we didn't ever see him, so I was pretty sure she wouldn't tell him.

She stood up and straightened her skirt. I saw a tear sneak out of her eye again.

"Mama?" I said.

But she had already turned and was walking toward our old brown station wagon. She opened the creaky front door and threw her purse onto the seat.

I looked back at Piper, who was playing again, not realizing that Mama was leaving.

"Mama?" I repeated louder, walking toward her, tears pressing at the backs of my eyes.

But Mama got in the car and slammed her door, accidentally dropping her brown tube of Sunrise, Sunset lipstick onto the street. It was her favorite.

I reached the sidewalk and knelt down to pick it up. I thought maybe if I showed her, she'd want to stay.

Holding it in the air, I cried, "Mama! Look!" It seems funny now that I thought a dumb old tube of lipstick could have that much power over a person.

She looked at me and mouthed the words "I love you," then blew me a copper-colored kiss and drove away.

I reached up and pretended to catch her kiss in my hand. And, unlike every other kiss she had blown me in my life, I pressed the captured kiss into my chest and collapsed on the sidewalk in a flurry of tears. Immediately, a sharp pain shot through my right ear, and I sniffled through the hurt.

Arch ran out of the house and scooped me into her arms while I looked down at all I had left of my mother—a brown tube of lipstick.

"When is Mama coming back?" I remember asking Arch a few nights later. Mama had never left us there for so long before.

Arch was sitting on the side of my bed pretending to put makeup on my face. It was a tradition we had when we spent the night with her. She would delicately whisper the words *blush*, *eye shadow*, and *lipstick* while tracing the areas of our faces where one would apply the real thing. I don't know about Piper, but it always lulled me to sleep and soothed my troubled mind.

Even now, at sixteen, I still sometimes ask her to "play

makeover" before bed. There's just something about those soothing words and the feel of her fingers tracing around my face that calms me.

"I don't know," she said with tears in her eyes. Then she kissed my dimple, which lies to the right of my lips. And when she did, I felt a slight sting in my ear. That little reaction was the beginning—the first time it happened.

"Ow!" I said, reaching for my ear.

"What's wrong, baby?"

I shrugged, no longer feeling the pain. "My ear just hurt for a second, that's all."

"I'm sorry," she said before leaning down and kissing my dimple again. "Sleep tight, peanut."

I winced. Within a split second, I saw it: a vision. In that teensy microsecond of a kiss, I saw her conversation with my mama—the one that made Mama cry.

I inhaled sharply, feeling the vision develop in my mouth. I was having trouble swallowing it. Their conversation felt spiky and stuck in my throat. And the *taste*—their conversation, at least in Arch's memory, tasted like dark chocolate: comforting, complex, and bittersweet, all at the same time. Mama was crying and asked Arch to take care of us. She said to make sure we didn't marry a loser like she had.

Arch was scared, too. Scared of keeping us, of being unwed with children. Her fear tasted like pickled jalapeños, green onions, and cilantro. But she was also scared *for* us with a love I haven't tasted since. It was this feeling, this *love*, that lessened the bite—kinda like when Luke's mom mixes these same fiery ingredients into buttered sweet potatoes, making them warm, spicy, and wonderful.

Within those few short seconds, I knew exactly how my

aunt felt. And, after swallowing it, I knew Mama was never coming back.

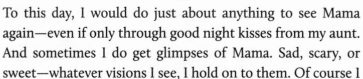

To this day, I would do just about anything to see Mama again—even if only through good night kisses from my aunt. And sometimes I do get glimpses of Mama. Sad, scary, or sweet—whatever visions I see, I hold on to them. Of course I never thought that when I grew up, I'd have to train myself to withstand the images in order to kiss a boy.

CHAPTER FOUR

Innocent

On Valentine's night, just as a bright bolt of lightning sets my room aglow, I'm hit with a similarly intense idea—one that enters my head as a full-blown science fair poster. (I've clearly been reading *way* too much.)

OPERATION LIPLOCK

PROJECT FOCUS:

1.) Make better grades by studying with a hot boy.

2.) Learn to kiss said boy without being traumatized by visions.

MY HYPOTHESIS:

If practice test taking (and studying) helps one perform better on actual tests, then practice kissing should do the same.

THE GOAL:

A calculated appointment with Sawyer Thompson— science project winner, AP English whiz, mathlete, and charter member of what Trina and I like to call "The Ivys": those brainy types destined for the Ivy League.

THE METHOD:

Not only can I ask him to help me study, but I can try to kiss him! Who better to practice on than a quiet boy who doesn't talk to any of my friends?

MATERIALS:

Innocent lip gloss and swag.

PROBABLE OUTCOME:

As soon as I master the skill of normal kissing, I will ask Vance to study with me. And we shall fall in love over English sonnets and geometric formulas just as Trina envisioned. Yes, with this foolproof way to practice, I will emerge with a black belt in romance and much better grades.

I'm feeling smarter, having just come up with this killer idea. If only real science posters were as easy.

The following day, before first period even starts, my poster plan is already under way. I turn the corner and see the door to the science lab glowing in the distance. He's in there all right, sitting at the right front table with his eyes permanently affixed to a microscope, I'd bet. I can picture him right now with his pale-brown buzz cut, his shirt tucked into his pants, and his thin, red lips, scrunching as he calculates whatever it is science and math brains calculate.

As I walk toward the lab, I think about Trina's bumper sticker again. "To conquer your fears, face them. At full speed!" My feet might be sluggish, but my heart is thumping so hard I can feel it in my throat.

Holy cow, what am I doing?

Shaking my head with determination, I pick up the pace. *Stick to the plan*, I tell myself. Stick. To. The. Plan. Practice-kiss an Ivy, master the art of ignoring my gift, learn the subtle art of flirtation, and score a boyfriend. And with all the happiness-juice Trina says will course through my veins, I will be more motivated to study—which equals better grades and a permanent place at Haygood Academy.

Bada boom!

Looking into the small, square window on the door of the science lab, I spot him. He is alone and peaceful looking, at home with his microscope, dead frogs, and petri dishes—a perfect practice-kissing partner. It's the "alone" part that makes him the perfect choice. For this mission I need guaranteed privacy.

But wait. *What if he's really stiff and proper and won't kiss me?* He doesn't know what I'm doing, after all. I chew on my bottom lip. I should have thought about that.

Maybe . . . ?

Maybe I should approach a real player like that sleazy guy in my English class. *Yes!* What is his name?

I turn away from the window.

But then again . . . I turn back. Fighting off *his* memories and thoughts might be harder. I might be battling years of Playboy bunnies.

Oh, mother of pearl. Just go in there.

Sensing my presence, Sawyer looks up and waves. He twists his hand like a homecoming queen on the back of a Mustang. I try to ignore this, as well as the fact that his pants are as tight as my new skinny jeans and his shirt has math symbols on it.

While my heart continues to slam around in my chest, I notice that my hands seem to be forming condensation. *Gross.* Wiping them on my pants, I wonder if I should just bag this idea.

No, I decide, reaching for the doorknob. *This is a good plan. It really is.*

Looking behind me, I scan the hallway of gray and blue lockers to make sure no one has seen me. The paper hearts on the February bulletin board catch my eye and seem like a blessing from above. Confirmation of my newest endeavor: Operation Liplock.

While turning the knob, I smile at him through the window. This exchange is commonplace for us, because he is always there, and I am always here. I hold the prestigious position of Hallway Monitor, which is Haygood Academy lingo for "unathletic girl desperately in need of something extracurricular to put on her high school transcript."

The monitor's primary job is checking on the classrooms

after school. But once a week I have to check the halls *before* school, like today. I'm supposed to make sure thugs aren't spraying graffiti around the place, which is totally ridiculous, because Haygood Academy doesn't have thugs. We have academic decathletes. Our school is the proud home to a plethora of academic-loving Ivys, well-groomed daddys' girls, thick-muscled hotties, and a handful of kids like me whose parents never went to college (like Arch) and who want their children to experience something better. Haygood Academy is *the* place to prepare for the college of your parents' dreams. It even says so in the brochure.

"Busted any bathroom fights?" Sawyer asks as I walk in.

I toss him a practiced smile, but sweat is quickly moving from my hands to my armpits.

"Nah," I say, my voice cracking. "Whatcha reading?"

He tilts his book toward me, and I see what looks like a bunch of calculus formulas.

"Math?" I ask.

"Kind of," he explains. "The velocity and acceleration of a rocket my after-school science team is building."

I consider asking him what that means, but I won't understand his answer anyway, so I sputter something that sounds like "Meuh." Great. I'm that guy in *Pride and Prejudice* who tries to woo Elizabeth Bennet and is a miserable failure. Come to think of it, I am probably the least-prepared flirt in the entire sophomore class. I don't have a clue how to effectively hit on a guy. What am I thinking? *Abort! Abort!*

I turn around to leave when he says, "How can I assist you this morning? Might I interest you in some practice equations for our test tomorrow?"

I *should* be thinking about the fact that I have somehow forgotten we have a test tomorrow, but all I can register is his use of words like *assist* and the fact that he just said "Might I interest you in some practice equations" as if they were the catch of the day.

"Emerson?"

I look at his ginormous calculator and remind myself that this is it: fear facing. "Yes," I confirm. "The test."

"Stupendous," he says, holding me in his gaze like a snake charmer.

Focus, Emerson!

Shaking my head, I break our little stare-off, but a piece of my hair gets stuck in my lip gloss. "Uh-oh."

"My, my," he says. "That gloss is adherent!"

"Yeah. I like the color." I pull the strand away from my lips, and he watches me with fascination.

"I'd love to try some of that on the interior of my model rocket. We've had a terrible time getting the control panel to attach to the base."

"Are you kidding?" I ask, but he's clearly not, so I laugh it off and insist we start the geometry lesson. Grabbing a stool, I sit next to him. Nothing like a little fractal foreplay, right?

Leaning over the side of his stool, he removes our yellow geometry textbook from his backpack while I nervously smush my Innocent lip gloss around my lips with my finger. Then he lays the book open on the long, black lab table in front of us. There's barely any room next to all of his equipment, so he sets his motion equations in the sink and begins to speak.

And talk.

And explain.

And teach.

And it's all very nice. But after listening to him go over who-knows-what for who-knows-how-long, I still don't understand.

Staring at his mouth, I try to imagine what it might be like to kiss him—what my full lips pressed against his thin ones will feel like. Can fat lips kiss thin ones? Do people take this into account when they are choosing potential mates? Does lip size matter?

It's only a kiss, Emerson. Easy peasy. French people do it all day long. And he's a boy. You love boys, remember? Think Mr. Darcy, Edward Cullen, Prince Caspian, that dreamy Brit Daniel Deronda.

"Are you okay?" he asks.

Batting my eyes, I realize he's been staring at me for like a fortnight. "Huh?"

"Are you okay? Do you understand? Not to be rude, but you look sorta . . . sick."

"Can I kiss you?" I blurt out, desperate and terrified.

He snickers, making me feel like a sushi-grade loser. I should have asked my sister how this is done. She's had a boyfriend since preschool. I'm not lying. Arch loves to tell this old story about Piper and her first little beau sharing their Play-Doh.

"Geometry turns you on, huh?" he asks, continuing to chuckle.

"No," I say a tad too forcefully. "I just . . ." I stand up to leave and accidentally knock my stool backward. It slams into the vinyl flooring with a clatter. "I have to go."

"Wait! Wait!" he says. "You were serious?"

With my back to him, I walk to the door and put my hand on the doorknob, talking to the air in front of me. "No. I mean yes. I'm sorry. I wanted to practice."

"I'm your practice guy?" he asks from behind me, obviously confused. "Practice for what? You're like . . . popular."

I don't know how to answer this because he's right, and the

whole idea seems so absurd now. So I just shrug and twist the knob to leave. But then he puts his hand on my right shoulder and turns me around to face him. "Hey, you. Wait."

A ginormous zit smirks at me from his chin. *He needs Stellar's Acne Blaster,* I think. *Maybe I'll bring him some.*

Closing his eyes, he leans toward me, and I feel his narrow lips touch mine, gentle and smooth.

Yowza. It's not so bad. Maybe even kinda nice. But then lightning strikes my right ear, forcing me to pull away abruptly. "Ow!" I reach up and grab my ear as a mess of images spills into my mind in a tangle of pain and numbers. Fractions and formulas. Holy moly, it's his homework. *Uh . . . this is a first.*

"That bad, huh?" he asks, backing up.

"No. No," I assure him, and this is true. It wasn't nearly as jarring as when I'd kissed Silas. But there was no way to ignore all of the numbers that flew out of Sawyer's mind like carnival confetti. Thank goodness it was just a boring mess of homework.

"Can we try one more time?" I ask, my ear still throbbing.

Grinning like a kid on a carousel, he leans his head to the right and says, "Perhaps we should tilt our heads to a firm forty-five degrees like this."

I can't decide if I should laugh or cry, but I tilt my head the required forty-five-ish degrees and squint hard, hoping it will help me ignore the images.

It's no use. I start coughing. I think I just inhaled a quadratic formula.

Lessons learned:

1. I suck at vision-blocking.

2. Practice-kissing a nerdy Ivy is safe and not scary—at least as far as images go. He is chock-full of boredom.

The taste of the vision lingers in my mouth as a twisted

mess of sesame noodles flavored with peanuts, soy sauce, carrots, and ginger. A complete Asian masterpiece. And Sawyer's not even Asian. I guess it's not often you taste math and science formulas mixed together.

"Maybe one more time?" he asks, making me feel a bit icky.

"No thanks. I have to go. Might need to stop a cat fight in the junior hall." I turn the doorknob and look back at him one more time. "Don't tell anyone I needed practice, okay?" I feel like a five-year-old saying this, but still. . . .

His eyes brighten as he lifts his hand and pretends to turn an imaginary key around his lips, "locking" our secret away. Then he walks over to the silver trash can in the corner of the room and makes a dramatic spectacle of throwing away the invisible key.

I should be comforted by this little display, but instead my cheeks burn with shame.

CHAPTER FIVE

Nervous Nellie

My hands are still shaking a few minutes later as I reach into my purse to find a piece of gum—the kind that's so strong it borders on spicy and makes my eyes water. The type I think might erase the taste his memory left on my tongue. I'm relieved that at least it wasn't scary. The truth is, it was sorta fun—being kissed in secret and all. But suddenly I feel even lonelier and worried that I'll never be able to control my gift.

"Ace!" I hear Luke yell from behind me.

I whip around to see six feet of Poker-Loving Fun stroll up—otherwise known as my next-door neighbor, Luke Baldwin.

"What are you wearing?" I reach out and grab his shirt. "Jorge?"

Luke has a love of vintage shirts. And not just any vintage shirts. Luke likes the ones with names on them. Think old gas station uniforms with IRWIN on the pocket, or his favorite: a green polyester get-up with TOUGH TONY stitched across the back in shiny black thread. I'm not kidding. It's the definition of groovy.

"You like?" He smiles, and his smattering of cinnamon freckles crease under his bright blue eyes. "I got it at Flashback. It's classic Chevron."

"As in the gas station?"

He nods. "Where ya going?"

"History. Come on!"

"Why are we going this way?" he asks, but follows my lead. "It's on the opposite side of the building."

I shrug my shoulders. "I dunno. Taking the scenic route." But I *do* know. I want to go in the opposite direction of Sawyer.

Luke's lips curl into a smile. "Guess what?"

I chew my gum and wait for his answer.

"Party at Frances's house tomorrow."

"Really?" I ask, slightly bugged. Frances is, like, my least favorite person in the entire world. In fact, if I had to choose between kissing Grady "Fish" Cromwell (reigning king of Dorkopolis) and hanging out with Frances, I'd pick kissing Fish nine times out of ten.

Frances Hudson is as fake as my aunt's sugar substitute—with her fake boobs, fake blond hair extensions, and fake way of pretending to still be my friend. As far as I'm concerned, she and I *used* to be friends—*before* she decided I was no longer cool enough, or whatever she thinks. This is what she told Trina when Trina asked her why she dissed me all summer: "Emerson's so childish. She's totally awkward around boys." Thank goodness Trina never liked Frances that much anyway. For Trina, the fact that Frances wears way too much perfume is reason enough, and I'm inclined to agree. There's nothing worse than a fragrance overload. Arch battles this problem in old women on a daily basis.

"Yep," Luke says. "I'm stoked."

"Sounds good," I reply, reaching skyward to muss up his ginger hair. "Man, you're getting tall. I can barely reach your hair now."

He snickers and messes with mine. "And you're still as short as always."

We turn the next corner, and I think about how much of our lives are based on appearances. Some of this is good, like wanting to appear well-groomed, glossed, and healthily fit. But some of this appearance business is bad. For example, as much as I can't stand Frances, Trina and I "appear" to like her. In this regard we're just as fake as she is.

We will go to her party tomorrow with smiles on, not because of *her* but because of the fact that everyone *else* will be there, including Vance. Conversely, Frances wouldn't dare *not* invite us, because she will want to "appear" to be inclusive, not to mention want to rub in our faces that she is hosting the first party of the new semester. It's pretty twisted, but that's life.

We head down another long hall before I see Sawyer up ahead. He's standing in the center of the hall twenty lockers down talking to Edwin McNeely with exaggerated hand motions. I stop dead in my tracks. *What if he's telling Edwin I kissed him? What if that invisible key was just an act?*

"What are you doing?" Luke asks. "Come on! We're gonna be late."

"I forgot something," I lie. Dropping my backpack, I unzip the front pocket and pretend to look around. My face feels hot, which means it's probably beet red, too. Damn my pale, can't-keep-a-secret skin! "Go ahead," I say, careful to keep my head down. "I'll meet you there."

"What? Why? I'll wait."

I swallow and unzip another pocket. "My lip gloss."

"Huh? Who cares?"

I keep my face down as I dig around in my backpack. "It's the new Nervous Nellie. And it's Arch's. It's not in here, so I guess I left it in the bathroom."

He pats my head. "All right, Ace, but hurry up! You know Mrs. Parker gets mad if we're late."

"Uh-huh," I say without making eye contact. If there's one person who has the potential to see a lie, it's Luke. He spends all his free time studying the Art of the Bluff.

After he leaves I stand up and rush back toward the senior hall to take an even longer, more circuitous route. The nurse's office beckons me like a trip to the Pedicure Palace, so I swing by to complain of a stomachache (which is true) in order to kill some time. She gives me a peppermint—all she's allowed to dispense—then asks me to take a seat while she finishes her phone call. Judging by the clock on her wall, I'm dangerously close to being tardy, which is not good, so I interrupt her, motion to the clock, and ask for a tardy note.

"There's still time," she says, shooing me out of her office. "Go on now."

Turning the next corner, I run into Trina, who is glowing. For *real*. Like a glow stick. I must tell Arch that Tantastic really works, even though Trina looks a little ridiculous being as tan as our UGGs in February. She's been using it daily since the day we made our resolution to get boyfriends.

"Hey, you!" she says, stopping my rush to class. "Where'd you get that blush?"

Reaching up, I touch the sides of my cheeks and realize that she is referring to my visible shame and not to some new Stellar color. "It's A Shame," I tell her, hoping she doesn't ask me for a sample.

"It looks great. Perfect for the party!"

I laugh nervously, feeling like I might vomit. Not only have I just kissed a grade-A goob, but I've lied to both Luke and Trina. How on earth will I ever handle a real crush like Vance?

True to her reputation, my history teacher, Mrs. Parker, has just finished putting the sophomore project information on the board when I rush into first period. It's a famously large project that crosses over several subjects. Good ol' Edwin McNeely is standing by her side, blocking the doorway and making it so I have to stop and wait for him to move before I can get to a desk.

I clear my throat to alert them to my presence.

"Oh, sorry," he says casually, stepping aside for me to pass—but not before shooting me a crooked little grin and a wink.

Does he know? *DOES HE KNOW?!*

I swallow and try hard not to stare at his lips.

Mrs. Parker turns to look at me, then down at her watch, silently reprimanding me with her eyes. "Do you have a pass, Miss Taylor?"

Edwin steps in front of me awkwardly and addresses her like a sixth-grade teacher's pet. "It's my fault, Mrs. Parker. I asked Emerson to help me carry in some of the band equipment. I'm sorry."

Band equipment? My jaw drops in horror. I know he's only trying to help, but band equipment?! I guess that's what I get for nicknaming him Band Man in middle school. In my defense, he did play his horn during lunch period, which was weird times ten. He doesn't do that anymore, thank goodness. But he still keeps to himself, spending most of the school day in some corner with his headphones on.

Arch periodically mentions his "dashing looks," but that's just because he has good skin and she notices things like that. She told me once that Edwin and I were as tight as ticks when we were in first grade, but I don't believe her because I distinctly remember him never allowing me into his dumb Swords and Soldiers game at recess. And not to be mean, but the only kids who played that goofy game have all gone on to become legendary losers. Some of them even still play it online, discussing it in the halls as readily as the athletes talk sports.

"Oh, well, in *that* case." Mrs. Parker smiles at him, then redirects her attention back to me. "Miss Taylor? Your note?"

"Yeah. Uh. . . ." I am still stunned by Edwin's wink and subsequent defense of me.

"Yes, *ma'am*," she corrects me, and in my confusion I see she's got hot-pink gloss on her teeth, probably Insanity. A bunch of the teachers recently ordered it from Arch.

"Yes, ma'am," I repeat running my tongue across my own front teeth in uncontrolled lip gloss sympathy.

"The note, Emerson. I need your note, please."

"I don't have one."

She puts her eraser down in the tray under the board and raises her eyebrow. "Don't let it happen again."

"Yes, ma'am," I reply, glancing again at Edwin, who has moved to his seat and is writing in his notebook—probably working ahead on the homework.

After sitting down at my own desk, I get out my textbook and make sure to keep my eyes on the page. No more boys for me this morning. I'm fasting.

"All right, class," Mrs. Parker starts. "For this project you will be writing a paper on the social conditions in a preassigned decade. In fact, this year your project will focus on anything and everything that happened in that decade."

The class lets out an audible groan, and she calls up a student to pass around a small wicker basket from which we each take out a tiny piece of paper with our assigned decade. I get the 1920s. Looking across at Luke, I hold out my piece of paper and say, "At least it's not the Great Depression."

"Don't be so sure," he says. "That stock market crash was in twenty-nine."

Great.

Mrs. Parker adds, "And for those of you who are interested, you can get extra credit if you can think of a way to enhance your project with another class."

"No thank you," Luke says with a chuckle, whereas I have the opposite reaction. I need all the extra credit I can get. Just then my phone vibrates in my pocket, so I wait for Mrs. Parker to turn her head before I check it.

It's Arch. **Be home late tonight. Potato soup is in the fridge. Let Piper know.**

After shoving my phone back into my pocket, I look across the room and notice something rather awesome. Vance Butcher is staring right at me. *My Vance!* I ease out a smile but within a microsecond feel my nose twitch—a full left nostril flare. *Dammit!* I can't even manage a durn smile without screwing up my expression. I'm as doomed in Boy Interaction 101 as I am in every other class I take.

CHAPTER SIX

Peach Perfection

"Can you cover for me?" Piper asks me after class. She's leaning against my locker looking as polished and perfect as ever. "I have plans and won't be home till later."

"Don't worry about it. Arch just texted me and said she'd be late. She has a makeup party." Opening my locker, I toss in a few books.

Arch's makeup parties happen at least twice a week at night and last anywhere from two to three hours. Being chauffeured around in a blueberry is mortifying enough, but her job also forces her (she swears she can't control it) to occasionally insist that the checkout girl at Kroger "stay away from bronzer" or tell the waitress at the Mexican restaurant to "refrain from wearing green eye shadow." Yeah—embarrassment central. But, I have to admit, she's usually right. She didn't get that car for nothin'.

"Is that Tantastic?" Piper says, having spotted Trina at the top of the hall.

"Yes." I snicker.

Piper rolls her eyes. "Bad idea." (She'd never fake a tan.) "But this isn't." Reaching into her backpack, she pulls out a fashion magazine and flips it open to a giant two-page ad for Stellar's newest line of glosses, Crystal Craze. "Do we have these yet? Aren't they awesome!"

I'm already familiar with them, of course. If there's one thing I *am* capable of studying, it's Arch's catalogs. So I know for a fact that this particular compact isn't going to be available until spring. "Yes, awesome. But not available till mid March."

"Bummer. I saw something in *French Vogue* like it."

I smile. Piper likes to think we look European with our petite features, dark hair, and fair skin. She supports this theory with the aforementioned *French Vogue*, her drug of choice. Though whether or not we do is debatable. But I still like it when she says this because the opposite—blond hair, tan skin, big boobs, and fake perkiness—seems to be *the* style in high school, regardless of what her magazines say.

I remove another textbook from my locker and toss it into my backpack while she hangs hers over her shoulder. "Look," she whispers. "It's your lucky day."

Turning around, I spot Vance at the far end of the hallway entertaining a throng of drooling girls. Frances is front and center, wearing a shirt that is just short enough to reveal a thin line of her stomach. Nice. She laughs obnoxiously at something he says, then waves flirtatiously at him as he turns to head toward his next class, which just so happens to be right past my locker.

I look at Piper and clench my jaw in anxiety.

"Relax," she adds. "You've got this." She floats down the hall in the opposite direction, seeming not to have a care in the world. I envy her confidence. Will I *ever* feel that way?

After shutting my locker, I squat down and pretend to get

something out of my backpack for the second time today. Honestly, I need some new moves. My hair falls into my face, and I brush it away when Vance's shoes appear a minute later.

"Hey, Emerson."

"Oh. Hey!" I jump a little, trying to act like he's caught me by surprise—but I'm not sure if it worked or not.

"You going to Frances's tomorrow?"

Fact: If he is going to be there, then of course I'm going.

I stand up and casually sling my backpack over my shoulder as if I have to think about it. "I dunno. You?"

"Yeah." He pushes his blond bangs back, and I admire his natural tan. Talk about Tantastic—his picture should be on the bottle.

We stand there for a few awkward seconds while I nervously twirl a long strand of my hair, trying to remember the history question I thought of as a good icebreaker. Vance, on the other hand, casually adjusts the straps of his backpack. "You should go," he finally says.

Ohmotherofdrool. Forget the question. Is this a meet-me-at-the-party kind of date?

"I mmiigghhttt," I say as slowly as I can. Trina always says slow-talkers seem more in control.

"Great! I hope I'll see you there." He spins on the ball of his foot to leave, so I grab the opportunity to say something interesting.

"Whatdecadedidyougetinthehistoryproject?"

Too fast! Too fast!

He turns back around. "Umm . . . I didn't get all that. Huh?"

"Notthhing," I slur. "I'll see yyou at the parrtyy. Thatt souundds grreeaatt!"

"Cool," he says, then gives me a once-over, making me feel both sexy and self-conscious.

"Cool," I repeat, suddenly wondering how the heck I can pass that geometry test tomorrow. It'll be crucial to my being able to go to the party. Because, Lord knows, if I fail, Arch the Grade Nazi will ground me.

Later that day, on my way into the cafeteria, I run into Edwin again. We pick up some silverware and head toward the moving caterpillar that is the cafeteria line. As I walk beside him, I can smell him. It's a good smell—one that reminds me of Vance, or Luke: a musky combination of pine, sweat, and courage. I didn't expect the courage part, but it's definitely there. What detergent do these guys use? I smell the sleeve of my shirt, but it just smells flat—like bread or wood. I make a mental note to freshen up my closet. Maybe a hanging sachet? Or a Stellar perfume?

Pushing his tray forward, Edwin says, "I'm excited about that history project."

No wonder he and those brainy guys are friends. "Um, yeah. It's cool," I say. "But I have the twenties."

"Sweet. The Jazz Age!" He knocks out a quick beat with his silverware on the side of his plastic tray, making me chuckle.

"The Jazz Age? For real?"

He nods and picks up a chocolate milk.

"Nice. I was worried I'd have to write about the Depression."

"There was some of that Depression stuff building, but you don't have to focus on that for your report." Our eyes meet for a second before I pull mine away. His are green with brownish edges, reminding me of old velvet. For a minute it feels as if he can see clear through to my bones, and I suspect he knows about The Kiss.

"I think I'll have the salad bar," I say, certain that Sawyer has broken our pact. He must have, or why would Edwin look at me like that?

Two minutes later, after drowning my salad with rémoulade dressing, I head over to Trina.

"Geez louise. What's up with you?" she asks as soon as I sit down.

Is it that obvious?

"You're not sick again, are you? Did you fail something else?"

I raise my head and calmly lick my Perfect Score Pink lips before allowing a ginormous grin to explode across my face.

"What? What? You're worrying me."

"It's nothing." I take a bite of a cucumber. "Did you hear that Frances is having a party?"

"Sheesh, I thought someone had died or something."

"No. No death."

"You're not telling me something." The gears in her brain are clearly clicking away in diagnosis. "What's going on?"

I open my mouth to tell her, when all of a sudden, Frances herself appears, boobs blazing. And her perfume is so powerful I have to swallow to be able to use my mouth for breathing and seal my nostrils from the stench.

"Hey, y'all!" She sits down on the other side of the table and rearranges the food on her tray so that it's all nice and neat. "So, have you heard?" She begins wiping down her utensils with a napkin. "I'm having a party tomorrow. My parents are out of town."

"Mmm," Trina mumbles.

"I just heard about it," I say, then nudge Trina under the table with my knee.

Trina widens her eyes and says, "What?" but Frances keeps talking. "I just love February! A new semester is under way;

the weather makes me want to snuggle . . . so much promise."

"That's exactly what *I* think," Trina says, now scowling at *me* as if she and Frances know something I don't. "I've declared this year the Year of the Boy."

"That's genius!" Frances squeaks. "I'm in total agreement, but I'm calling it the Year of Vance Butcher." She pops the top of her soda with her long, fake French tips and takes a dainty sip while I cough and bang my chest with my fist. *Did she just say Vance? Frances Hudson has her sights set on Vance?*

"Are you okay, Emerson?" Trina leans over and smacks my back hard with the palm of her hand.

"Ow!" My eyes turn red and watery as I regain my composure.

"Vance does that to me, too." Frances laughs.

"Did you just say he asked you out?" I ask her. *Please say no. Please say no.*

"No," she says. "But I'm working on it. Oooh, look! There he is!"

Turning my head toward the table in the corner, I feel my stomach drop like the Gravitron ride at the Neshoba County Fair.

"Who is *that*?" Frances asks, staring at the new guy sitting between Luke and Vance.

"Hellooo there, handsome," Trina says, entranced. "It's Silas!"

Can this day get any worse?

"He's gorgeous!" Frances practically shouts.

Does he go to school here *now?* I wonder.

"Em? Can you believe it?" Trina gushes, struggling to breathe. "This *is* going to be the Year of the Boy after all."

Luke waves.

"Why is he *here*?" Trina continues, her eyes now glazing over. "He goes to Saint Joseph's, doesn't he?"

"You *know* him?" Frances asks in disbelief. "Who is he? He's so hot my eyes are burning."

"Step off, Frances," warns Trina, no doubt remembering seventh grade and their dual crush on Tommy Bartlett. "He's mine."

"Oh, fine," Frances says. "But who is he?"

He's the spawn of Voldemort, I want to say.

"That's Silas Martin," Trina coos before her head thunks the table.

Just kidding. Her head doesn't really thunk the table.

Mine does.

CHAPTER SEVEN

African Sun

Safely in my room at home, having rushed straight from lunch to the nurse's office, I lie back on my bed and try not to have a Nervy B.

Facts:

1. Fragranced Frances is out to ruin my most promising chance at love.
2. Silas Martin shows up midsemester like some kind of cruel ghost of Summers Past.
3. In faking sick and going home, I have skipped the very necessary geometry review, which means a D at best.
4. I kissed Sawyer. Enough said.

Hours later, something hard hits my butt. "Ow," I mumble.

"Are you okay?" Piper asks, picking her shoe up off my bed. "Trina said you left school early."

"What time is it?" I rub my eyes and roll over to look at my alarm clock.

"Five."

"Crap! I'm late for jazz!" I jump off the bed and open my top dresser drawer. The word *jazz* sizzles in my head. The Jazz Age . . .

"So what's wrong with you?" Piper asks.

"Nothing," I say. "I'm trying to figure out a way to get extra credit for school."

"You're gonna need it. Arch is downstairs on the computer right now."

I pull out a T-shirt. "I thought she had a party today!"

Piper shrugs. "She changed her plans."

"Ugh!" I shimmy down my jeans, then look under my bed for my leotard.

"Your room is disgusting," Piper says, curling her lip in revulsion.

"Whatever," I say. "See if you can find my shoes."

She walks over to the closet, sticks her toe in, and kicks my clothes around as if my closet is a murky lake full of piranhas. "Got any ideas to help your grades?" she asks.

"I'm not sure." I'm waist-deep under the bed now but can see one of my shoes. "But I got one idea for history. The Jazz Age has something to do with jazz, right?" I wriggle back out. "And I take jazz dance after school. Maybe I can get art credit or something just by taking lessons?"

"Mrs. Parker loves that sort of stuff."

"Exactly, right? She told me after class that I could get extra credit *if* I combine my topic with another class, and dance is an art. So . . ."

Piper finds my other shoe and throws it to me—but not before Arch enters my room. "Not so fast, Emerson. I just got a call from the school nurse." She walks into my room and shakes her head at the mess on my floor.

I pull out my bottom dresser drawer to put away my pants, but it sticks; and when I pull it harder, my favorite eye shadow trio crashes to the floor, shattering into a million brown and gold flecks all over the carpet. Reaching down, I pick up the plastic case that used to contain African Sun and feel water pressing at the backs of my eyes. African Sun is no longer available, and as inconsequential as it seems, it feels traumatic in that moment. I was going to wear it Friday night.

"I wasn't feeling well," I tell her. "Can we talk about this later? I'm already late for dance."

Arch shakes her head in disappointment. "Girls who play sick and cut school can't go to dance."

"What? I have to." I stuff my head inside a navy sweatshirt and grab my dance skirt. "I need the grade."

"What grades?" she asks calmly. "You don't have any grades worth mentioning according to my computer."

Can we please not go there right now?

"But I can get extra credit for my history project," I tell her while I regloss my lips. "I need to see if Ms. Alvis will let me do a dance or something for it." I look to Piper for help.

"It's gonna be awesome," she says, and I'm surprised she's being so nice.

But all of a sudden Arch gets up in my face, and I can see that her lovely red flush is not bronzer—it's flaming hot anger. *Yikes.*

"Have you forgotten our little talk? Either you improve your grades and act more responsibly or I am pulling you out of Haygood Academy."

"What?" Piper gasps.

"I know. I know." I feel intense panic building in my belly. Not now. Not after the love of my life has just sorta-kinda asked me out. "I promise I'm working on it. And this dance class will *improve* my grades." I make sure to heavily accent the word *improve*.

"How are you working on it?" Arch asks.

I clench my teeth. "I, uh . . . I'm going to study with some brainy people."

"That's what I thought. You haven't done a thing."

Leaning against the side of my closet, I cave into the waterfall that has been building behind my eyes. And at that exact moment, my phone rings.

"And I'll be taking that for the night, too," Arch says, walking over to my desk and picking up the phone. She looks at the screen. "Who's Vance?"

Vance is calling me!

"A boy," I reply.

"Not just any boy," Piper adds, giggling.

"No phone tonight," Arch says. "You need to get rid of distractions, young lady." She sighs and puts the only link to my boyfriend-to-be in her pocket. "Like I said, no boys, no dance, no nothing until these grades come up. And, by the way, you just failed your Spanish test. I checked online." She walks out of the room, and I drop my head in defeat.

This means no going to Frances's party.

After weeping on my bed for what feels like forever, it's clear that there's only one thing I can do: schoolwork. It seems like an easy thing, but I can assure you it's not. Schoolwork is a struggle for me—always has been. While Piper has sailed through school making nothing less than a B, I have to work my butt off just to keep a C. School just doesn't interest me. At all.

Opening my geometry textbook, I begin to study for the test tomorrow, praying I can stay awake long enough to learn it all. Numbers typically put me to sleep.

Something catches my eye on the right-hand side of the page: a long equation. I tilt my head, narrow my eyes, and carefully read the fine print in the column, then the entire page, and then the next one.

This can't be, I think. *I haven't read this before. I missed the review.*

And yet . . .

I know this. I KNOW this. I KNOW THIS!

"Oh, sweet Georgia Brown," I whisper, barely able to contain my excitement. This is the confetti of numbers I saw fly out of Sawyer's head. This is the vision. The sesame-noodled concoction I tasted this morning. The exact information that flooded into my mind when I kissed him.

Oh joy, joy, joy.

"I KNOW THIS!" I scream for joy. "I KNOW THIS!" I shout.

Standing now, I crank up my music and twirl around my room in excited circles, imagining the newer, smarter Emerson Taylor dancing around the school, surrounded by every brainy boy she knows. Numbers, formulas, and history dates are whizzing around their heads before falling like the snowflakes pictured on the Stellar cosmetics labels. Falling and landing gently inside her brain.

MY brain.

And as far as tomorrow goes, every last geometry fact is locked down tight.

In.

My.

Head.

All because of a kiss.

Holy mackerel, I'm gonna ace this test!

CHAPTER EIGHT

Super Red

The geometry test is laid out before me like the Look What's New section of the Stellar catalog. I understand *everything*! So *this* is what it feels like to be smart. No wonder the Ivys love it so much.

Dr. Cox puts on some classical music, probably thinking it will motivate us. I have to give him props, because it does. Maybe it's helping me envision the flash mob of Ivys again, twirling around me in glorious, number-filled circles. I can't believe this! I have to breathe deeply just to keep myself from giggling all the way through the test. *Why don't I ever see Edwin laughing his way through tests?* I wonder. *Or the English whiz, Grady?* It's true: knowledge really *is* power.

Who knew?

After answering a few more questions, it strikes me that I've never done this well on a test, or anything that's judged, for that matter. Not even in a dance performance. I can never nail perfection. There's always room to improve. But here?

It's black or white. Right or wrong. And today it's right, baby! I know every last answer. This is insane. I feel as though I might scream. Or sing the "Hallelujah Chorus."

Ten minutes later, with more time to kill than imaginable, I glance over at Oliver Foreign-Language-Loving Magee. He is furiously writing. Edwin is, too. Wow, I'm almost finished even before any of the geeky guys. As I continue to scan around the room, Sawyer catches my eye and winks.

Yikes. My high is immediately reversed, and that feeling comes over me again—the bad one. The one that makes me wish I was Catholic and could go to confession. Or at least rub some beads or something.

"Emerson?" Dr. Cox motions for me to keep my eyes on my paper.

I smile apologetically and turn the page to look at the last section of formulas.

After writing the first answer in the blank, I quickly scan the rest.

Piece o' cake.

"Ten more minutes!" Dr. Cox shouts.

I look back at the questions and feel a strange new form of adrenaline kick in. Ducking my head, I ignore the awful feeling that I've stolen these answers and get to business finishing this thing with flair.

Take that, geometry beast!

Sawyer approaches my desk. "Hey, you."

"Hi." I try not to look him in the eyes. I don't want to lead him on or anything.

He clears his throat "You, uh . . . I just . . . What I'm trying to say is, if you need to practice some more, that's cool with me. I mean . . ." He doesn't know how to have this conversation any better than I do, and he begins to rock back and forth on his feet.

"Thanks," I say, packing up. "I'll think about it." I press my lips together and smile at him, grateful for the gift of his knowledge and sorry about the way I got it. Next time I'll pick someone I don't know at all, like Oliver. Kissing Ivys may not be my proudest achievement, but it's genius. Operation Liplock is going to be about way more than practice kissing. And if I apply myself, I won't have to do it for very long.

Suddenly, I'm struck with the urge to tell Trina about it, but there's no way. She'd never understand. This must be what Peter Parker feels like. Supercool superhero trapped in a web of silence.

Speaking of Trina, she has texted me no less than seven times with things like:

I love Silas <3

Silas turns me on.

Silas just smiled at me. Swoon...

Have you seen my juicy boyfriend today cuz he's hawt!

Ew. Talk about obsession. And I thought Frances was bad, pretending her pencils were making out in middle school.

Leaving class, the front-office secretary sticks her head out into the hallway and asks if I'll take a letter to Mr. Wheeler in the music room.

"Why sure," I say from my new perch on cloud nine.

Pretty music spills out of the band room and flows down the hallway like a peaceful stream. Although I always hear the music, today I want to take a sip, drink in the sounds, and savor my geometry victory like sweet wine. That sounds goofy, but I feel as if I have heightened senses or something. Everything sounds better, feels sharper, looks clearer.

Seriously. Why read books when you can read minds?

Mr. Wheeler is not here, so I look around for the best place to put the envelope. There's a metal music stand in the corner that looks like as good a place as any, so I walk toward it and lay down the note before picking up the conductor's stick. Slicing it through the air, I pretend to conduct pretty music like a goofy band person. What if I kissed some fabulously talented musician? Would I be able to play an instrument?

The possibilities are endless. I am so clearly under the influence of my new drug, it's insane.

"You have talent," Edwin says from the doorway.

Instantly mortified, I put down the stick and suppress an awkward giggle.

"Are you going to join us?" he continues, walking into the room.

"Nope." I hold up my hands as if to surrender. "I can't play anything."

He is wearing a black T-shirt with SIT DOGGY, SIT written on it. Judging by the picture, it's probably some random band that guys like him listen to. His jeans are faded and have a few holes in the thigh region—the kind of jeans girls now call "the boyfriend" and pay hundreds of dollars for. But his look is genuine, and I wonder what he's been doing to produce thigh holes. Holding one of those massive violin things between them?

"I bet you could if you tried," he says, getting a little bit too close to me.

My cheeks flush. "I don't think so." I start walking toward the door, thinking about the fact that he's one of *them*— an Ivy. What if I kissed him? What would I learn? Spanish? English? Math? Thigh-holing techniques?

"Wait." He walks over to me, bringing his clean, warm scent

and noticeably awesome boots with him. "You're leaving?"

"I . . ." I'm realizing that I am strangely attracted to him. But that can't be because Edwin and I have nothing in common and ninety percent of me thinks he's a nerd. But the other ten percent wonders if this is what it feels like when werewolves imprint? Very strange, I assure you. Must be due to the heightened-senses thing.

"I was just dropping a note off for Mr. Wheeler," I tell him.

The left side of his mouth raises in a small smile. "Come here. I want to show you something." He walks past me toward the windows, and I follow. *What am I doing?*

He waits for me to get close, then walks over to a stereo in the corner and hands me some oversized headphones like the guys who direct airplanes wear—the soundproof kind.

"Put these on," he instructs.

"What am I going to hear?" I take the headphones from him.

"You'll see." He picks up an identical pair, and we put them on. Then he reaches over and pushes some buttons on the stereo. A cool tune slides out of the stereo and into my ears. It's mellow and groovy, and I feel myself sink into relaxation mode.

He looks at me without speaking. I'm not really sure what to do or how to proceed; but before I can decide, he reaches over and lightly brushes my face. Whoa. A thousand hairs on my arms stand on end, and I instinctively pull back a little.

He glares at me as if to say *Trust me, silly!* then touches my eyelids in an effort to close them.

This feels mega strange, but I obey and close my eyes, totally and completely hypnotized by this boy.

After T minus two seconds, I open my eyes again and look at him. His long, black eyelashes are resting on his face, spread out like a mascara advertisement. Beautiful. I'm not sure I've ever been this close to a boy without kissing him, and that's only happened twice; so this is beyond butterfly inducing. It's like squirrels are jumping around inside my rib cage.

I notice that his sandy-brown hair is shorter than it used to be but still kinda shaggy. I always thought he looked like he had bedhead, but now I can see that it's just adorably wavy. *Did I just say* adorably? *THIS IS BAND MAN, EMERSON! SNAP OUT OF IT!*

And then, with a flutter, his eyes are open.

And locked onto mine.

We freeze for a moment before he smiles and mouths the word *"Jazz."*

"Oh," I mouth back. "Perfect." And although I mean the song is perfect for the dance I plan on asking my teachers about, I'm suddenly worried he might think I meant something else entirely. *"Cooool,"* I add, glad I didn't try to kiss him.

Now his eyes are closed again, and he's moving his head with the beat. I watch in half amazement, half horror. I can't decide if he's the weirdest loser I know or actually kind of wonderful. But just then something shifts in my peripheral vision, and I turn around.

Luke, Vance, and Silas are all standing in the doorway, laughing. Just seeing them shocks me back into the reality that I am madly in love with Vance—not this Edwin guy. *What am I doing? Oh no!*

Ripping off the headphones, I run my hand through my messed-up hair.

"What are y'all doing?" Vance asks. I can't tell if he's mocking us or just genuinely confused. But all I can think is, *Why can't I go to Frances's party? Why? WHY!*

Edwin calmly takes off his headphones and looks up at

them. His peaceful gaze hardens into a protective shield.

"Nothing," I say, avoiding Silas's eyes while projecting my best puppy dog eyes at Vance.

"It doesn't look like nothing," Luke says.

Dammit, Luke.

I head for the door, unsure what to do.

"Ace! Wait!" Turning around, I can see that Luke and the guys are following me. No sooner do I make eye contact with Silas than I am hit again with the vision from his kiss two years ago. "Remember my friend, Silas?" Luke asks.

I toss back my hair. *Do I remember him? Um, yes!*

"Emerson?"

I grunt and stand still, feeling as if I might implode in front of all of them. And Silas, of course fully aware that we've met, looks at me as though he wants to eat me or something. I can smell the heady scent of something I can't quite name, like a tropical berry that lures you in with its beauty only to poison you minutes after you pop it in your mouth. Hot or not, he creeps me out.

"Silas," Luke begins. "This is Emerson."

"Nice to see you again," I play along, ready to get to my next class.

"The pleasure's all mine," he says, smiling wickedly while the pigment in my Super Red blush drains from my face.

CHAPTER NINE

Shock Me, Stop Me

As I pull into the driveway, Mrs. Wilson rushes out onto her front porch wearing an orange muumuu with a yellow towel wrapped around her head. "Emerson! Emerson, sugar! Can you come here?"

"Ma'am?" I ask, walking toward her. Her eyes are darting around like she's just escaped prison, and I wonder what she's gotten herself into this time.

"Pumpkin, I've gone and done something real bad." She continues to look around nervously.

"Oh no," I say.

She leans forward and slowly unwinds one side of her turban to reveal a stringy mess of PINK hair. We're talking Cotton Candy Confection—a perfect spring color for *nails*, not hair.

"Oh, wow!" I say in shock. "That's not good."

"Not good? Child, it's awful!" She peers around me and looks across the street in search of Arch's blueberry car.

"It's . . . ," I start.

"It's pink, baby. There's no hiding it. Lord, help me. I was going for auburn, but something went wrong. And I can't possibly go up to the salon like this. It's Friday, and half my bridge club is in there on Fridays." She exhales a frustrated poof of air. "What on earth is Mr. Wilson going to say when he sees it?"

I smile. I may not be able to solve most science problems, but a beauty dilemma I can fix. "Hold on," I tell her. "I'm sure we can fix this."

"Really?" she asks. "I've got to work at the antique store tomorrow. And there's no way in you-know-what that I'm going to show up looking like some kind of pink oompa loompa."

"Come on," I tell her, grabbing her hand and leading her across the street. "Arch isn't home yet, but I think I saw some hair-stripping shampoo in her closet. Ladies turn their hair blue all the time. I'm sure this is the same."

"You're the best, doodlebug."

Piper is in the kitchen snacking on cheese straws when we walk in. "Whoa there!"

"Don't you say anything, Piperoni. I'm well aware of my condition," Mrs. Wilson says.

They crack up, and I head to Arch's closet and locate the hair-stripping shampoo. A dorky hat with earflaps catches my eyes, and I bring it out just in case.

"Here ya go," I say, handing her the bottle. "I think this'll do the trick. But you're still gonna need to put some color back in it." I hand her the hat. "And you can wear this if you need to go to the store."

She hugs me and giggles while putting the earflap hat on

for her walk back across the street. "What would I do without you girls?"

"You'd rock pink hair," Piper says with a chuckle.

"Yeah. Maybe I'd finally get to be in a *real* rock band," she jokes while strumming an air guitar.

A few hours later I'm sitting on a stool in the bathroom watching Piper get ready for Frances's party. "Make sure you tell Vance I'm sick or something," I say. "But not anything gross like throwing up," I add. "Just say I have a headache."

"Gotcha."

"I'm worried he's going to start dating Frances before I really have a chance to . . . you know, be around him."

"There is no way he'd ever choose Frances over you," she assures me. "And if he did, he's crazy."

"Thanks." I sigh, rearranging our makeup drawer for lack of anything else to do. "So are you going with anyone?"

She brushes some powder across her face. "Kinda."

Reaching over, I pick up the flatiron, feeling the sudden urge to straighten my hair. "What do you mean, 'kinda'?"

Piper stops and looks at me. "Can you keep a secret?"

"I guess so."

Digging around in a drawer, she finds her Shock Me, Stop Me blush and runs her Kabuki brush across it. I admire the brush's short, chunky shape. I need to get one of those.

"I sorta have a date." She blows on the top of the brush before freshening up her already-glowing cheeks. "But I'm not ready for anyone to know about it yet." She smiles at herself in the mirror, pleased with her appearance.

"Who?" I ask, taking another long strand of my hair and searing it flat.

She stops and looks at me with the same excitement she displays when she's made a new dress she wants to show off. "Promise you won't tell."

"I promise."

She goes on. "I don't want anyone to know yet. It's still new, and I don't want to jinx it."

"I promise I won't tell. Now who?"

"Silas Martin."

"But he's Trina's crush!" *And he's evil!*

The charred smell of something fills the bathroom, and I recall the flaming vision of Silas's obsession with fire. *I didn't hear her right. Surely my own sister isn't dating that creep. Surely . . .*

"Emerson!" Piper shouts. "You're burning your hair!"

Staring in the mirror, I see the flatiron in my paralyzed hand twisted around a smoking chunk of my hair. I watch Piper grab the iron and pull it out of my hair while shouting at me in a bizarre sort of slow motion. Then Arch runs into the room, no doubt summoned by our screams. In the mirror, I see my mouth spew a string of curses as long as the bathroom counter. Words are flying out like a swarm of angry bees. I can see all of this happening, but I can't hear a thing.

An hour later, with a blue hair masque saturating my scalp, I feel as far away from Vance and that party as I am from the Australian Outback. Arch grounded me further to my room (thanks to all the cussing), so I'm stuck in here, staring blankly at my textbooks, imagining Vance hanging on Frances's every word, his arm around her shoulder, and later putting his lips to hers instead of to mine.

Damn my stupid grades.

Arch is totally overreacting about all this grade stuff.

I mean, I aced that geometry test today, and she knows it. But at this point, I'm more concerned about Piper dating Silas than about my grades. What is she thinking? And as if *that* isn't enough to worry about, Piper made me promise I wouldn't tell Trina. *Oh, the injustice!*

The clock on my bedside table reads 9:16. When will this night end? The TV beckons me, and I finally cave in to whatever reality show might be on. I still can't believe I am sitting here on a Friday night prohibited from partying.

A commercial for Budweiser comes on after an ad for *So You Think You Can Dance* and then it hits me. I know *exactly* how to get extra credit for my twenties project, and it's so durn brilliant that I rush downstairs to impress Arch.

Holy smokes! Arch isn't watching a *Seinfeld* marathon, a Lifetime movie, or even a *Hoarders* episode like I'd assumed she was. She is standing in the kitchen amid *hundreds* of shiny blue gift bags. HUNDREDS. There are boxes of lip gloss samples, gobs of miniature mascaras, loads of body butter samples, and a gazillion fragrance vials all scattered across the kitchen counters.

"Why didn't you ask me to help you?" I almost beg. "I love making these!" I walk over and start taking samples out of each box and putting them into the bags, being sure to withhold a few for my pockets.

"I thought you were sick," she says, pretending to pat the blue masque on my head.

"Not anymore," I say. The healing power of Stellar makeup fills the room with promise, and I rake my fingers through the box of mascaras, feeling the tiny tubes play against my fingers. "Who are these for?"

"I have a couple of big parties coming up. What have you been doing?"

"School stuff." I prepare to wow her with my genius. "Wasn't Prohibition that thing that happened in the twenties?"

She lights up, amazed that I've really been studying upstairs. "Yes. Yes, it did. It gave rise to the speakeasy."

"Wait. What's that?" I ask.

She hands me a stack of small bags, and I get to work loading them with samples.

"It was an illegal nightclub," she explains. "In the twenties, alcohol was prohibited, which made people mad, so they created nightclubs where they could sneak in alcohol and dance their stress away."

I think about how *her* prohibition of my partying is bothering me. *Let it go,* I tell myself. "Okay, good. That's what I thought. So jazz was there, huh?"

"Yes." She drops a tiny paper square of eye shadow into a gift bag and looks at me with curiosity.

"*That's* why I need to go to my dance class, Arch." A warmth courses through my body at the sheer brilliance of this idea. "I want to do something with my jazz class for the best extra credit project Mrs. Parker has ever seen. I want to choreograph a dance as if it happened in one of those speakeasy things."

She smiles. "That is really smart, Emerson. Really, *really* smart. Why didn't you tell me that the other night?"

"I tried, but I hadn't totally figured it out yet. It's great, right?"

"Absolutely!" She sets down her bag. "Come here. Let me take your temperature. You seemed warm when I felt your face after the hair scorching." She gently touches her lips to my forehead.

"I think you're good," she says, as if taking temperatures with lips is the most normal thing in the world.

I put down the samples and look at her. "Why do you always do it like that? Most moms use one of their hands."

"I don't know." She drops a handful of mascaras across five bags. "I guess when you girls were little I was always kissing your foreheads, and I just learned to sense your body temperature through my lips. It's the only way I can tell. Same as your mother."

"My *mother* did it this way?"

She stuffs another bag. "Mmm-hmm. I used to watch her when you girls were itty-bitty."

Her comment makes me wonder if her sensory lip thing is somehow related to mine, so I ask her, "Can you do anything else weird with your lips?"

She laughs. "Like what?"

"I dunno. Can you *tell* anything else with just your lips?"

She thinks for a minute and then says, "Your mother used to claim she could read a person's mind in a kiss."

WHAT?! I drop the little blue bag I'm holding like a stick of dynamite and calmly ask, "What did you say?"

"I said, she claimed she could read a person's mind in a kiss." Arch chuckles in a can-you-believe-how-crazy-that-sounds kind of way. Then she looks at me, and her face falls. Sparks are probably shooting out of my chest.

"You look a bit shocked, baby. Why don't you sit down?"

Little does she know.

"Your mom was sick, Emerson. You know that. We tried to help her, but in the end we couldn't. It was her own decision."

I grasp my chest, half expecting to feel a visible hole from the bomb she just dropped. *Is this thing genetic? Will it kill me, too?*

"I used to tease her that it must be from that lipstick she insisted on wearing all the time. You know the one? You have it now—the brownish one? Sunrise, Sunset?"

I know the one, all right. I've kept it in my bedside table drawer like an old photo.

I nod, and Arch continues. "I never dreamed she was serious. That she really *believed* what she was saying. Not until later anyway, and by then it was too late to save her." She looks away in sadness, and I don't know what to say. If I tell her that I can do it, too, she'll panic. Take me out of Haygood for sure. Probably commit me to an insane asylum for fear I'll kill myself just like my mother did.

"I will always miss her," Arch says, putting down a bag and looking at me with sad, soulful eyes. "But it does us no good to focus on the negative." She goes back to stuffing her little bags while I silently pray that kissing won't make me as crazy as Mama. Was *kissing* the cause of all her problems?

Poor Mama. She confessed her secret, and no one believed her. I can't even imagine how horrible that would be.

Hours later—3 a.m. to be exact—I am *still* awake. And so hot I can't sleep. I think back to that day when Mama ran past me to our old car and the brown, cracked tube of Sunrise, Sunset lipstick fell out. It haunts me. Unable to bear it anymore, I roll over and mentally retrieve a happier memory of Mama—one of the hundreds I've seen in Arch's mind since that day. When Arch and Mama found some kittens in the woods behind their house, Mama was always singing to the little white one as she walked around, rocking it in her arms. I try to remember the song but give up and focus on one memory of Mama baking. According to Arch, my mother loved to cook, and it's clear from Arch's memories that Mama knew her way around the kitchen. It was the one place she felt in control, creative, and at peace.

Finally, I feel better and decide to study. I want to give my English homework my best effort. Sitting up, I get out of bed and walk over to my desk. After turning on my lamp, I pick up the novel we've been assigned and read a few paragraphs while the sun rises. My heart sinks. By paragraph two I know I'm in trouble. I don't comprehend what I'm reading without backtracking twenty times. It's beyond boring—horribly dull. And I have a quiz on it in two days. If I bomb this one, Arch will never let me go out with Vance, and there's still the chance she'll pull me out of school altogether.

At that thought, my mind is overrun with everything I have to do: the dance routine, the project paper, the tests. Oh, all the tests. They fly into my brain like a murder of crows, feeding on my sanity and confirming that I just can't do this alone.

I *can't*.

I need my lips.

CHAPTER TEN

Red Pepper

"I missed you," Vance tells me before first period Monday morning. He is wearing a thick black North Face jacket, looking super handsome and huggable.

"You did?" I feel my cheeks bloom as red as my Red Pepper supergloss while he leans against the wall outside our chemistry class.

"Mmm-hmm."

He missed me! Seven thousand birds sing "He missed me!" in my head as I race to think of something cute to say. "I was sick" is my winning reply.

"Yeah, your sister told me. It was no big deal. You didn't miss anything."

I nod and practice being normal, which is harder than it should be. For some reason talking to him feels artificial, like I'm interviewing for a job or something. But I guess I am—the job of his girlfriend.

"Cool," I add, frustrated by my total lack of vocabulary.

My chemistry teacher, Dr. Allen, is old-school. He has been teaching for a hundred years and is a strong believer in memorization. He assigns tons of homework, makes his classes take loads of notes, and has frequent oral pop quizzes. In other words, his class sucks. But suck or not, it's one I need to master for Project Grade Domination.

I walk into the room, still enjoying my little love hangover, only to notice that the one remaining open seat is right in between Edwin and Oliver, the straight-A, foreign-language-loving video gamer I've been eyeing for a potential kiss. (He's in my Spanish class, too, which is a subject of concern this week.) Vance is seated in the back, forcing me to spend the next two minutes trying to make sure my back looks perfect. I smooth down my hair, my sweater, my pants, and anything else that might be out of place before deciding I am a lunatic and Vance is probably not staring at my back as if it is his favorite sitcom.

"Hey," Edwin says warmly. I smile at him, letting myself linger on his eyes a millisecond too long. I almost have Vance's boy-friendly attention, and here I am staring at a brainy boy. I know I have to kiss more Ivys to ace my classes, but still. . . .

"Emulsions," Dr. Allen begins, and not a minute too late.

I quickly start turning pages in my textbook before glancing over at Oliver's book to see what page we're on.

"Emulsions are significantly stable suspensions of particles of liquid. They are of a certain size within a second, immiscible liquid."

W.T.H.? Rewind! I feel my pen start to doodle, and my bad side is already thinking about who I can kiss this information out of.

"They are widely used in industry, car polish, skin lotions, and personal care products, as well as in pharmaceutical applications."

I write down the words *Emulsions—found in skin lotion and personal care products*. Now *that* I can remember.

"Does anyone know what is needed to make an emulsion?" Dr. Allen asks us.

Mallory, a quiet girl in the back, raises her hand, and I turn around to listen. Vance catches my eye and smiles at me.

"Water, oils, waxes, or emulsifying agents," she says.

"Excellent, Miss Davis!" Dr. Allen says, then writes another formula on the board. "When an emulsion breaks, it separates into an oil phase and an aqueous phase. Does anyone remember what *aqueous* means?"

"Water," says Oliver.

So Oliver's good with chemistry, too. Nice to know.

"Well done, Mr. Magee. Water."

I write this down in my notebook next to the puffy heart (with a *V* in it) that I drew there absentmindedly.

"So then, what factors affect an emulsion's stability?" the teacher asks.

Edwin slowly leans back in his seat and raises his hand.

"Mr. McNeely?"

He takes the pencil he's been chewing out of his mouth and casually says, "Uh . . . temperature, properties, pH, viscosity."

"Right. And can anyone give me an example of an emulsion being affected like this?"

I look down at my notes and mutter, "Yeah. Like when my lip gloss separates if I leave it in my car all day."

"What did you say, Miss Taylor?" Dr. Allen asks.

I raise my head in complete embarrassment. "Nothing."

"No," he says. "I think you mentioned your lip gloss and heat?"

I nod my head sheepishly.

"Great example!" He goes to write on the board. "Miss Taylor deduced that some types of lip gloss must be emulsions because when they get hot, they separate into two messy liquids."

I straighten up. Maybe this isn't as hard as I thought. I raise my hand. "Is that why beeswax makes a better base than, umm"—I flip some pages—"petroleum?"

"Yes! Yes, Miss Taylor! You are correct."

I smile awkwardly at the teacher, and Oliver nods in approval.

However, that's my only moment of genius. Forty-seven semiconfusing minutes later, I feel drained and more determined than ever to kiss a nerd. And, with Vance walking around in a sexy polar fleece, blabbing about missing me at Frances's dumb party, I had better get my head in the game.

CHAPTER ELEVEN

Fish Lips

Grady "Fish" Cromwell is the goobiest Ivy in the entire school. Just his nickname makes me squirmy, especially since I have no idea what it refers to. Fish lips? Fish breath? Fishy smell? But marine life aside, he has the highest GPA in every subject he takes. One of which is English with me. So, fishy or not, he's the perfect person to kiss in order to understand the novel I started last night.

I find him sitting in his usual spot on the tattered green sofa inside study hall right after lunch, looking seriously nerdy. In addition to some new rose-gold, rimmed glasses reminiscent of my late Grandma Ethel, he has on a T-shirt with the cover of a Charles Dickens novel on it. Where he finds these things, I will never know.

Placing myself strategically to his left, I sit down, pull out a book, and wait for an opportune moment to ask him for help. I am close enough to decide that he doesn't smell fishy, and his lips look normal.

"S'up?" he asks, smelling instead of licorice and innocence. He pushes his glasses proudly up his nose. "Did you hear the news?"

"No. What?"

He leans over and whispers as if we're all in some kind of secret society. "Microwaves."

Before I have a chance to ask him what "microwaves" mean, or even bat my eyelashes flirtatiously, Trina walks up and totally ruins the moment. "Eww," she says. "Why are you sitting on this thing? It's as old as the hills and smells like feet."

I glance over at Fish, still in his spot on the sofa. Much to my surprise, he is staring at Trina, his pupils morphing into visible hearts.

"No it doesn't," I say, leaning down to sniff the battered sofa arm. "Okay. Maybe it does, but it's supercomfy. Have a seat. Fish was just telling me something."

Trina wrinkles her nose, takes a seat, and instinctively begins bathing her hands in hand sanitizer, apparently horrified to be so close to Fish without some sort of germ barrier.

"Microwaves," he repeats louder, looking around to make sure no one else is listening.

I wait for him to tell us how he has discovered that microwaves are faster than television waves or something equally scientific, but he just licks his lips and adds, "In the cafeteria."

"Huh?" Trina is clearly annoyed and shifting uncomfortably in her seat.

"We can use them now." He kisses his fingers in a distinctly *Bon Appetit*-ish kind of way. "I just enjoyed a *warm* Pop-Tart with my lunch."

Trina flashes me eyes that say, *Why did you start talking to him? Now he's gonna want to talk to us all period.* But I'm fired up. "Microwaves? Really?"

"I thought you were talking about electromagnetic radiation," Trina says with an air of know-it-all-ness.

I start laughing that she even *knows* those words, but Grady's lips are spread across his face like the adoring words on a birthday cake. "No, but there is a section on that in the decathlon manual." His heart-shaped eyes remain big and excited.

Trina looks bored out of her tree.

"Tomorrow I'll be dining on steaming Hot Pockets, and next Monday"—he raises his eyebrows and tilts his head—"I've arranged a little feast."

I chuckle. "A feast?" Heaven knows what *that* involves. "Of Pop-Tarts and Hot Pockets?"

"Don't judge," he says. "It's a microwaveable Thanksgiving. Like Christmas in July—we're doing Thanksgiving in February. Oliver is bringing mashed potatoes, Edwin's in charge of the turkey—which is really just some chicken fingers from KFC. And I was thinking about something green."

"Chevron green beans?" I suggest. Our gas station has a kick-ass hot-lunch bar. I'm not kidding—it's been written up in several magazines.

Trina rolls her eyes. She's not a fan.

"Brilliant!" he gushes. "You want in?" He points his finger at us. "You two can be in charge of microwaveable cheese dip and chips."

"I guess Thanksgiving wouldn't be Thanksgiving without cheese dip and chips," I say, trying not to laugh.

"My thoughts exactly." He reaches down and unzips his backpack. "We'll do it again next month. A Thanksgiving every month. It *is* my favorite holiday, after all."

Trina is making faces at me now and itching her arms.

He continues to stare at her. "So, what's new with you?"

"Silas Martin," she says flatly.

Oh, Trina. Give him a break.

Grady bites his lip, and I can only imagine what he's thinking. "Silas is a jerk."

My thoughts exactly. Hmm . . . maybe these Ivys aren't as bad as I thought.

"What do *you* know?" Trina says, standing up to leave. She is being so rude that it's almost making me mad. But at the same time I completely understand her view of Grady. It used to be mine, too.

Grady looks down awkwardly before shifting his attention to me. "Have you finished *The Canterbury Tales* yet?"

"No. You?"

"I just finished. It was impressive."

Impressively boring, I'm thinking.

"I'm going to get that magazine for Arch out of my car," Trina says, totally ignoring Grady. "You wanna come?"

"I'll be there in a minute."

After she leaves, Grady looks at me. "I shouldn't have said that, huh?"

"Maybe not."

"I know some guys who go to Saint Joseph's. He used to hide their clothes every time they had PE."

"Yeah," I say, all too familiar with the inner workings of Silas.

"He's an ass," he adds, opening the novel on his lap.

I'm trying to listen to him but my thoughts begin to merge into this icky mess of compassion and grade lust. Subconsciously, I run my tongue across my teeth almost tasting how sweet it will be not to read that awful book.

Grady moves his finger down the page while I nervously scan the room. The proctor is leaning over a desk helping a girl with her homework, and a group of three boys is working on something in the far corner. This covert kissing thing is far riskier than I would have thought. I feel like some kind of undercover operative seeking answers in a foreign war zone full of enemy soldiers. Gotta watch out for a gossip bomb, too.

Just thinking about the horror of having someone discover my mission makes it hard to breathe. What would Trina or Luke say if they found out I sucked face with Fish?

My phone vibrates, and I shriek in terror. I was so focused on bombs and war zones that I thought a bomb went off in my pocket.

"Are you okay?" Fish asks.

I burst out laughing from the sheer stress of it all. "Yeah. My phone."

He smiles. "You have to be careful with those things."

Looking down, I see a text from Trina. u need rescuing from Micro-Grady. Say it's ur aunt and u have to go.

"Sorry about that," I tell him. *I'm running out of time.* Before rational thought can take over, I say, "Can I kiss you?" And then, before he can respond, I lean over and kiss him hard on the lips, reassuring myself that Europeans do this all the time and it means nothing.

My eyes are open and he blushes, turning so purple that he looks like an eggplant with glasses.

I feel at least half of the novel's plot lock down inside my cerebellum as the pain takes over.

"Are you okay?" he asks, jaw gaping and pulling away from me. He practically falls off the couch.

I hold my hand up to let him know I hear him while trying to swallow the aftertaste—it's especially convoluted, making me cough. My ear is pounding. But it was worth it. I mean, good gracious, I could have *never* read and understood that one alone.

"Emerson?"

I ignore him and scan the room. Free and clear. No one saw it. Standing up, I put my phone in my purse, then sling my bag over my shoulder. "I'm fine. I have to go."

"Wait!" he says, inching forward. "Why did you kiss me?"

I shove my tongue into the gap between my back molars and think.

Leaning even farther forward on the sofa, he silently waits for my answer.

"I . . . uh." I don't know what to say. *I am sick and need your help in English? Kissing you is easier than reading? I have a superpower I'm practicing? I'm like a kissing vampire who needed to suck on your mind?*

I settle on "I'm just really sorry about Silas. You're way nicer."

"Wow. Thanks." He awkwardly settles back into the sofa and adjusts his glasses, which are now resting rather crookedly on his nose. "Do you think you might feel like kissing me again someday soon? Like maybe this weekend?"

Oh boy. I'm flattered by his attention but also sickened by it. "I don't think so, Grady." And then I flee the scene like the traitor I am.

CHAPTER TWELVE

Pleased as Punch

As the week goes on I keep waiting for someone to find out about my dirty little business, but no one does. Those Ivys sure can keep a secret. Just in case, though, I decide that the safest way to proceed is to get organized, and no one is better at this than Piper. So I adopt her fail-proof method of "charting." Twenty-four hours later I have little chart of my own:

OPERATION LIPLOCK
Grady: English
   (good with novels—reads a lot)
Martin: English backup (try for poetry)—
   good with history, too
Sawyer: Chemistry and geometry
   (in lab before first period)
Malcolm: Geometry backup
Oliver: Spanish and chemistry
   (teacher's pet)

Juan: Spanish backup
Edwin: History
    (knows about Jazz Age)

Too bad all this charting takes away from the time I should be studying.

❦

Ms. Alvis agreed to let me work at the studio, choreographing a jazz dance for a group of eight little girls. But Arch has now decided that since I came up with such a creative way to improve my twenties project, I must have the potential to be as wonderfully innovative in the rest of my subjects. She has all but decorated the house with math symbols and English quotations in an effort to create an intellectually stimulating environment.

She's so happy with my geometry and English grades that on Tuesday she hangs a banner over the stove that says, COURAGE DOESN'T ALWAYS ROAR. SOMETIMES COURAGE IS THE QUIET VOICE AT THE END OF THE DAY SAYING, "I WILL TRY AGAIN TOMORROW."

On Wednesday she gets up bright and early to make pancakes in the shapes of trapezoids and rhombuses. And on Thursday she begins playing classical music at breakfast. This is after she placed a sticky note on my mirror that says, "Every accomplishment starts with the decision to try." I swear, with all this pressure, the house feels as if it might spontaneously combust.

But the low point of the week is reached when I stop by Piper's locker Friday afternoon, and Silas and I have this weird little conversation.

Piper is nowhere in sight, but Silas is standing next to her locker, beaming his tall, dark, and handsome all over the place. "You're looking mighty sexy today, Emerson."

Sexy? No one's ever called me sexy before, and I feel myself swoon a little before hating myself. *THIS IS THE GUY YOUR SISTER'S DATING, YOUR BEFFIE'S CRUSH, AND AN UNCONVICTED ARSONIST!*

I think my hair is standing on end.

He points to my skirt, tilts his head, and smirks. "You should lend that skirt to your sister this weekend. Or maybe your lipstick."

Ew. He is truly disgusting. However, I'm happy to know Pleased as Punch is such a great color on me.

"Cat got your tongue?" he asks, forcing me to speak. But speaking isn't happening. My words have left me, leaving me in a puddle of lost syllables. This is worse than with Vance. *Say something, idiot!*

Reaching over, he holds both of my shoulders and presses me against Piper's locker. I wonder if he's about to kiss me again, and my pulse quickens. *Does he remember our first kiss? Would he dare? Why is he doing this?*

"Let me help you." He leans over and whispers in my ear, and I can smell his strong scent: a musky combination of wood, moss, and lust. "You were saying, 'Silas, I want you.'"

I take a step sideways—more like a trip—and remind my eyes to stay in their sockets. Who does he think he is?

"I'm just kidding, Emerson." He laughs and lets go of my shoulders.

I reach up to rub my shoulders, struggling to think, to relax, to figure out what he is saying. Is he kidding? Or not? Is he flirting with me?

"Piper?" I squeak out. "Have you seen her?"

"Nope." He shifts his weight and grips the straps of his backpack with both hands.

"If you see her, can you tell her I need her?"

The corner of his mouth raises in a sly smile. "Anything for you."

Anything? What does anything *mean?*

When Piper finds me later, I am still wondering if I should tell her about my conversation with Silas. I decide, yes. She needs to know.

"So," I begin casually. "I saw Silas earlier, and I think he was flirting with me." I laugh nervously and chew on the inside of my cheek.

"You're kidding, right?"

I shake my head. "Not really. It was pretty sick. He said I looked sexy and should lend you *my* clothes. As if." I force a giggle before adding, "What a jerk."

She stops walking. "What did you just say?"

"I said, he said you should borrow my skirt." I point down to the skirt in question.

"No. After that."

I tilt my head in thought but then remember. "He's a jerk?" I bare my teeth in an I'm sorry? kind of way. Bad word choice, I guess. But he is!

She shakes her head. "I should have known you'd pull something like this. You're such a little wannabe. I can't believe you, Emerson! You're just jealous."

"Jealous? Of Silas? I am not! I hate him," I say. "He's such a dick."

"Whatever, Emerson. Stay away from my boyfriend."

Great. So now he's her *boyfriend.*

CHAPTER THIRTEEN

Melon Madness

Piper's words ring in my ears as I skid around the corner. I can't stand it when she's mad at me—especially when I've clearly done nothing wrong. But . . . maybe I'm overreacting. I'm sure Silas was just kidding. He had to be, right? As I pass through the senior hall, I realize I've been way too concerned about kissing boys lately. It's time I focus on someone else for a change: my sister.

Piper's adviser, Mr. Bondurant, opens his door within seconds of my knock. He is the tallest man in the school and makes me feel like an ant in his presence. "Helloooo, Emerson," he booms down at me. "How can I help you?"

"Actually," I squeak, "I was hoping *I* could help *Piper*." I silently wonder if this is a stupid idea. "Help her with her college application," I clarify.

"I'm sure you can, but why aren't you asking her?"

I back up, momentarily winded by the volume of his voice. "I had this idea." Grabbing a chunk of my hair, I begin to twirl it nervously, then stop. It's a really good idea, and I know it. So I straighten up and address him with the kind of confidence Arch displays at her cosmetics parties. "I was thinking Piper could help me with my history project, and it could help her, too."

His eyebrows raise. "Are you trying to get your sister to help you get an A?"

"No. I mean, yes, sir. But not like you think." I speak a little louder. "I have permission to choreograph a dance number for extra credit. It will represent the Jazz Age; and I got this thought that maybe Piper could make the costumes for me, and you could use it somehow on her college application."

He walks to his chair and sits down, then leans back and rubs his broad chin with his massive hand. "That's a pretty good idea, Emerson. Have you mentioned it to Piper yet?"

"No, sir. I wanted to make sure you'd allow it first." I toss him my best, most convincing grin in the hopes that he will agree. If he does, Piper will be ecstatic. She spends all her free time playing around on her sewing machine and is desperate to go to Parsons School of Design in New York.

Reaching over, Mr. Bondurant grabs a stack of file folders off the edge of his desk. He sits them in his lap and begins to thumb through them with his giant, hot dog–sized fingers. "Let me see . . ." He locates Piper's and opens it on his desk. "Ahh, yes. She's my Parsons's girl. I think costuming might be the perfect addition to her application. We could even film it. Tell her to come see me immediately."

"Really?" I swear I could hug the giant!

He smiles. "It's so odd that you came to see me today," he adds. "I just overheard a few of your teachers talking about their most improved students, and your name was among them."

Now I really do hug him.

He turns as red as a crawfish and shoos me out the door,
where I run smack dab into Vance. "Whoa there, hot stuff!
Watch where you're going." He grins before running off
toward class.

He called me hot stuff!

This calls for some chocolate. My project is going to be
fantastic! Just the kind of thing Piper's been looking for to
make her college application stand out.

But right then my phone alarm dings, reminding me of
my "tutoring" session with Oliver. I'd scheduled it earlier this
week. The Spanish test is this afternoon and like it or not, I
desperately need a kiss to pass it.

I screech to a stop outside the door to the language lab,
pull in a long, deep breath while straightening my skirt, then
press my lips together to spread out my Melon Madness lip
gloss. (I ditched the Pleased as Punch after my run-in with
Silas. Too dangerous.) Before I go any farther, I pull out the
kiss list I made last night and cross off Oliver (and Grady) (and
Sawyer).

OPERATION LIPLOCK
~~Grady: English~~
   ~~(good with novels—reads a lot)~~ (not fishy)
Martin: English backup (try for poetry)—
   good with history, too
~~Sawyer: Chemistry and geometry~~
   ~~(in lab before first period)~~
Malcolm: Geometry backup
~~Oliver: Spanish and chemistry~~
   ~~(teacher's pet)~~
Juan: Spanish backup
Edwin: History
   (knows about Jazz Age)

Smiling, I push my hair back and take hold of the doorknob. Once again I peer through the small glass window in the top of the door. Edwin is sitting in the corner with his headphones on. *What's he doing here?*

His chair is cocked back and leaning against the wall, and he has our purple Spanish book open on his lap. *Where is Oliver?* I wrench my head to the side to see if I can spot Oliver while I slowly turn the doorknob and walk into the room.

Edwin leans forward, forcing his chair to make a loud thud against the tile floor. "You're late."

Huh?

I'm caught off guard by his hair again. It's messy—not his usual bedhead messy, *cute* messy. "I was supposed to meet Oliver here . . . to study Spanish," I tell him.

Edwin takes off his headphones and sets them on the windowsill before moving the purple book to the desk. "He's sick, so I said I'd help you." He's wearing those jeans again and a green T-shirt with THE DIRTY RAZORS on it. His signature leather jacket is hanging off the back of his chair.

"Really?" I ask. "But I just saw him first period." My heart sinks, and I feel a slight panic coming on. *I was going to kiss Oliver! Not Edwin! I'm not prepared for this!*

"That was three periods ago, and he threw up in between. I told him I was free, so he asked me to help you. Anything else?" Edwin's voice is deep and throaty—I've never noticed it before.

I stare at him, unsure what to do. The test is this afternoon, and I haven't even learned the *first* few chapters yet. But spending every weekend watching old *MacGyver* reruns with Arch will ruin my life. My eyes get wide, and I chew on the tip of my fingernail so I can think for a minute.

He stands up and takes a couple of steps toward me, then

reaches out his hand as if this is a business meeting. "I'm Edwin McNeely."

"I know." I take my fingernail out of my mouth and rub it against my thumb, then shake his outstretched hand. "And I'm . . . uh, Emerson." *AWKWARD. Is he kidding? I feel like such an idiot.*

"That you are." His eyes brighten, and a small smile cracks across his face, erasing his previously annoyed gaze. *Stupid, Emerson, he was kidding.*

He turns to the desk next to his and pulls the chair back for me, making a loud scraping sound against the floor.

"So . . ." I take a step toward him. "Oliver isn't coming back?"

He shakes his head, and I slowly take a seat.

It's official: I'm screwed.

I set down my backpack on the floor wondering if maybe I should just ditch. Edwin's not like the other ones. He's cuter, and he smells like heaven.

Focus, Emerson! You can do this. He's not Vance. He's BAND MAN! A boy who used to play Swords and Soldiers way after it was remotely cool to do so. (Actually, it was never cool to do so.)

I can't kiss him.

Yes, you can.

I haven't prepared for this.

My head itches.

This won't work.

Just do it.

What is wrong with me?

Vance is probably roaming the halls.

Vance . . .

"Do you have your book?" he asks, hurtling me off my mental seesaw.

"No." I scratch my neck. "Is it hot in here?"

He laughs. "Then how'd you plan on studying?"

I look at the desk and try to think of an answer. "I was late. And I fo-forgot. I FORGOT my book," I say louder and more awkwardly than I intend.

"Easy there, tiger." He smiles.

I feel my face flush. "Sorry." *Get a grip, Emerson!*

"No worries. You can just use mine." He tilts his book toward me and scoots his chair closer, bringing his freshly scrubbed boy scent with him. "I think we covered the vocabulary in class yesterday, so let's do the verbs."

I look at the page, dizzy from the fear of needing to kiss him—and wanting to. But being scared to death to do so.

Still . . . I don't really know him. I've barely spoken to Edwin, so this might be even *easier* than kissing Oliver. Oliver and I are hallway friends, so I was prepared for an awkward month of Oliver-avoidance. But if I kiss Edwin, I can get the information I need and then go back to ignoring him. Yeah. He can just think I'm the ditz who asked him to kiss me one day in the most whack tutoring session ever.

"Emerson?"

"Mmm-hmm?" I look at his face for the first time since sitting down. I mean, *really* look at it.

"Did you understand what I just said?"

He has full, pink lips, teasing me to imagine what it might feel like to kiss him and what his thoughts might taste like. I can't even venture a guess.

"Emerson?" he repeats.

I pull my thoughts back. "No, can you repeat it?"

"Sure." He slowly repeats himself, and I notice how sincere he is. He really *is* trying to help me. And for a minute I hate myself.

But it's kiss or fail. He's my only hope.

Just as I'm gathering the courage to kiss him, the doorknob turns and in walks the janitor. *Oh no. This will never work. I can't kiss him with an audience.*

The janitor stops and looks at us.

"Mr. T!" Edwin says enthusiastically.

The janitor smiles. "Edwin! My main man!"

"You don't mind if Mr. Thibodaux cleans the room, do you?" Edwin whispers to me.

"Cleans the room?" I look over at Mr. Thibodaux, who is already sweeping in the corner.

"He cleans the language lab this period, but he's quiet. I promise it won't matter to us. I study in here sometimes when he's cleaning."

Our eyes meet for a second before I pull mine away. That icky, guilty feeling slinks its way through my veins like a disease. *Go away!* I order it.

"Can we just be alone?" I ask, trying to soften my gaze.

His emerald-brown eyes narrow, and he knits his brow while pulling his head back a little as if I've shocked him. Crap.

"I have ADD," I lie. "And the janitor moving around will distract me. I just do better with quiet. Ya know, so I can focus."

His shoulders relax, and he leans back toward me. His hair smells coconutty. Yowza, I feel like I'm in sensory overdrive and I haven't even kissed him yet.

"Let's go down the hall," he says. "I'm sure there's an empty room somewhere."

"Great." I'm relieved. "You lead the way."

We pick up our backpacks, and I follow him.

CHAPTER FOURTEEN

Ice Balm

He opens a few doors before he finds an empty classroom. I study him while we walk. He really isn't as weird as Trina and I always thought. Just quiet. Okay, maybe a little weird. He sometimes wears strange hats and occasionally dresses like he just rolled out of an old fifties' movie. I analyze the crinkled worn-out look to his leather jacket. Maybe *that's* his smell: leather, like a new car.

If I asked her to, Piper could give him one of her signature makeovers and he'd be a dead ringer for the high school quarterback. Of course, I wouldn't ask. She'd die if she thought I'd ever be interested in a guy like Edwin. Besides, as soon as he pulled out his tuba, or whatever horn he plays, he'd blow his cool-guy cover (literally).

"How's this?" He opens a door on our right and motions me over to a couple of desks in the corner.

I mumble in agreement.

We sit down, and I get out a pencil, pretending to be

serious about my studies. He sticks his hand into his pocket and retrieves a blue tube of Ice Balm. I'd recognize that tube anywhere. I wear it to bed. He rubs a smooth line across his lips before opening the purple textbook again. I can't help but get a teensy bit excited about my plan, twisted as it is.

Glancing at my watch, I see that I have forty-five minutes to secure the kiss. Plenty o' time.

We talk vocabulary for a while before I check the time again. Twenty minutes left. *Durn.* I watch him write a verb conjugation chart in his tiny, compact print style. I've spent too much time faking interest in verb tenses, and now time is running out. Leaning in a little closer, I say, "Edwin?"

He glances up from the chart and his Spanish textbook— something I haven't looked at the entire study session.

"Nevermind," I say.

"What?" he asks.

I look down at the book while rubbing my pencil between two fingers. "You'll laugh," I say, remembering Sawyer.

"No, I won't. I promise," he assures me with eyes that smile. "Look, it took me a while to conjugate the progressive tense, too."

Oh boy. He definitely isn't feeling it.

Putting down the pencil, I lock his gaze with what I hope is a *Come hither, baby* look. I invented it last night and have practiced it no less than thirty times in the mirror already this morning. "I wasn't wondering about verb tenses."

He looks at me like I am speaking another language—and not the one he's been trying to teach me.

Ack! Now I really *do* feel idiotic. *Come on, Emerson. You've done this before. Just do it!*

I swallow and look into his eyes. "I was wondering if you had a girlfriend."

He looks down and speaks to his notebook. "No."

Forcing a confidence I am definitely not feeling, I say, "Then kiss me," causing him to freeze.

"I can't believe you just asked me that." His cheeks turn a rosy shade I'm certain matches mine.

"Are you mad?" I ask, now completely regretting my decision.

He laughs. "No."

Thank goodness! I giggle and bat my eyelashes a little while ducking my chin.

He slowly raises his right hand to the side of my face, and heat floods my body as I tilt my head to meet it. His eyes are locked onto mine. Then he gently leans forward and kisses me.

On the cheek.

I smile at him, almost from a strange sense of relief. *You don't have to do this,* I tell myself. *You* can *study.*

"No," I whisper. And then before my heart has a chance to stop my brain, I touch my lips. "Here."

"You're making me nervous, Emerson," he says, glancing around the room.

"You make me nervous, too," I tell him. And good gravy, that's the truth.

He leans toward me again, but this time I hold his head in my hands and direct his mint-laced mouth to mine.

Our lips touch slowly and gently.

We kiss for maybe four whole seconds (as in one Mississippi, two Mississippi, three Mississippi, four Mississippi). *Way* longer than Sawyer or Grady. I don't know what's come over me, but I don't want it to stop. Our tongues touch. He is a surprisingly good kisser—not slobbery at all. My ear starts to buzz immediately, and as wrong as it is to use boys this way, I resist the urge to stop the kiss. And then, like tiny television pixels merging together, the vision comes into focus. Or at least it kind of does. Hmm. I can't see the Spanish notes. I can't even see band practice. Or his memories.

Is that me I see?

Where is everything?

There's no landscape of images to choose from this time. There's only me.

Starting to sweat, I pull back. *Why is this happening?*

He looks at me with that same intense gaze, questioning my actions with his eyes. Poor guy is no doubt wondering why the heck I'm kissing him. He probably thinks I like him—or that I'm a slut.

Suddenly I feel ill. Maybe this is exactly how a slut feels—like her kisses have an alternate purpose. Like she has no power without them. Does this make *me* a slut?

Too late to worry about that now. I've already committed. I need those notes, so I quickly lean in before I lose my nerve (or get hyperanalytical) and let my lips touch his again.

One Mississippi. Two Mississippi.

Me again—I see myself in Piper's long white coat now, the one I wore yesterday. I have to strain to see anything else. He must be one focused dude.

Three Mississippi.

I let my tongue enter his mouth and focus hard on all things Spanish. But all I see is *me again.*

Me in Spanish class.

Me in the cafeteria a few days ago.

Me laughing with Trina.

And finally, him begging Oliver to play sick and let him tutor me.

Me—in the center of a blurry haze.

Four Mississippi.

Me. Me. Me.

Edwin "Band Man" McNeely has a major crush . . . on *me*?

He pulls his head back and looks at me. My eyes, I'm sure, are huge and bug-eyed. I may not be able to see the vision very well, but I can taste it: sweet like Mrs. Baldwin's banana cream pie or the Wilsons' rose garden. Running my tongue over my teeth, I try to scrape off the sweet residue; but it tastes good, and part of me wants to suck on the vision like a Christmas peppermint.

The earache is in full force now, radiating down the right side of my neck. But it feels stronger this time—soul splitting. I wrinkle my forehead and wince at the pain, temporarily letting go of the vision.

"You okay?" he asks.

I notice that he looks almost as shocked as I do, which is understandable, considering. I blink in slow motion, trying to stop the room from spinning. The reality that I'm going to fail the test *and* be grounded next weekend suddenly hits me. *"Sí,"* I say. *What in the world? Did I just answer him in Spanish?* I feel my face flush, then press my palm to my ear. "I have an earache."

"I'm sorry. It's me."

"No. No. It's not you," I say. But it *is* him. "It's . . . I just have this ear problem."

He reaches over and gently touches my hand. His fingers are warm.

"I'm sorry," he says again.

I have to get out of here. "I don't feel so good." I shove

my pencil into my backpack and zip the bag up. "I'll see you around."

He smiles awkwardly as I bolt from the room.

In the bathroom, I grip the sink and look into the mirror. I can still see the lie in my eyes. I close them, trying to erase what my brain knows I've just done; but it's too late. Too late for me to ace that dumb test and too late for Edwin. I know his secret now.

Mind reading isn't all that it's cracked up to be, even if you're kissing while doing it.

CHAPTER FIFTEEN

Kick A$$ Crimson

"He's looking at you again," Trina whispers on Tuesday in English. She's referring to Edwin, of course. Vance isn't as blatant with his attention. "He's so strange," she adds. "But it's kinda cute. I wish Silas would look at me like that."

I need to pay attention in this class after I got that C– on the Spanish test Friday, but the mention of his name irritates me. "I heard Silas's dating someone," I tell her. This is the first time I've mentioned it, so I'm careful not to add that the girl in question is my sister.

She huffs.

Glancing over at Edwin, I try to figure out how I feel about him. Arch is always preaching about purity and love, and most of the time I just nod and ignore her. But this kissing business has gotten me thinking. Don't I want it to *mean* something when I kiss someone? Heck, with all the play my lips are getting, by the time I finally get to kiss Vance, it'll feel like a high five.

"Get your phones out," Mrs. Beenie says, interrupting the purity pep rally in my head.

I look around to see everyone talking excitedly.

"I didn't say you could *talk*," she continues. "I said to get your phones out."

Trina raises her shoulders in confusion, but we follow orders and take them out.

"I don't have one," says Vance.

Mrs. Beenie smirks and raises her eyebrow. "Don't worry, Mr. Butcher. I'm not taking them away; I just want to try something. Since you people don't seem to be paying attention today"—she looks right at me—"I thought we'd do something *different*. I'm going to ask you a question, and the first person to *text* me the right answer gets a piece of candy."

Seriously? In-class texting? Is she for real? We all giggle, and Vance sheepishly removes his phone from his pocket.

"See, English isn't so bad now, is it?" Mrs. Beenie reaches down and grabs a large bag of candy out of her purse. Then she deposits it in the center of her desk and turns to face the board.

"Sweet!" Vance shouts. He is *so* adorable.

And I'm seriously boy-bipolar. Just sixty seconds ago I was thinking about Edwin.

"All right," Mrs. B begins. "Get your phones ready." She pauses. "What does Geoffrey Chaucer's name mean?"

I stare at my phone, thinking. Is it basket weaver? Shopkeeper?

"Excellent!" she says less than four seconds later. She is holding up her phone and reads from it. "Shoemaker is correct. Whose number is 551-7643?"

Edwin raises his hand and strolls confidently up to her

desk to pick a piece of candy. On his way back to his desk, he looks at me again. Just looks. No smile. No nothing except intense pupil lockage. After unlocking my eyes from his, I glance at Vance and back again, feeling more confused than ever.

She writes his phone number on the board and puts a (*1*) beside it. "Next question. What did Chaucer *write*?"

Oooh! I know this. I frantically type **Canterbury tales**, but before I can finish, Martin has already won.

"Next question. Text me one character Chaucer appears to like, followed by one character he appears to dislike."

Everyone's head drops to type. Everyone's head, that is, except Edwin's. It's firmly twisted in my direction, his eyes on me.

Maybe it's the power of my Kick A$$ Crimson lip gloss—a known power enhancer, with a cinnamon sting—or maybe in-class texting has made me flat crazy; but whatever the reason, I text him. His number *is* on the board, after all.

Hey you. Quit looking @ me. Emerson (Don't ask me why I did this. I don't even know.)

And I suddenly regret my decision.

He's typing.

What if he didn't get it? What if I'm wrecking his chance to score the most points in class? Will he be mad at me? Does he hate me for leading him on?

My phone vibrates, and I'm scared to look down.

Ur beautiful u know

Whoa!!!! Talk about butterflies. Who says that? I expected "good answer" or "I'm whipping you at this game" or "what time is lunch?" but *"you're beautiful"?!*

"Another one for Mr. McNeely!" Mrs. Beenie says.

Another one for sure.

"What was the question?" I ask Trina while texting him back. **Thx.** I can't think of anything else to say.

Trina shrugs.

My phone vibrates.

Wanna go with me sumwhere?

Is he asking me out? Uh-oh. This is bad.

Where? I text back.

"Approximately how many medieval manuscripts exist of *The Canterbury Tales*?" Mrs. Beenie asks before my phone vibrates again.

I look down. **It's a secret.**

"That's right!" Mrs. Beenie says. "Eighty-three. Good job, Miss Strickland!"

I look up and grin at Trina. She blows on the top of her phone as if she's just shot a bullet out of it and then pretends to holster it.

Turning around, I see Edwin staring at me, questioning me with those eye-daggers of his, and my phone vibrates again.

So u wanna come?

I wrap my jacket around myself, feeling chilled. Then I text him back. **Like, to study?** (It is Tuesday, after all. And he's an Ivy. What else could he want to do?) **When?**

2morrow @ 7. You'll c.

K.

K. Okay. *Okay.* Did I just say OKAY?

He never turns around again, and I don't see him for the rest of the day; but when I get to my car, there's a note on it. "Later Gator" is written in his tiny, compact, boy scribble. Okay. I'll admit it. He's growing on me.

I'm lost in a fried-okra daydream when the phone rings.

"Is Piper the girl you were referring to today?" Trina asks.

"What?" I drive past the Wilsons', wondering if it would be rude to ask Mrs. Wilson to make me some. She loves to cook and is always offering to whip up my favorites.

"Piper!" Trina says. "Is your *sister* dating Silas?"

The okra dream poofs when I realize she's referring to our conversation in English. *Why did I tell her he was dating someone?* I consider lying, but since I've been doing far too much of that lately, I just tell her the truth. "Yes, but she asked . . ."

"Thanks, Emerson. You could have told me instead of letting me look like a monumental idiot, flirting with him all month long."

I laugh. "You did not."

"You were my best friend!" she shouts.

Yikes. She's using the past tense.

Putting the car in park, I turn off the ignition and explain. "She's my sister, Trina. What was I supposed to do? She asked me not to tell anyone. And anyway, he's kind of a jerk."

"How do you know he's a jerk? Oh, wait. I know. He's probably been having dinner over there every night."

I get out of the car, determined to end this conversation. If I know Trina, she's just hormonal and will forget about this as soon as *Celebrity Rehab* comes on. "I'm sorry, T. I wanted to tell you. I really did. I'll call you later. I have some homework to do before Arch gets home."

She starts to say something else, but I've already hung up the phone. *Whoops.* I text her on the way into the house to say I'm sorry again.

She never replies.

CHAPTER SIXTEEN

Promise Me

Penelope is naked.

I stop in the hallway outside of my sister's room and stare at the life-sized dress form standing in the corner of her room without clothes on. This is bizarre. My fashion-obsessed sister *always* has something on Penelope. If it isn't an outfit she owns, it's one she's working on—has been that way since Mrs. Wilson gave her the silly dress form and taught her how to sew.

Wait! I know what she can put on Penelope: the costumes! I've been so preoccupied with grade lust, and keeping her secret about Silas, that I've forgotten to tell her about the dance project! Mr. Bondurant is probably wondering why she hasn't come by.

Bouncing into her room, I find Piper sitting in her desk chair, staring out the window. She's picking the polish off her fingernails, obviously upset.

"What's wrong?" I ask, my excitement fading.

"Nothing," she says flatly.

"Penelope is naked," I point out with a chuckle, but she doesn't think it's funny.

"I wanted to talk to you about my dance project," I add.

No response.

Uh-oh. She and Silas must have had a fight. I'd recognize Post Traumatic Fight Syndrome anywhere: glassy eyes, detached personality, brittle emotions. Trina suffered it weekly during her short-lived relationship with Ben the Butt last year.

"Is everything cool with Silas?" I ask slowly. Hesitantly.

She turns her head abruptly. "Yes. Why? Do you want me to break up with him? I know what people are saying, and it's not true."

"Huh? What are they saying?" I ask.

She rolls her eyes and looks back out the window. "That he's cheating on me."

"I haven't heard that," I tell her, which is true.

"It's just that there are girls," she begins. "Girls who like him."

Girls like Trina? Yeah. Tell me about it.

"But he's promised that nothing's going on." She looks at me with desperation in her eyes. "I trust him, Emerson."

I've never seen my big sis like this over a guy.

"Right," I say, opening my palms toward her in submission. "You know him better than I do." And then I do the unthinkable. I start sticking up for the little rat—gushing all kinds of crazy comfort—telling her how I'm sure he's wonderful and loyal and would never be so stupid as to wreck what is clearly the love affair of a lifetime. *Change the subject, Emerson. PRONTO!*

Clearing my throat, I add, "I was actually coming in here

to tell you that I got permission to teach a jazz dance to some girls at my studio for school credit."

She nods her head. "Good."

"We're going to perform it at the Spring Follies."

"Cool," she mutters, her voice falling as flat and matte as Arch's new Promise Me lip blush.

I step a little closer to her and proceed with my good news. "I asked Mr. Bondurant if you could help me with it."

"Why would you do that?" she snaps.

Good grief.

"I thought you could get credit for it, too," I say. "And maybe use it on your college application." I tilt my head in annoyance and glare at her.

"Use *your* dance on *my* college application?"

"Oh! I forgot to say that your part will be to design and make the costumes. Cool, huh?" Puckering my lips, I strut toward her like a model. "Bondurant said we could film it for your application to Parsons. He thinks it will be just the thing to make your app stand out from the rest."

She shakes her head and stares out the window. "I'll think about it." Then she looks over at Penelope. "I haven't made anything in a while, and I have to study."

My excitement fizzles like a dud firecracker. And I blame you-know-who.

Back in my room, I know I need to study, but what the heck am I gonna do about my stupid costumes without Piper? And what about Silas? *Is* he cheating on her? For a second I ponder the fact that I *could* find out if I wanted to. I'd just have to lock lips with him. . . .

STOP, Emerson! No. Way.

I shake my head to clear it of such an awful thought and

get out my books. Then I take a seat at my desk. (Luke says studying at a desk increases productivity.)

Hold up. Why didn't anyone tell me my nails were looking so shabby? I can't study like this. I need to polish. Getting out my favorite new winter color, I paint one nail, then

Two

Three

What should I study?

Four

Five

Six

I blow on my nails for a sec while checking my phone for missed texts.

Nothing.

Seven

Eight

Nine

Ten polished nails.

Much better.

I blow on my hands again, then open my spiral to write something down.

Hmmm.

CHAPTER SEVENTEEN

Kudzu

Crap. Ten minutes later, all I have written is:

Mrs. Vance Butcher
Emerson Butcher
Emerson and Vance Butcher
Mr. and Mrs. Vance Butcher
Emerson McNeely

My pen hesitates on the last name, and I slowly retrace the looping letters before quickly scribbling black lines through them with my Sharpie until I can't see the name at all. After that I draw large, curlicue hearts around the rest of my hopeful names.

Here's the deal: I know I like Vance. I've liked him for forever. But there's something about Edwin that I can't shake, and it's driving me crazy. He's become like the leafy green kudzu weed that covers trees with its vines, quietly choking them to death. Durn if Edwin isn't covering *my* thoughts with something new—something potentially deadly. I find myself staring at him in class, sometimes without even knowing it. And to make matters worse, I haven't been able to bring myself to kiss anyone else since kissing him last week. Yes, this vine is going to kill my grades, if it doesn't kill me first. If only I could talk to Trina about it. But there's no way I'm calling her back tonight.

I can't even *think* about my poetry assignment that's due tomorrow.

Leaning down, I open my drawer and locate my headphones. Maybe I can concentrate better with music on.

But I wanna kiss him again.

I put the tiny earbuds in my ears.

Velvet eyes.

I madly scroll through my songs and select a loud one, intended to blast these ridiculous thoughts out of my head.

Pink lips.

Pressing my own lips together, I turn up the volume, preferring an ear bleed over this foreign feeling taking root in my chest.

Banana cream pie . . .

Dang it! I give up and pull the buds out of my ears.

"Emerson!" Arch yells from behind me. "How can you study with that music so loud? I could hear it standing right here!"

"Sorry."

"No wonder you performed poorly on that Spanish test last week. I can't imagine trying to memorize verb tenses with rock music booming in my ears. There's no way you can concentrate like that. And you'd been doing so well."

"All right. I get it. No music."

She hands me a piece of paper. "Here is the address of my party tonight."

As I take it from her, she looks down at my notebook and points to one of my hopeful names. "Who's that?"

"Oh. That's just me being dumb," I say, shutting the notebook.

"Who's Vance Butcher?"

"Just a boy."

"He's the boy who called a couple of weeks ago, isn't he?"

I nod while drawing kudzu leaves on the squiggly lines on the cover of the notebook.

"Oh, Emerson!" she says, hugging me from behind. "Don't worry. I used to do that all the time." She looks out the window and goes all dreamy eyed. "Phillip Teegarden . . ."

I grin. "Who is Phillip Teegarden?"

She chuckles. "He was this older guy I used to see at summer camp. I loved him."

"Arrcchh." I laugh.

"He was a . . . what is it y'all say? A hottie?"

I nod and snicker. "He brought some heat, huh?"

"He sure did."

For a minute she looks young, even pretty. Strange that I never think of her as a girl—a girl who has probably felt all the things I've felt.

Before leaving my room, she leans down to kiss my dimple goodbye with a smile. I blink and pull back, feeling hot. Something's not right. The vision I see isn't soothing. It has a distinctly *different* taste—the flavor isn't balanced. It's like fish but super overwhelmed by the strong flavors of garlic, capers, lemons, and kalamata olives.

And too much salt. Much too much salt.

Ahhh. I clench my teeth. I taste *desperation*—a feeling I'm all too familiar with.

The vision is splintered, too. Rather than seeing Mama, I only see *Arch*. She's at the Wilsons', having coffee, telling Audrey that she's having trouble paying all the bills—our school bill primarily. Makeup sales have slowed over the last year, and our schooling is her biggest expense. But since my grades have started improving, she doesn't want to sacrifice the opportunities this school has presented. And the school guidance counselor said that if I keep it up, I'll be eligible for an academic scholarship. A scholarship she desperately needs me to have. Then she mentions Piper and how morose she's been this week. Audrey comforts her.

It all happens in a second, then it's gone, leaving me rubbing my aching ear.

One thing is clear: Arch blames herself, thinking she hasn't been a good role model.

Well, that does it. Piper may be hormonal, and I might be in the early stages of becoming a pseudo-slut; but I am not gonna let Arch down.

First up: English. I have to study some poet named Langston Hughes. After consulting the Web, I find out he's famous for none other than *jazz* poetry from the twenties. Great. Now all I can think of is Edwin.

"I'm home," Arch calls.

I walk downstairs a few minutes later and find her already in her bed with home-decorating magazines spread over her lap. "I'm beat," she says from behind her cute little black glasses.

I smile but feel sorry for all the work she has to do to keep us at Haygood.

"You okay?" she asks, moving some magazines off her lap.

I stand in the doorway and try to look happy. "I'm

fine. What are you looking at?"

She pulls a magazine out from under her mess and turns it toward me. "What do you think of this color?" I see a photo of a pale-green kitchen.

"Are you redecorating the kitchen?"

"I need to fix some of the plumbing, and it means they'll have to cut the wall behind the sink. So to make myself feel better about it, I thought I'd focus on the fact that I get to repaint."

"I like it," I say with a smile.

Arch inherited this house from my grandparents after they died. It's an old bungalow.

Most of our neighbors have already renovated their homes much more than ours, especially the gay guys who bought the old Barrett house. You should see it. It's our new fave. They did an incredible job, tearing off the front porch and totally redoing it. We've never been inside, only on the steps when we brought them a welcome-to-the-neighborhood coffee cake, but I can only imagine how superfine it is. They own a consignment store in town, so you just know it's filled with interesting pieces. Arch and I plan to casually "visit" if the *Southern Living* magazine photographers show up. She heard it's being photographed for the holiday issue.

"You wanna do some drive-bys soon?" she asks. Sometimes we drive around looking for ideas to give our home more curb appeal. Arch doesn't plan on selling it or anything, but she thinks a well-kept house is as telling a sign as a well-kept face. It usually takes us a while to find something we can do because she has to do all of our "fixin' up" by herself. She does a pretty good job (as long as Mr. Wilson helps her).

There was that time, though, when she got cocky. Sure enough, she went and got herself electrocuted. Luckily, the electrician she had to hire to repair the black hole in the ceiling was engaged to be married. He traded his services for Arch's, and she did the makeup for his fiancée's six bridesmaids the day of his wedding. Arch threw in some extra products for the women and scored an office internet-wiring, too.

"Drive-bys sound good," I reply.

"I met a plumber's wife at the party tonight," she says with a smile.

"Does she need a large supply of nail polish?" I tease, but secretly hope I'm right.

"Maybe . . ."

"Well, just let me know when you want to go. I'm gonna turn in." I lean down to kiss her good night.

She kisses my dimple, and I'm reminded why I love this ability. I see my grandma tucking Arch and Mama into bed. I never knew my grandmother, but Arch's memories of her are sweet and comforting, like warm corn bread, fresh out of the oven.

"I love you, Arch," I say.

"I love you, too, baby."

CHAPTER EIGHTEEN

Mayonnaise

A crusty fever blister stares at me from Martin's upper lip, and my mind races to come up with plan B. Of all the days for Martin to have a fever blister, it's today? The day I wanted help with poetry?

Ew.

"What'd you want?" Martin asks me as I try to shift my attention from the honking red abscess.

"Do you know where Grady is?" I ask, quickly changing plans.

Martin sticks his hand in his pocket, removes a tube of Carmex, and then smears it across his lips while saying, "The gym. He's working in the weight room this period."

"You know . . ." I point to the blister. "I could probably get you something for that. A cream maybe? My aunt reps a great line of skin care."

He continues to smear the greasy ointment across his lips. "No biggie. It'll be gone soon. I get 'em all the time."

Note to self: cross Martin off the list.

I find Grady leaning over a pile of dirty laundry in the weight room, separating the T-shirts from the towels and the shorts. The room has the distinctly earthy smell of mold and metal, and I feel my nose wrinkle as I approach.

"Milady!" he says when he notices me. "Hello." Standing upright, he adjusts the massive armload of sweat-soaked clothing, and I wonder how I can possibly lean over and kiss him with all that laundry in his hands.

"How may I serve you?" he asks while I estimate the exact distance from the top of my head to his. He's around six inches taller, I determine.

"Actually," I begin, "I was wondering if you understood that Langston Hughes stuff."

"Understood it?"

I scan his mouth for blisters and am pleased to find he is squeaky clean. But I'm thinking I should have asked something else—I'm not sure what. These poems Mrs. Beenie's been giving us are all over the place. Half the time they don't even rhyme, and the sentences (if you can even call them that) break in the middle of a thought. What's so beautiful about a choppy, disjointed stream of partial phrases? Why can't we study a real poet like Dr. Seuss?

"I savored it. Drank it up like fine, aged wine," he says, smiling at his comparison.

I shake my head, moving my hair out of my eyes. "Savored it like wine, huh?" That's got to be good.

He repeats himself, thinking I don't understand his comparison. "Fine, aged wine."

This conversation feels so awkward and forced I hardly know what to say next. "If only I could kiss you and taste it on your tongue," I blurt out, trying to be cute but shivering at how close to the truth it really is.

A deep red blush overtakes his face and he says, "I thought you'd never ask."

I giggle, hoping I seem equal parts funny (as in ha-ha joking) and desirable. I have no idea if he's being serious or not, but I sure hope he is.

Without another word, he drops the dirty laundry in a pile at his feet and takes a step closer to me, bringing the dank smell of perspiration and his LORD OF THE RINGS T-shirt with him.

Our eyes meet, and an awkward three-second silence fills the room. But at the same time, I am surprised and thrilled with how easily this is all happening.

He looks longingly into my eyes and then gently grasps my waist like a professional boyfriend.

Our lips touch.

Then separate as the door behind us bangs open.

We fly apart like two north-ended magnets resisting each other. Grady leans down and reaches with his arms—only seconds ago around my waist—to the lump of stinky laundry on the floor. I take a few more steps backward while trying to come up with something "normal" to say. I want to make sure Grady knows the whole thing was just for fun—the funny, ha-ha joke we were just talking about—but my loose lips freeze, and the words I *want* to speak stay imprisoned in my mouth because—

Vance enters the room.

I feel a rush of color erupt across my entire body. Talk about a fever blister. I have become one.

"What up, guys?" Vance asks, twirling his baseball bat as if it's a baton.

"Not much," I say. "IwasjustaskingFishaboutourEnglish quiz."

Too fast!

Grady chuckles like we have a private joke, and I want to kick him in the shin for being so stupidly obvious. The words *We kissed* are probably written all over my face, tattooed on my eyelids for the whole, wide world to see. What if he says something he thinks is humorous, like *Emerson and I were just feeling the depth and breadth of a poem together.*

I scan the room for the exits. This plane is going down.

"Cool," Vance says, then winks at me, making me feel utterly depraved.

Grady opens his mouth, and before he can say anything, I rush into the girls' locker room to regain my composure without blacking out.

Hurrying across campus to English class, I want to kick myself. I was so panicked about getting caught that I didn't even really talk to Vance. This is crazy. He's never going to want to date me if I keep running away every time I see him.

And I had hoped kissing Fish would suddenly make me into some kind of prolific writer, but now all I can think about is mayonnaise. That fine, aged wine he was bragging about wasn't what his kiss tasted like at all. Rather, a creamy concoction of old English—as oily and dense as mayonnaise and as hard to understand as Arch's King James Bible. A lotta good that'll do me.

Unlike other subjects, English, I now realize, isn't even a subject a kiss can help—at least not in the writing department. Writing requires something unique to the individual. I should have known this. There are no formulas.

I pull out my chart before I walk into class and cross off

Martin's name, making a notation never to kiss for English class again, at least as far as creative writing is concerned.

OPERATION LIPLOCK
~~Grady: English~~
   ~~(good with novels—reads a lot)~~ (not fishy)
~~Martin: English backup (try for poetry)—~~
   ~~good with history, too~~ NEVER!
~~Sawyer: Chemistry and geometry~~
   ~~(in lab before first period)~~
Malcolm: Geometry backup
~~Oliver: Spanish and chemistry~~
   ~~(teacher's pet)~~
Juan: Spanish backup
Edwin: History
   (knows about Jazz Age)

I can't bring myself to cross Edwin off the list.

Luckily, Mrs. Beenie gives us time to work on our poems during class. Chewing on the end of my pen, I retreat into my psyche in an effort to "dig deep"—said in Mrs. Beenie's squeaky voice. "Dig deep, children. Peel back the layers of your essence until you find the one thing that remains at the center. Find that piece of your soul and embrace it! Love it! Write about it!"

Ugh.

Mayonnaise.

But twenty-two minutes later, I have a first draft. Kooky, yes. But a poem nonetheless. One that rhymes—like all good poems should. I walk up to Mrs. Beenie's desk and turn it in.

She picks it up and reads it while I stand there watching a peculiar grin ease across her face. "I asked you to write about versatility, but I never envisioned a poem like this."

I shrug.

"How did you think of it?"

This is not a question I'm prepared for, and I am certainly not telling her I tasted it while kissing Fish. So I say, "My sister uses it all the time."

"It's very creative, Emerson. Very creative indeed." She puts it off to the side of her desk and asks if I've started the nonrhyming poem that's due soon.

I shake my head. "No. That assignment seems harder. I barely understand the examples in the book. They're so random." I leave out the part about how I think nonrhyming poems should be outlawed.

"Lemme give you a hint," she says, leaning forward. "Ignore the fact that you are writing a poem and let your honest feelings flow." The word *flow* rolls out of her mouth like music before she says, "Look to your pain. Sometimes that's where the best poetry nests."

I smile at her comment. A poetry nest. I like that image. I like thinking about it that way because *this* I get. I know what she means.

And boy is *my* nest big. Big and thorny, covered with tiny bits of Vance, little conversations with Edwin, several dirty kisses, and a few clean ones, too. My nest is woven with the threads of my aunt's tender care and gray clouds from the loss of my mother. All tangled up with one another in a bed of deception, hope, yearning, and life. *Hey, I better write that down before I forget it!*

"May I read this to the class?" she asks, interrupting my thoughts.

"I guess so," I reply.

"Class?" she begins. "Look at me for a minute. Emerson has

written a great example of a rhyming poem about versatility. I want you to listen and take note of how it's not what you would expect. It's personal to Emerson and her likes and sensibilities. *This* is what I want you to do."

I take my seat and smile, proud of my paper, and amazed that I did it on my own.

Versatility

Spread it on bananas
Or crackers and cheese.
Casseroles need it,
As do salads with peas.

With tuna or shrimp,
Horseradish or dips,
There's a satisfying flavor
It imparts to your lips.

Between slices of bread,
Makes tomatoes taste swell.
It's eaten in high places
And low ones as well.

For conditioning hair
It's now quite the craze.
This versatile product's
Of course mayonnaise!

CHAPTER NINETEEN

Sunlight

I don't see Edwin for the rest of the day, but it's a good thing, because I need space to mentally prepare for our study-date-thingy tonight. However, I don't see much of Trina either. And she hasn't replied to my last three texts. Hmm. Since I'm early to the dance studio, I pull out my phone and text her one last time before rereading Edwin's messages again. *He thinks I'm beautiful?*

Piper is late, which is no surprise since she's consumed with Silas. But while most of me is fuming, a small part is concerned. She's different since she started dating him. And the change feels bigger than your typical Post Traumatic Fight Syndrome or the obvious Senior Slump. But it's subtle at the same time—as barely there as my Sunlight lip gloss. It's like when you first get braces and you stare at your teeth night after night, desperately looking for change but seeing nothing. Convinced the teeth aren't moving at all, you decide that surely the dentist has made a mistake. He is going to show up on the six-o'clock news as a total orthodontal hack. But *then*, time passes and he's *not* on the news; and before you know it, your whole smile is different.

I would bet that no one has even noticed the change in Piper, but I see it. And there seems to be nothing I can do to stop it.

The fact remains, however, that my dance in the Spring Follies is only a month away—at the end of April—and I need to get to work. This dance is an excellent opportunity to increase my GPA without doing too much, and it involves NO kissing, thank God—just a few encouraging hugs for the girls who will be dancing my original jazz dance.

After reading Edwin's texts one last time and trying to decipher if this is a date or not, I walk inside, apologize to the girls for Piper's absence, and run some exercises. Then I go through the little bit I've choreographed so far. All is good except I haven't really chosen a song yet. I am simply working them through an eight-count routine, hoping I can match it to a song pretty easily.

Piper never shows. Figures.

An hour later, I walk to my car while texting Trina to tell her that I'm headed to her house. I still have time before my thing with Edwin. As I open the door, I see something sparkle on my seat: a CD.

PLAY ME is written in black Sharpie on the front, and I recognize the writing immediately as Edwin's. My heart rockets up into my throat. Did he actually drive over here and leave me a CD? *Is that creepy? Or adorable?*

I start the car and push the silver disc into the stereo. The same slippery tune I heard in the music room with Edwin that day fills my car, melting me into a puddle of wax. Literally. My heart is racing so fast, I almost feel faint. *Why can't this be Vance?*

I press NEXT. The following song is faster, but it has that same slippery feel I now recognize as jazz. I imagine him sitting in his room making me this CD. How long did it take? Are the songs random? Or are there subtle messages in the lyrics? I press NEXT again and listen to the words all the way to Trina's house. I'm at full capacity with this Edwin confusion. I *have* to tell someone. But I'm really hoping Trina won't laugh. This *is* Band Man, after all.

What I need is a sofa counseling session. This business with Vance just isn't happening as easily as I'd hoped, and my kissing project is screwing things up. (Can't tell her *that* part, though.)

Right before I get to Trina's, I call Piper but get no answer. Her pseudo-husband, Silas, is probably monitoring her minutes. Ew.

After taking a left onto Trina's street, I turn into her driveway and happily notice her watching me from her window. So I park and hop out of the car.

"Don't think we're okay, because we're not!" she shouts out the window before I can say anything. Her words fall onto the pavement sharp and angry, like glass.

"Are you still mad about Silas?" I ask, looking up at the window. *Was she avoiding me all day?*

"What do you think?"

Uh-oh. She *is* mad.

I take hold of a piece of my hair and have to physically resist the urge to twirl it. *Why didn't I tell her? She's my best friend. But Piper . . . she's my sister.* "What do you want me to say?" I shout back.

"I saw them today," she says. "All leaned up against each other after school. It was gross."

"I said I'm sorry, Trina. I swore I wouldn't tell." And this is true. I *promised.*

"Whatever, Emerson!" She reaches up and takes hold of the top of her window. "You know, you didn't have to fake not liking him all the time."

"But I *don't* like him. I . . . I . . ."

Slam! And just like that, I watch our friendship close.

"Trina!" I beg. "Wait!" But she's not at the window anymore.

A large blue box covered in diagrams of ice crystals is leaning against the back door of my house when I pull into the driveway. But for the first time since I was eight years old, I walk right past it and whatever magic it contains.

I call Trina when I get upstairs, but she doesn't answer the phone. I call Piper, too—about a hundred times, but she won't answer, either.

With no one to talk to, I get out my history book and look at my homework. But I can't concentrate. I feel like my world is on tilt and I have less than an hour before Edwin comes over.

Pretty soon Piper arrives, and right away I confront her.

"Not only did you ditch my dance class, but Trina hates me now!" I say. "And it's all your fault!"

"Puh-lease . . . Trina never had a chance." She walks into her room and throws her books on her bed.

"What's happened to you, Piper? You've changed since you started dating Silas."

"Leave Silas out of this, Emerson. I love him."

"You *love* him?!"

"Are you seriously going to sit here and act like you know

anything about love?" She laughs. "You wouldn't understand. You've never been in love."

That hurts. I look at her, hot tears burning the backs of my eyeballs. "Since when did you become such a . . ." I pause and clench my teeth, not wanting to cuss out my own sister.

"A what?" she shouts.

I growl, unable to speak with words anymore.

"Get out!"

She may as well have added "of my life" because that's what it feels like.

CHAPTER TWENTY

An Old Ivy

Mr. Wilson is in our garage when I head outside to the car. "Howdy, young lady. I'm glad you turned up. Max and I need your help."

He's holding "Maxwell," his magic bird "seeder," which is no more than an old broom handle with a Maxwell House coffee can screwed onto the top. He invented the contraption as an easy way to fill Arch's giant bird feeder—a miniature version of our house that is mounted high up on the tree outside our kitchen window. We can see it from inside the house, but it's out of reach from the yard. Max allows Mr. Wilson's feet to stay firmly planted on the ground while he lifts up the torch-like pole and dumps the seeds into the tray, or the "carport," as he calls it. It's pretty smart, actually.

I take Max from him and hold it straight while he goes to the corner of the garage and gets the ginormous bag of birdseed.

"Where ya headed?" he asks.

"Nowhere," I tell him. I leave out the part about how I'm mad and just wanted to drive around. He'd think "cruising" was a waste of gas and probably lecture me on the economy or something. "I can't find my tap shoes and thought I might have left them in my car."

"Oh good, because I've been thinking about something. You know you girls are like daughters to me, and"—he reaches into the bag with a plastic cup, then brings it out and dumps the first cupful into Max's head—"I saw a young man come visiting the other day."

I chuckle. It was probably Silas.

"Do you have a boyfriend?" He's not really looking at me while he talks, so I wonder if he's nervous about asking.

"No. Not really," I say. "I mean, there's this one guy I really like"—(*or is it two?*)—"but . . ."

"He hasn't tried anything, has he?" Mr. Wilson dips the cup back into the bag.

"No! No. But I don't know. I'm not sure if he really likes me. I mean, I think he does, but . . . well . . ." This is harder to talk about than I thought. Little does Mr. Wilson know he's about to show up!

He looks at me and smiles. "Just know this. You are a beautiful young lady, and what they say about boys only being interested in 'one thing' isn't true of all boys. There are plenty who are looking for love, just like you. They may have stronger hormones, but that doesn't mean they only want one thing." He pauses. "So I guess I'm saying, don't feel like you have to give in to their demands. The ones who want love will be willing to wait." He rolls down the top of the birdseed bag and carries it back to the corner of the garage.

I nod. He's not saying anything I haven't heard before. But I don't have a father or anyone else to discuss boys with, and as much as I adore Arch, it's not like she's had a lot of success in this area.

"I'm not very good around them," I add as we walk out of the garage and around to the tree. "Sometimes I can't think of anything to talk about."

He laughs. "Oh, that's par for the course. When I first started seeing Mrs. Wilson, I was a blathering idiot. Had no clue what to say. So I did the reverse and talked *too* much—told her about all of my inventions, my favorite books, random sporting statistics." He starts laughing. "Can you believe I'd quote football stats to her? It's a miracle she gave me the time of day."

I love the idea of the Wilsons dating. "What was she like?" I ask.

"Oh, she was popular," he tells me. "And she was a looker, too. Still is." He takes Max from me and lifts it up high toward the birdhouse. "But I was the exact opposite. Always had my head in a book."

He's like an old Ivy. Ha!

"Audrey used to say the best men are in disguise."

"What does that mean?"

"Sometimes," he says, "the ones who are meant for you are waiting on you at the grocery store, or cutting your grass, or heck, I don't know what you gals do, but sometimes they're found where you'd least expect to find them."

I ask one more question. "What's the best way to get a boy's attention?"

"Just be yourself, baby. It'll all work out in the end. I promise."

We start back for the garage and he adds, "But boys like a challenge. So don't be one of those girls who chases them all over the place. You just be you and focus on your own interests. A girl with a life of her own is irresistible to a boy. Don't you worry. He'll come calling."

A girl with a life of her own? That sounds harder than it should. Now I have to go out and get a life. Blerg.

CHAPTER TWENTY-ONE

Love Potion No. 9

An hour later, I run downstairs to borrow some of Arch's perfume.

"So who's this guy coming over?" she asks me as I pass through the kitchen. She is standing next to the stove with a candy thermometer in her hand.

I hesitate, knowing how she'll respond. "Edwin. What are you making?"

"McNeely?" She stops stirring her pot. "Cheryl's son? But I thought . . ."

"He's helping me with my history project."

She looks at me curiously.

"What are you making?" I repeat, not wanting to work myself up right before my big date-thing.

"Fudge," she says, now beaming. "I thought you could use some after you talked to Piper. She's a mess, that one."

I huff. "Did she tell you Trina won't speak to me?" I pull out a stool and sit at the counter.

"No. What happened?"

"That Silas guy she's dating is Trina's crush."

She sighs. "Mmm. That's hard."

"Trina thinks I betrayed her because I didn't tell her."

"Well"—she pours the hot fudge into a buttered glass dish—"Piper's your sister, and family comes first."

"I know, but Trina's my best friend." I knead my stomach. I feel like I have heartburn.

"If I know Trina, and I think I do, all you have to do is wait until she finds another crush, which will be sooner than later."

I smirk, doubting it'll be *that* easy.

She takes a sip of her coffee and sits down next to me. "I promise, as soon as she gets her mind off Silas, she'll forgive you." She stands up. "Wait here. I have an idea." She walks out of the room. When she returns, she has the large, blue shipping box in her hands—the same one I passed up this afternoon.

I peer inside, and my heartburn clears in an instant. There truly is magic in makeup. Whoever denies this simple truth is nuts.

Our hands dig through what feels like hundreds of tiny rectangular boxes, then she picks up a small one and hands it to me. "Here it is!"

I take it from her and look at the name on the tiny circular sticker on the bottom of the box: Strawberry Twist. "I've been wanting to try this one!"

"Go on. Put it on," she says. "You'll feel better."

I hug her. "Thanks, Arch." I love this woman.

Opening the box, I slide out the sparkling tube of gloss, unscrew the top, and pull the wand through the thick red liquid before smearing it on my lips. "Mmmm." I can smell the faint strawberry scent. Yum.

"So, where are you and Edwin going tonight?"

"I'm not sure. The library maybe?"

"How nice. You have a lot to study."

That's an understatement. With about a month behind me, I've brought up the majority of my grades. But I'm beginning to think this kissing-Ivys thing might not be the answer.

Just then my phone vibrates. I can see it's Edwin, so I walk outside to answer it.

"Hey," he says, his voice alone giving me chills. The thought almost makes me mad. Vance is the guy who is *supposed* to be calling me—not Edwin. Vance is the one who should be making my knees weak—not Edwin. Edwin shouldn't be doing anything to me, except schooling me, I guess.

"I told my aunt we were studying, right?" I'm not sure how to find out if this is a date.

He laughs. "Not exactly. You'll see."

Oh Lord, this sounds like a date. What am I doing?

"Then I'll see you in a little while." After hanging up, I make a few loops around the house. To process.

Good gravy, it's Wednesday, and I'm about to have my first date-thing with an Ivy!

Edwin picks me up on time, but he won't tell me where we're going. I honestly can't even begin to imagine where a guy like Edwin will take me on this strange Wednesday night outing. His interests are so varied compared to most of the guys I know. He loves jazz and politics, history and astronomy. I picture him taking me to the science museum or something. *Oh, gross. Please don't take me to a museum. Please.*

I am wearing my dark-blue skinny jeans, black patent leather flats, and a gray top I stole from Piper's closet—don't want him to think I'm going all out or anything. My goal was to dress only slightly better than I do for school.

When he arrives, I walk down the stairs and see him in the kitchen talking to Arch. Suddenly I'm nervous and second-guess my outfit. *And what do I do with my hands?* I begin to fidget with my jeans.

Edwin looks up at me and smiles. "Ya ready?"

"Emerson!" Arch gasps. She looks like she's just seen a ghost.

"What?"

"Excuse us, Edwin." She leads me into the dining room. "Have you seen yourself?"

I glance down at my outfit.

Leaning over the dining-room table, she grabs her purse. "I mean, I know you're only studying, but . . ." She reaches in and retrieves a tube of Love Potion No. 9. "Your lips are *naked!*"

Instinctively I gasp and throw my hands up to touch my nonglossed lips. I must have been so nervous that I forgot to apply gloss after brushing my teeth! But Love Potion No. 9 seems a bit bright for a date like this. "Love Potion?" I say. "Ya sure?"

She hands me a mirror. "I'm sure. You need a little pop of color."

"Thanks." I apply the gloss while she walks around the corner to occupy Edwin again. When I walk back into the kitchen, she is beaming. She's been bragging to Edwin about the dance I'm choreographing at the studio. For all I know, she's invited him to the event. Lawsy.

"Bye, baby!" she says with a wink. "Y'all have fun!"

I grab my coat off the back of the chair in the kitchen. "Bye."

"Stay out as late as you want," she adds after the more normal "Study hard!"

I wish she'd be quiet. She's starting to embarrass me.

Edwin and I walk down the sidewalk to his car. "You look really pretty," he says.

"Thanks." His attention is making me self-conscious. But at the same time I get the feeling I could have worn a potato sack and he'd like it.

"Are you curious about where we're going?"

"Yes. Very."

"I think you'll like it." He walks around to open my door for me. *He opened the door for me!* I know I should be impressed, but I'm really kinda weirded out. Who does that? Mr. Wilson is the only male I've ever seen open a door for a lady.

We drive for a while in an awkward silence before he asks, "So how is your jazz project coming?"

I laugh. "Edwin . . . you know it's not really a *jazz* project. I mean my art credit is a jazz dance, but the rest is boring old history."

"I know. But I like to emphasize the jazziness of it."

I giggle. "Thanks for the CD, by the way. I like it."

"Good," he says. "So your aunt was telling me you dance. How long have you practiced?"

"Since I was five."

"You must be good."

"Not really."

"But I get to see your work soon? At the Spring Follies, is it? Your aunt told me you were choreographing a twenties' dance for some kids." He smiles, and I shrink into my seat. It's one thing for him to know about it, but it's another thing entirely for him to come!

"Mrs. Parker is giving me extra credit for it."

"I can't wait to see it."

I'm a tad uncomfortable and a tad excited at the same time. "Where are we going?" I ask, changing the subject.

"You'll see."

CHAPTER TWENTY-TWO

Beautiful Chaos

After a few more turns, it's clear we're headed downtown. Edwin parks in front of Liquid Bar and Grill, which leaves me more stumped than ever. I've never pictured him to be the bar type. But before I can ask him the plan, he reaches for his door and says, "Let's go!"

"Wait," I say, grabbing his arm. "I don't have an ID."

He looks at me like he's got it all under control. "No worries. You don't need one."

Once again he gets out of the car and walks around to my side to get me like a southern gentleman. A beefy-looking bouncer watches us from the front door. But when we approach, instead of asking us for IDs, he gives Edwin a half hug and some kind of secret handshake with a fist pump. *Really?*

I can't believe it. Edwin McNeely has taken me to a bar on a Wednesday night.

Inside, it's loud, not to mention stuffy, and smells like beer.

A jazzy-sounding band is pumping out loud music, and there are loads of people. I assume this must be some pretty hot and famous local band, judging by the size of the crowd. But I have never really been to a real bar before, so I'm not sure. It's exactly like I imagined a nightclub would be: smoky, loud, and hot. I feel as if I am in another country, or on another planet. Even the people in here look unlike most of my friends from school. I mean, I know they're all older, but they don't resemble my friends' parents, teachers, or anyone I can think of. They're cooler, and I'm feeling cooler, too—like *way*.

Edwin seems completely at ease. And he looks handsome— even more so in this environment. He puts his arm around me and moves us through the crowd toward the bar. I'm amazed at how comfortable we are together. I feel as if I've known him forever, and yet so far I know almost nothing about him.

"You okay?" he yells.

I nod, feeling safe within his arm.

He leans against the bar, and I think I see him nod to a few people as if they're friends. "You want a Coke?"

"Sure," I yell over the din. I would have agreed to a beer— or milk for that matter. This is all so freakishly fun.

After we get our drinks, he takes my hand and pulls me toward a small table in front of the stage. The band is jamming, and I figure this is why we're here. The jazz. My project. The fact that he is doing this for me, for my project, excites me so much that I can't stop smiling.

A waitress brings over some chips and salsa, and we watch the band, marinating in their music. When the song ends, I look to Edwin, smiling and clapping. But before I can ask him about the band—who they are and all—he says, "I'll be back in a minute" and jumps up onto the stage.

Let me repeat: EDWIN IS ONSTAGE!!!

"Tonight, I want to welcome back a special guest," the dude with the sax says. He puts his arm around Edwin and shouts, "ED-MAN MCNEELY!!"

The crowd goes crazy. They *know* him. Edwin may be the one onstage, but *I* suddenly feel like a rock star. Even better—the rock star's date.

I watch him walk to the big piano at the right of the stage, and before I can register all that's taking place, he starts playing the most insanely beautiful and wicked cool song I have ever heard. Then he looks up at the saxophone guy, who signals the whole group to start.

It. Is. Awesome.

Edwin's whole body is moving and pulsing to the sound of the beat, his notes spilling out of the piano, all over the floor, and into the crowd of rabid fans, who are lapping it up like hungry animals. And here I sit, in the middle of it, feeling like I am resting in the eye of a musical storm. It's beautiful chaos, I tell you. Beautiful chaos.

On the way home, Edwin explains that his uncle owns the bar, and he has grown up playing in it. He knows all kinds of famous musicians as well as many local celebrities. He has even played with the great Mississippi Barnes! I feel a little silly, but I almost beg him to take me back again sometime. He just laughs and says I'm cute. *I'm cute! Swoon . . .*

"Are you going to pursue music?" I ask him.

"I don't know. I don't think so."

"Are you crazy?! Why not? Seriously, Edwin, you have real talent. And you love it!"

"Like your dancing?" he compares.

"No. I'm average. You're great!"

He pulls into my driveway and stops the car. I lick my lips

instinctively, feeling a kiss in the air, but stop myself. This is Edwin. The fact still remains that in the morning my dreamy rock star date will silently morph into the class band loner. *Oh, why do I care so much?*

"You're anything but average," he says.

Chills spiral around my chest. Who cares about his inevitable Clark Kentish transformation? I bravely turn toward him, but it's too late. He's already got his hands on the door and is on his way out of the car.

We walk up to the door in semi-awkward silence before he says, "Thanks for coming. I had fun."

"Me, too." I meet his eyes and wait for his lips to touch mine; but he shoves his hands into his pockets, turns around, and walks back to his car.

"See ya!" he hollers over his shoulder.

"Yeah," I say, puzzled.

CHAPTER TWENTY-THREE

Swords and Soldiers

"I want everyone to know I'm choosing you to wear my heart," Vance says as he strolls up to my locker Thursday morning wearing a festive red-and-blue shirt underneath his Haygood letter jacket. He's been coming by my locker a lot lately, but today he's especially pumped. It's the varsity baseball team's first game, and it's all he's been able to talk about.

In his hand I see a large red sticker in the shape of a heart with his baseball number on it in blue: #14. Sometimes the faculty will promote a game by having stickers printed for the student body to wear around in support of the event. Our school colors are red and blue. Today, I guess it's hearts. I'm not complaining.

Vance is sporting a furtive grin under his signature baseball cap and looks even more *stellar* than his reputation. Reaching toward me, he places the sticker on the front of my shirt for all the world to see.

I lift my hand and put my palm against the heart, as if

safeguarding it from a swarm of female hands. "Thanks!" I wasn't prepared for this romantic display.

"No," he says. "Thank you." Flashing his hundred-watt grin at me, he tosses his hair and adds, "You headed to chemistry?"

A girl across the hall watches us in what I assume is total jealousy. I wish someone were videotaping this.

"Yeah," I reply, then proceed to walk down the hall next to one of the hottest boys in school, my new brand blazing: Owner of Vance's Heart. Whoa.

Later, as I'm heading to geometry, I'm having a hard time staying focused. The sticker seems to have developed a syncopated throbbing. But it's not just that. At lunch I spotted a brunette in the hall making googly eyes at Vance. And as I passed her, I saw it: another red #14 heart sticker beaming at me from *her* chest. *Maybe it's a coincidence? He wouldn't.* But apparently he would, because as I'm packing up to leave my last period class at 3:30, I catch sight of a third—on Frances's sleeve. It appears she is literally wearing his heart on her sleeve.

Frumping down into my desk chair, I discreetly tear off the sticker. What a letdown. A baseball hero he may be, but he's giving "playing the field" a whole new meaning. I'm not sure I want to run the bases with him after all.

Still . . . I can't help but wonder if the most-fun-I've-had-in-a-long-time outing last night with Edwin was nothing more than an I-think-I'll-take-Emerson-to-see-me-play-the-piano outing? I'm so torn. If Trina and I were still friends, we'd have analyzed it last night over the phone for hours. And I mean *hours*. If there's one thing Trina's great at, it's analyzing boys and their behaviors. Man, I miss her.

My mood is still hanging around in Dumpsville the next day. In English we have to work on poetry again—a needed distraction. I can only hope our assignment today is as much fun as the mayonnaise one was. At least I feel pretty good about my creative writing abilities now.

I squirm around in my seat like a bird trying to settle comfortably into its nest. I take out a fresh piece of paper and run my hand through my hair. My hand gets stuck in a tangle and I whimper, angry that even my hair feels like a mess.

Tangled.

Hmmm . . .

Taking out my pen, I write the word *Tangles* at the top of my paper. And before I know it, half the poem flows from pen to paper, as slip-slidey as Edwin's jazz. I follow my teacher's advice by being honest and raw with my emotions, which, I have to admit, feels like a release. However, my poem is depressing. A life in tangles, dangerously close to knots.

Looking up from my paper-o'-pain, I meet Edwin's smiley eyes, which, of course, make everything better. *How does he do that?* I smile back, then pack my things while he walks out of class. I *so* don't understand this guy. *Did he see my sticker yesterday? Would he have cared?*

Trina sits at our usual spot in the lunchroom. Deciding I'll brave the storm, I start making my way toward her—but she shifts in her seat and turns away from me to talk to *Frances.* I'm sure Trina knows how this makes me feel, but I realize I'm not mad at *her.* I blame that stupid, face-sucking Silas for leading her on with all of his chatty hotness.

Risking public humiliation, I sit down with Fish instead. I need a friendly face.

"Hello, fair maiden," he says.

"Hey, Grady." I cut my salad into small bites and take a sip of tea.

"The decathlon announcement is nigh," he says.

I nod and take another bite, totally disinterested in things like decathlons, as well as all things "nigh." I look back toward my regular table, but no one's even looking at me. Or looking *for* me, which basically sucks. *Does she miss me at all?*

"Emerson?" he repeats. "Aren't you excited?"

"Nah." I stab a large tomato. "I'm not good at game shows."

He laughs. "Game shows? The mighty decathlon is nary a game show, my dear. It's a fantastic mental competition!"

"I guess you're wanting to be on the team?" I ask with a smile.

"Damn straight I am! I aim to be captain!"

I nearly spit out my salad. His comment sounds so normal and the opposite of what I thought he'd say. "So how do you get on the team?" I ask.

"The faculty decathlon board decides who gets to compete. But you have to have achieved near-perfect grades or at least show incredible promise by the time the board meets. Of course, you can always let them know you *want* to participate."

I'm sure he's made them well aware of his desire to compete. "So you have to be headed toward the honor roll," I say, thinking of Arch's deepest desires for me.

"Yes," he says, and I notice something black stuck in his teeth.

I get ready to tell him about the black thing, but before I can speak, Edwin sits down across from me.

"Hi," he says happily. "I didn't expect to see *you* here." He glances over to my regular table, and it feels as if he's looking from Mississippi to Arkansas.

"I, uh . . . I was asking Grady about the decathlon." I clench my jaw, wondering if it's a good idea to sit next to two boys I've kissed for schoolwork.

Fish nods while chewing on a massive hunk of hamburger.

"Did you ask to compete?" Edwin asks me.

Ha! As if. I shake my head and wrinkle my nose.

Edwin opens his drink. "You'd be great at it."

I risk glancing into his velvets and feel my heart thumpity thump thump. He's beaming at me. "I'm not that smart," I say.

He smirks and tells me with his eyes, *You most certainly* are.

Woo wee. This guy makes me feel like I can do anything.

Nah, I answer back with my own eyes and a shake of my head. After which, I feel a bit embarrassed, so I play around with my fork, stabbing random vegetables while Edwin takes a bite of his sandwich and asks Fish something. I look back at Trina, who is standing up to leave.

"I have to go," I tell the boys, gathering up my lunch.

"But you just got here," Grady says.

I can see that the black thing is gone, thank goodness. "I have to talk to Trina," I tell him.

"See ya later," Edwin says with a smile that could light up a Christmas tree. And once again I'm left all befuddled.

CHAPTER TWENTY-FOUR

Sock It to Me, Plum

"Your deal," Luke says, passing me two decks of cards. "Now remember. Hold the decks closer when you try to shuffle them. It looks more professional that way."

I take the cards from him and carefully cut the deck.

"So what's the latest with Vance?" he asks before popping a toothpick into his mouth. "I feel like I haven't talked to you in forever."

I try to pack the cards together tightly.

"I can tell something's up," he says. "You're doing that thing where you gnaw on the side of your cheek. It's so obviously a guy."

I roll my eyes, annoyed by how right he is. "I don't 'gnaw' my cheek, Luke. That sounds cannibalistic."

"Yes, you do." He offers me one of his toothpicks. "Here. Chew on this. It'll calm your nerves."

"Right." I wave him off.

"Seriously. It does. I plan on dominating the World Series with a mouthful."

Luke is crafting his "character." He says the best poker players are as good at acting as they are at playing cards. They hide behind carefully planned disguises and fake personalities in order to throw off their opponents. Luke has chosen "hillbilly-chic." The Chevron shirts, the toothpicks, the holey jeans—it's all supposed to make the players think he's a simple-minded novice. It's pretty brill if you ask me, because he *does* look idiotic; and yet when it comes to cards he is a genius. See? Brilliant.

"Be careful, Jorge," I tell him. "I know you like to be in character and all, but most girls don't wanna date hillbillies."

"True that, Ace, but my kinda girl will love it."

We laugh.

"So Vance?" he reminds me.

"Not really into it anymore." I want to say more. Or maybe I just *wish* I wanted to say more, but I don't. Instead I say, "Arch threatened to take me out of school last month."

"What?" he asks, grabbing the decks from me. "That shuffle sucked." He knocks the decks on the table, and I watch him expertly lock the cards in place. "She wouldn't do that."

"She would!" I say with frustration. Of course, I can't tell Luke that I have seen the desperation and fear in her mind.

"Okay. Okay. She would."

"She can't afford it if there's no payoff, she says."

"So study harder. You hold all the cards, you know."

"Huh? I do not. You're holding them."

"What I meant is that *you* have all the power with your grades. The outcome is in your hands. You hold all the cards."

Taking the cards back from him, I separate them into both of my hands. "Easier said than done." I start to shuffle again. I know he's right, but I don't want to talk about me anymore. "What's new with you?"

His eyes go crossed and loopy, and I swear he starts to sparkle, which is totally not Luke. He's acting like a girl.

"What?" I ask, dealing the cards.

He flips the toothpick to the opposite side of his mouth with his tongue. "I think I might have found my woman."

"Your *woman*?" I laugh. "Who says that?" I bat him with my cards. He falls backward dramatically, then rolls over onto his side, laughing.

"So spill it," I say. "Who is she?"

He sits back up and fans his cards into a perfect arch. "Guess."

I put down my cards. "Stephanie."

"The beret-wearing girl whose beauty mark moves around? No way! Pick up your cards."

"Frances," I say jokingly.

He gives me the *puh-leese* look.

"Come on. Give me a hint."

He lays down a six of spades. "Full lips."

"Full lips, huh?" I scan my cards, squinch up my own full lips, and think. "What else?"

"A tad neurotic, but totally cute." He removes his toothpick, so now I know he's serious.

I put down a two of hearts. "Sterling?"

"Sterling? She walks like a horse. Come on, Ace, think!"

I wrack my brain trying to think of cute, big-lipped girls with a normal stride; and all I can think of is either me, or that brainy friend of Edwin's from my chemistry class, Mallory.

"Mallory?"

"Bingo!"

"You like *Mallory*?"

"Dude. Yeah."

I throw my cards at him. "Get out!"

"I'm tryin' to get in." He laughs.

"Oh, gross."

Mallory's nice and all (and wears a hot shade of gloss few can pull off called Sock It to Me, Plum) but I can't really see Luke wanting to date her.

I start picking up the cards. "But wouldn't you be hesitant to date her? I mean, she's not really like"—I pause—*"us."* He knows that I mean she doesn't hang out in our same swirl of people.

He sits up and puts the toothpick back in his mouth. "If she's weird, then I'll just break up with her."

I'm surprised by how easily he says it. Dating outside of our circle is simply not the norm. Not at all.

"Seriously, Luke, I have no problems with Mallory. I really like her." I pick up my cards. "But can you imagine if I started dating someone like *Edwin?*"

He looks at me, and I fan out my cards again. "So?" he asks.

"So, duh. Our friends would probably make a big deal out of it. Trina and Piper would never let me hear the end of it."

"Are you interested in McNeely, Ace?"

"Gah . . . no . . . ," I say, while reaching up and twisting a large strand of my hair.

"STOP!" he shouts. "You just twisted your hair and bit your lip."

I laugh. "I did not." It was so subconscious that it takes him a minute to convince me I actually did.

"That's a *tell*," he explains. "All poker players have one."

I suddenly feel as if I have made it as a professional poker stud.

"It means you were lying," he clarifies.

Oops. Not a stud.

"Lying?" I ask. "About what?"

"About Edwin."

I resist the urge to yank another strand of hair and realize that he's right. I totally twirl my hair while lying.

"You like Edwin McNeely!" He jabs me.

"Stop!" I giggle. "I do not."

He puts down his cards. "Emerson, you can't fool me. I am a professional human shit detector. You like Edwin McNeely."

I exhale heavily and frown. "No, I don't."

"You might *think* you don't, but you really do."

Oh my gosh. How did I end up with not one, but two of the most psycho-analytical friends on the entire planet. (If I can still consider Trina a friend.)

"He's weird all right but, dude! That doesn't mean you can't date him."

"You just said he's weird." I sigh with a chuckle. "I don't want to be a weirdo-lover." Fact: I hate this about myself, but it's true. I worry about what other people think. People other than Luke.

Luke leans toward me. "Maybe he's *not* weird. Maybe dating you will make him unweird."

I smile. I love that Luke loves me so much.

"Think of him as a makeover project," he says. "You're simply dating him to beautify and educate." He swirls his hands in an overtly feminine manner.

"People will think I've lost my mind."

"Who cares?" Luke stands up.

I throw back my head and groan in frustration. If only it were that easy for me.

He picks up my hand of cards and slaps them down on the table, then takes hold of my arm and lifts me up. "Come on. Let's go cruisin'."

I stand up and follow him, rolling the idea of dating Edwin around in my head like a sour ball: part sweet, but pretty tart, too.

CHAPTER TWENTY-FIVE

Tan in the Tropics

Principal Overton taps the microphone. "Attention! Attention!"

Frances, Trina, and Trina's new fake group of friends settle in behind me, making me feel like the Ivys I kiss. I scan the auditorium, planning to move my seat. But Luke is sitting with his football buddies near the back, and I can't see any open seats near any of my other friends.

UGH.

"Please settle down!" Principal Overton says. "It is my great honor today to announce our new academic decathlon nominees!"

"Ahhh . . . it's the dork fest assembly," says the guy next to me jokingly.

The principal continues. "As I announce the nominees, will you please come up onto the stage?"

I look around the room, wondering who will be asked to go up there. I will know every last one, I'm sure. Intimately.

"Our first member is Malcolm Reynolds!"

Okay, there's one Ivy I haven't kissed.

Clapping ensues before dude-on-my-left whispers, "Oh man, he is such a geek."

Malcolm struts proudly across the stage. He has a calculator sticking out of his back pocket where most guys keep their wallets or cell phones. Walking right up to Principal Overton, he grabs the mic and says in a perfect Elvis imitation, "Thank you. Thank you very much!" Then he hands the mic back and bows as the crowd erupts in laughter.

"Thank you, Mr. Reynolds," the principal says, grinning.

I watch Malcolm salute him like an army general.

Principal Overton continues. "Next we have Oliver Magee!"

Oliver scuffles up the side of the auditorium staring at his shoes. He climbs the stairs on the left and flips his long hair out of his eyes.

I think about how I *could've* kissed Oliver, how Edwin begged him to play sick.

Fearing another mic steal, the principal backs up, but Oliver just stands quietly next to Malcolm.

"Okay, then. Give it up for Sawyer Thompson!"

I laugh at the principal's choice of words, and we all clap.

"He's kinda hot," I hear Trina say behind me, and I'm not sure if she's joking.

He sure is I think, smiling to myself. I remember how hot his last vision was—a total tongue burner.

"Don Yin!" Principal O continues.

Don walks gracefully forward and takes his place next to Sawyer. He, too, bows before readjusting his glasses.

"And our first girl, Mallory Davis!"

"Oh gawd," Frances says, which infuriates me. So I clap and cheer for Mallory, then look across at Luke, knowing he adores her.

"How many more are there?" I hear someone say from behind.

"Two, I think," replies Trina.

"Grady Cromwell!" says Principal O.

"Fish. Fish. Fish. Fish." The audience booms his nickname over more clapping while Grady rushes up to the stage. He trips on the steps and several people laugh. I, on the other hand, cringe that I have kissed him.

"Edwin McNeely!" Principal Overton shouts.

My heart seizes, and the memory of Grady's kiss evaporates in an instant. I look across the room to stare at the leather jacket and messy hair I've grown to adore.

"Whoa. Another loser," I hear Frances say.

She is seriously going to make me punch her.

I watch as Edwin strolls onto the stage, smiling. He looks out over the audience, and I wonder if he's looking for me.

"I guess that's it," says the girl next to me. She leans down and picks up her purse.

"And last but not least," Principal O goes on. "Our most improved student, Emerson Taylor!"

I freeze, petrified, my eyes nervously darting around the little section of "cool people" that I'm sitting in. I hope I don't puke.

I have kissed several boys on that stage, and the last thing I want to do is go stand up there with them.

CHAPTER TWENTY-SIX

Roses Are Red

Luke rises from his seat and turns around, scanning the room for me. "Get up there, Ace!" he yells when he finally spots me.

Without even seeing myself, I know I've turned Roses Are Red. Forcing an unstable smile, I slowly stand and wiggle my way out of the row and toward the stage. I climb the steps to the left and walk over to stand next to Edwin.

People are clapping, and Luke and Vance are now hooting obnoxiously.

I begin silently reciting the Stellar Cosmetics Creed in my head like some kind of yoga mantra meant to relax me and get me through this moment of Ivy stardom. *We pledge to present you with the finest cosmetics available, carefully prepared in our labs in Switzerland. . . .*

"As always," the principal begins, "the students you see in front of you have some of the highest GPAs in their class *or* are the most improved. We are proud to nominate them this year for our academic decathlon team! But these students must maintain their current grade point averages in order to compete in the decathlon itself. They are merely our nominees today." He chuckles. "Well, not *merely*. These kiddos are great!"

More clapping ensues, and I feel like such a fake standing up here that I can hardly bear it.

"Hey, Jazzy," Edwin whispers to me. "Welcome to the crew."

Did he just call me Jazzy? I look over at him, on the verge of nerd-girl tears. "Thanks."

Principal O continues. "Don't forget to bring in your old coats for the coat drive; and all of you in Mrs. Vaughan's homeroom please stay behind for an announcement before heading back to class."

Kids start talking and getting up before he even says, "You are dismissed."

A roar of voices fills the air, and I inhale and exhale deeply.

"Congratulations," Edwin says.

"You too," I say, embarrassed that he's congratulating me—a total poser. I know this was my goal. This was what I wanted. I know this, but now that I'm standing here next to all of these people who worked really hard to be here—these people who *deserve* to be here—I'm mortified.

What's worse: it's only a matter of time before everyone discovers I'm a fake. Unless, that is, I get back to work locking lips—the very thing I'd hoped to stop doing!

Oliver walks over and gives Edwin a high five. "Dude! Campbell is gonna be pissed!" I assume he means because Campbell wasn't nominated. Great. Not only did I steal all of their knowledge to be up here, but I probably stole Campbell's place as well.

"So when do we start strategizing?" asks Sawyer.

Strategizing? I think. What does *that* involve?

Fish steps in. "I'm game whenever y'all are, but let me suggest that we study after six p.m., which is the optimum hour for information retention."

I start to fidget. I don't want to do this anymore; but I can almost taste Arch's pride and desperation, and I know I have to. I look for Mallory, but she's talking to the principal.

Sawyer smiles at me and asks, "Do you want to study with me?"

"I, umm . . ." I start to bite my fingernails. *Study what? Like how do you prepare for this thing?*

"She's studying for the first part with me," Edwin declares to the group.

"Then I'll teach her the second part," Sawyer says.

"I think it would be better if I did," says Fish, coming out of his shell.

Ugh. I know exactly what they're all thinking!

Edwin looks across from Sawyer to me and then back to Grady. I'm suddenly worried he might have heard something, or can see what's going on.

"Uh, I, I have to go," I say in stilted segments, motioning toward the crowd. "I'll think about it. I have to get back to class."

CHAPTER TWENTY-SEVEN

Rock on, Rosie!

After school I head to the dance studio a bit discouraged. Vance hasn't come by my locker since last week, and though I tried to talk to Trina after the assembly, she acted as if she was in a rush and couldn't chat. Trina ALWAYS has time to chat. It's, like, her job.

"One more time from the top," I say to the girls, turning on the CD again.

My eight young dancers move through the routine with only a few snags. I decide to move Bridget in line with Anna. "Bridget, you stand here."

"I don't want to move there!" she complains.

"What's wrong?" I ask.

"I can't dance next to Anna. She slaps me when I make a mistake."

Bridget and Anna are sisters—a relationship I know only too well. My head starts to throb. Teaching kids is *hard*.

"Anna, is this true? Do you slap Bridget?"

"She slaps me, too!" Anna shouts. "All the time!"

"I'm going to get Ms. Alvis," I threaten. "And if you girls can't follow directions, you will not be allowed to dance in the recital. Do you understand?"

They all look toward the door, where Piper has magically appeared. I am both pleased that she's shown up and mad at how uncommitted she has been. But the truth is, I'm tired. Stressed-out, burned-out, scared-to-fail-the-decathlon-prep tired.

"Hey," I say as Piper walks into the room.

"Hey, guys!" she says enthusiastically.

I smile, wondering why she's so chipper today. "Thanks, Piper. I really needed you today."

She pulls out a large purple tackle box from behind her back. "Now," she says with a twinkle in her eyes, "can everyone sit down?"

The girls all get really quiet and sit in a tight circle. Anna pushes Bridget to get closer.

"I saw that, Anna!" I say, cutting my eyes at her. "You come sit over here with me." I flop down and put Anna in my lap.

Piper moves the tackle box to the center of the circle. I already know what it is. I have one that looks almost exactly like it, except mine is pink. PIPER is written in large paint pen letters on the top. "Do you guys know what's in here?" she asks.

They shake their heads.

"Well," she begins, "Emerson has asked me to not only work on your costumes"—she measured the girls last time she surprised us with an appearance—"but we also have to see what your *makeup* should look like."

"Is that makeup?" Margaret giggles, excitedly pointing to the purple box.

Piper nods and opens the tackle box to reveal drawer after drawer of glorious makeup. There are eye shadows in every color of the rainbow, as well as tube after tube of lipstick. Loads of shiny lip glosses and probably eight different shades of blush. There are applicators, tweezers, mirrors, Q-tips, foam smudgers, brushes, and powders of various shades, all meticulously arranged as only an OCD freak of nature could do. I must admit, it's a thing of beauty—pun definitely intended.

Excited hands and fingers reach forward, and Piper snaps the top shut. "Not so fast," she says, smiling. "I need to figure out how I am going to make your faces look like girls from the Jazz Age. So I want you to sit one behind another in a row, and I will do your faces one at a time. Emerson?" She turns to me and whispers in my ear, and I smile remembering when Arch came to my own class at just about this age. "Emerson will give you a gift at the end if you sit still and let me do your faces first." She hands me one of Arch's glittery blue bags.

They all get superstill and quiet. "Bethie," I say, "you can go first."

Bethie inches forward on her bottom and tilts her face toward Piper, ready to receive her beautification. After Piper finishes, I show Bethie a mirror and hand her her very own tube of lipstick to keep—Rock On, Rosie!

I decide to play a hand-clapping game with the girls while Piper calls them over, because "sitting still" is not happening.

Thirty minutes later, all eight have been made up.

"Tell Piper thank you," I instruct the girls.

"Thank you!" they say while waving their new tubes of Rock On, Rosie! in the air.

"Next time we'll be doing your hair, okay?" Piper tells them.

"Thanks, Pipes," I say, and I mean it. *I miss you.*

CHAPTER TWENTY-EIGHT

Family Pride

Our kitchen smells like Arch's famous chicken and dumplings when I get home. Yum! She must have made a big sale at work.

"Arch?" I say as I shut the side door and walk into the kitchen. But there's no answer.

"Piper?" I shout.

Nothing.

A large paper sign that says CONGRATS! is hanging from the lights over the island, and Arch has drawn hearts around the edges with lots of exclamation points and little red lip kisses.

"Arch?" I repeat, walking farther into the house.

She rounds the corner. "Oh, hey, darlin'! You're home early."

I put down my backpack. "Piper came to my dance class today."

"I know." She hugs me. "She told me."

"What's the sign for?"

She doesn't answer—just smiles and yells for Piper, who comes down the stairs looking bored.

"Well, girls," Arch begins. "A celebration is in order."

I look at Piper excitedly.

She shrugs, clearly as in the dark as I am.

Arch puts her arm around me. "We have a decathlete in the family!"

I blow a huge, panicked breath out of my mouth. "How did you know?" I ask.

Arch shakes her head. "Silly! Principal Overton e-mailed me this morning to tell me how impressed all of the teachers have been with your grades this semester. They want to give you a chance to really show the school what you know."

"I can't d-d-do it," I stutter.

"So modest," Arch says, hugging me again.

"I don't think I can do it," I repeat.

She kisses my dimple. "Yes, you can, baby!"

Her pride tastes overpowering, like wasabi; and I can see her envisioning me on stage, winning all kinds of awards. *Oh, lawsy.* It's such a lie that I almost double over with cramps. Me on stage, winning awards? Ha!

"Principal O said you'll have a team that studies together; but during the decathlon, you won't know exactly what questions will be asked, only the categories. It's kind of like *Jeopardy*, except that any team member can buzz in to answer the question. During the study sessions, each member usually picks a subject to specialize in."

"That's cool, Em," Piper says, laughing. "In a dorky way."

"Piper!" Arch says. But my sister's right. It's Dorksville.

"Sorry," Piper says. "I need to go stuhhh-deee. What time is dinner?"

Arch groans. "I was wanting some family-bonding time."

"We'll bond over Easter break," Piper teases.

"Oh, all right," Arch says. "But I'd like a little pre-Easter bonding over dinner, which will be in about an hour. I invited the Wilsons to join us. Until then, study."

After hugging me *again*, Arch gushes, "I am just over the moon, Emmie! Over. The. Moon! And the Wilsons will be, too!" She rushes for the phone.

Good grief, she's so excited she can't even wait until they get here for dinner? If I bomb this, I'll look like an idiot. Think, Emerson, think.

"What if I don't want to?" I ask tentatively.

Arch narrows her eyes at me while holding the phone to her ear. "You have to. I already told Principal Overton that you would accept. There's no better achievement on your academic transcript. I'm so, so proud of all of your hard work, Emerson. *So* proud!"

She's quiet for a second, then shouts into the phone, "Audrey, my baby is a decathlete!"

CHAPTER TWENTY-NINE

Grayce

"Jazzy?" Edwin pops his head around my locker Wednesday morning, my first official day of decathlon prep. "You wanna go with me to get some candy after school?"

"Candy?" I ask. I thought we were going to study?

He tilts his head and looks at me in this intense way, like he can see clear through to my secret grade-stealing alter-identity. "How can we study without Sour Patch Kids?"

"Are you serious?"

He wrinkles his forehead. "Don't tell me you're one of those girls who are always on some kind of diet."

"No." I laugh. "I've just never had a guy ask me out for candy before." In reality, I've never had a guy ask me out for anything until a week ago.

"Now, Jazzy . . ." He smiles at me with a lopsided grin that is part dorky, part sexy, and admittedly adorable. "You haven't lived until you've been taken out for candy."

"Well, then, how can I refuse?"

Six hours later, we're walking down the city sidewalk behind two moms and five little kids. I nudge Edwin, feeling like a kid myself. He grins before putting his arm around me and pulling me close. "Big kids can eat candy, too, ya know."

Yowsers. Edwin just put his arm around me in public.

Inside the shop, I look around the room, unable to believe I've never done this before. The pink-and-white-striped walls are lined from top to bottom with clear glass containers holding every kind of candy you can imagine. There are gummy bears, thirty-five different kinds of jelly beans, and chocolates galore. Not to mention gigantic swirly lollipops. And the air? It smells of spun sugar. As a matter of fact, it's exactly what I imagine Willy Wonka's gingerbread house might look like—if he had one.

Edwin, being a regular, makes a beeline for the jelly beans. He looks back at me as if to say *What are you doing? Dig in!* He hands me a small cellophane bag with a twisty tie, and I head for the sour cherries. No sooner do I have a bag bursting with cherry sweetness than I see a small plastic tub of what looks like candy lipsticks.

"Get out!" I say. "Candy lipsticks?" I pick up one and twist the bottom. A thick finger of sweet tart comes out of the top. Must. Have. Now.

"Those are old-fashioned," says the lady behind the counter. "You should get one for your mom."

"Good idea!" I say, taking a couple for Arch and Piper, and then hand them to her.

"Moms have seen these in their younger days," the lady says while putting my candy in a bag. "I bet it makes her smile."

I grin. "She sells makeup. She's gonna love this!"

Edwin pulls out his wallet and pays the lady. But before we

can get out the door, I stop in front of a large glass jar full of red wax lips. "Can you eat these?"

"Wax lips?" the lady says. "Of course you can! They're old-school, too. Take one for your mom. It's on the house."

"Thanks!" I reach in and retrieve a massive, goofy pair of lips. "This place rocks!" I tell Edwin on the way out the door.

He pops a jelly bean into his mouth. "Told ya."

Walking down Edwin's brick sidewalk, I remember the day a couple years ago when I delivered a catalog here, and Edwin was lying in the porch swing. The urns by the door no longer contain large ferns but small pine trees that spiral upward into beautiful, Christmas-like cones.

"Is it weird coming over to my house today?" he asks. "I mean you've been here before, but we didn't really know each other."

"Maybe," I say, but I'm really thinking, *YES! Über weird. Epic weird. Fantastic weird.*

He opens the door, and I am immediately struck by his mother's design aesthetic. It's not vintage like Arch's. It's colorful, artsy, and bright. "Welcome to Chez McNeely," he says, and I follow him through the foyer and the kitchen. We turn right and crash onto a big leather sectional sofa in the den.

"Your house is so pretty," I say. "I love it!"

Just then Mrs. McNeely pops in to say hello, and Edwin introduces me.

She is surprisingly young looking. Medium-brown hair, athletic build, same green eyes, and, of course, his perfect pores. She's wearing that cute new brand of jeans Piper loves, a black sweater, and a subtle shade of gray eye shadow that looks very much like Grayce. If I didn't know any better, I'd say she's in her early thirties—but, of course, that's impossible. "You're Mary Archer's niece," she says. "I just love your aunt."

"Thank you," I reply before she asks us if we need anything.

"We've got candy," Edwin says, popping jelly beans into his mouth.

"Well, that sounds better than apples, I suppose. Let me know if you need anything else. And, Emerson?" she asks. "I think I have a check for Mary, so remind me before you leave, and I'll give it to you."

"We will," Edwin replies. "Thanks, Mom."

"Yes. Thank you, Mrs. McNeely," I repeat.

"What does your mom do?" I ask. "She looks so young. Does she work?"

"She's a piano teacher," he says. "And she's forty-two. Come here." He stands up and takes my hand.

I follow him into the living room, where a large black grand piano sits proudly in the center.

"Wow," I whisper as if I'm in a library or something. There's just something reverent about a massive piano. "So this is where you learned how to play?"

He lets go of my hand and runs his fingers across the vast black surface. "Mmm-hmm."

I smile, looking around the room. If he wasn't standing here, I'd snoop like a mad dog. "I thought you played a horn?"

"I do," he says with an embarrassed chuckle. "The French horn. But I just play that because no one else can. This is my real love." He reaches over and plays a few notes.

I shake my head. "Amazing."

"So, you wanna see my room?"

"Sure." I answer like it's no big deal, but I'm thinking, *Are you friggin' kidding? Let's run!*

Once more I follow him from the living room into the

foyer, where I see a huge winding staircase. The walls are papered with a lush green vine design, making it feel as if we are preparing to climb up into the trees. At the top, the walls are lined with baby photos, and I laugh at how completely nerdy some of them are.

"Yeah, yeah," he says, chuckling. "You can show me yours next time I'm at your house."

"Not a chance," I say, but the truth is that we don't have any pictures of Piper or me before I was six. Arch told us that baby pictures were not a priority with our mother. This fact has always made me sad. What kind of mother doesn't take loads of pictures of her babies? I guess a semicrazy one. With as many pictures as Arch takes, it's hard to believe they were even sisters.

At the top of the steps we turn right and go down a long hall. Edwin's room is the last door on the left. I don't know what I expected—but it's so much better. Just being around his things thrills me. It's like the inner sanctum of *Edwin*. He has an insane music collection and several instruments lying around his room. He even has an electric guitar signed by some famous rock star hanging on the wall above his desk. And his books! Don't even get me started. This guy *loves* to read. I scan the rows of titles. Some of them are definite girl books. *Nice.* I giggle, picturing him curled up in bed reading *Twilight.*

Also cool is how neat and tidy he is. My room has shoes scattered everywhere and movie posters tacked to the walls. His room has framed art, bookshelves, and monogrammed pillows. Plus, my dresser has enough makeup, lip gloss, and jewelry to deck out the whole sophomore class. His dresser has a brush, a watch, and his phone charger arranged on top, spic-and-span perfect.

Sitting down on his bed, he pats the spot beside him.

I obey and bite the inside of my cheek. What will we talk about? Maybe he'll kiss me. But I'm not sure I'll learn anything. And if I did, I'd feel awful.

I never should have agreed to this.

He hints at a smile and licks his lips, sending butterflies zooming around my rib cage.

"So . . . ," I say, trying to fill the sexy silence.

Just then the door to his room swings open. "Edwin?" Mrs. McNeely sticks her head in the room. "Can I get you guys something to drink?"

Edwin smiles at me sympathetically. "You want anything?"

"No, thanks," I reply.

"Okay then," she says. "Y'all study hard."

Edwin reaches over the side of his bed for his backpack, and I feel our sexy moment pop like a soap bubble. "What chapter should we look at first?"

CHAPTER THIRTY

Icing

By Thursday morning, not only have I learned more history than I ever thought possible from one night, but I understand my geometry homework, too. All thanks to Edwin and *all* without a kiss. It's amazing how much I've learned lately. To be honest, it hasn't even been that bad. Some of it was rather interesting. I just wish I didn't have to showcase myself in this stupid decathlon to prove it.

But today, in honor of my successful study session, I grab a bright fuschia gloss called Icing and head to school early, stopping only once to pick up the Wilsons' paper and place it on their porch.

💋

"Hey there, Decathlete."

I turn away from my locker, expecting to see Edwin behind me—or rather *hoping* to see him—but finding Vance instead, blue eyes blazing. "Hey."

He leans up against the wall, and my knees tingle. Can't help it. It's *him*.

"Somehow I didn't peg you for the brainy type. Congrats."

"Yeah, well, I've been studying." Just saying this makes me wanna shrink.

He crosses his legs, still leaning back against the wall—the picture of confidence. "You wanna go out tomorrow?"

Holy smokes. Vance Butcher is asking me out. *But what about the stickers? Am I his first choice?*

"You *have* heard about Trina's party, right?" He gives his hair the toss Justin Bieber made famous. Chin down and swoop.

I nod. I'd heard from Luke, of course. *But why can't I speak?* This is something I have wanted and dreamed about for almost three years, and now that it's really happening, all I can think about is Edwin and his messy hair and pore-perfect skin. And the way he says "Jazzy" and his velvet eyes. *Snap out of it, Emerson! Snap out of it! THIS IS VANCE!*

I take a breath and smile. *What do I do? I'm not even sure I'll be welcome at Trina's, but what do I say?* I reach up to twist a piece of my hair but tug on it instead, transferring my pain and frustration to my scalp. "I'm going to Trina's," I say, hoping I can skate past his invitation with some sort of group invite of my own. "You should come."

"Right." He takes a step closer to me, and I see a crease of confusion form on his forehead. "That's what I'm talking about. I was wondering if you'd want to go to the party *with* me?"

Ring!

I am literally "saved by the bell." I never thought I'd be so happy to hear the bell ring in my whole life.

"I'm gonna be late!" I say, opening my eyes so large I'm surprised they don't roll right out of my head.

Grabbing my book, I start down the hall, leaving him standing there. "Call me later!" I shout. "We'll talk!"

At lunch I look across the sea of tables and spot Edwin talking about something with Grady and Oliver—probably strategizing. He's making motions with his hands as if he is telling them something HUGE. They're laughing, and I can't help wondering what he's talking about.

Edwin's funny in a cute, understated way. I want to know everything that flows through that head of his. Except I want him to *tell* it to me over hours of conversation and not just suck it out of him in a seven-second kiss.

On the other side of the cafeteria, Vance is hunkered down over his tray, eating. As boring as that sounds, he still excites me.

I look from one to the other until Trina plops down her tray next to me as if we aren't in the single biggest fight of our lives. "What's up?"

"Huh?" I ask. "I thought we weren't talking?"

"Yeah, well," she begins. "I'm tired of fighting with you, and I'm having a party tomorrow night."

I'm furious that she thinks she can just decide when we're friends and when we aren't. "You've been so mean," I tell her.

"But I miss you," she says, sticking out her bottom lip.

"Say you're sorry."

"I'm sorry," she replies with sincerity. "What about you?"

"I already told you I was sorry, stupid. Twice."

"Good. I'm unbelievably sick of hanging out with Frances. And although I don't have a sister, I get it. You can't betray her." She holds out her pinkie like we used to do as kids. "But no more lies, okay?"

"No more lies." I link my pinkie to hers, feeling a double

dose of guilt and relief. I finally have my friend back, but I can't really be honest with her about Edwin *or* this kissing business.

"Pinkie swear," we say in unison before she leans across the table with big, excited eyes. "I heard Vance is asking you out!"

I swallow a bite of my lasagna and chew, unsure of what to say.

"Okay. I'll be honest. I *have* missed you terribly, but when I heard he was asking you out, I just knew I had to make up with you because this is Vance! You can't possibly get ready for this date without me!" She takes a bite of her sandwich and goes on. "Also . . ." She removes a magazine from her backpack. "There's an article in here that I thought might help you with the twenties' project." She starts flipping through the pages. "It's about the Depression."

I look up and see that Edwin is leaving. "Uh huh."

"Are you okay?" she asks.

"Mmm-hmm." I nod and take another bite of my lasagna.

She turns to look at whatever was holding my attention. "Was that Band Man?"

"Edwin," I correct her as a seed of anger develops deep inside me.

"Since when are you on a first-name basis with *him*?"

"Since he helped me in class the other day, coolness." I know she disapproves of Edwin as a friend, much less a boyfriend.

"I heard he asked that girl in our PE class to hang out tomorrow night."

I drop my fork. "What girl? Who told you this?"

"The girl with the curves." She goes on about how perfect they'd be for each other because he's all into music and she sings—and before ten seconds goes by, I'm convinced my

relationship with him is doomed before it's even had a chance
to begin.

"Theresa Devlin? With the big butt?"

"That's the one!" Trina pops the top on her soda, then
cusses for breaking a nail.

*He's taking out the sexy, Irish girl who doesn't look a day under
twenty-six?* "I feel sick."

Vance looks over from his table and pins me to my chair
with his eyes. "Tomorrow?" he mouths, and without knowing
what I'm doing, I nod. One tiny subconscious nod, and I have
accepted a date I'm not even sure I want to go on.

"You're not sick," Trina says, oblivious to the real reason for
my pain. "You have a serious case of nerves over Vance. Hold
up." She raises her hand, palm facing me. "Has he already
asked you out? I thought it was going to happen later."

All of this makes me nuts. The fact that she has heard this.
The fact that she knows when Vance was planning on asking
me. The fact that Edwin asked someone *else* out. The fact
that I am quickly becoming a harlot. But the biggest thing
that's bugging me is wondering if Vance is the reason Trina is
making up with me.

"Yes," I reply. "He asked me out."

"I knew it! I knew it!" She's buzzing with enthusiasm.
"We have to prepare. Do you have any more of that tanning
spray?" She begins flipping through the magazine again, and
I push my tray aside.

"I don't know. Probably."

"He must think you're the ultimate challenge."

Me? A challenge? "Why?"

"You know. You're hard to get."

"Really?" I ask.

"Oooh!" she says, suddenly distracted by an article. "Did you know one in three teens is in an abusive relationship?"

I grab the magazine, a bit harder than I should. "I don't think of myself as hard to get."

"You're just hard to get to *know*," she says as if it's nothing.

Her comment makes me sad. Is *this* why Edwin hasn't tried to kiss me since that first Spanish tutoring session? "Really?"

She takes back the magazine. "Look. The Em I know is the bomb! It's okay to make him wait for the big kiss and whatever while he tries to get to know the you that I know. That's all I'm saying."

"Did you just quote *Seventeen*?"

"Yes." She laughs and then whacks me gently over the head with the magazine. "Did I mention that I miss you?"

She's right, and I know it. I think again about the guys I've kissed. I never really let them know me—not the real me. Vance doesn't know me, either. Maybe that's what's happening with Edwin—he's more interested in knowing me than in kissing me.

Well, that sucks, because I want to kiss him again, and I may have just lost my chance.

That afternoon, after eating my favorite snack (saltine crackers with Cheddar cheese and dill pickles), I check my phone for the thousandth time—as if the mere act of opening and closing it will generate a text from Edwin. Or a call.

But there's nothing.

Trina, on the other hand, has been actively texting—seven times, to be exact. She's asked what I'm going to wear, what Vance said, what time we're coming to the party, and four other equally pertinent questions. I have to admit, her insane interest and excitement is starting to rub off on me. This is Vance, after all.

Confession: I like having Trina back. And I like *finally* being the one we focus on, the one we dress, the one with a date. And if it took Vance to rejoin us, so be it. I should be thankful.

CHAPTER THIRTY-ONE

Touchdown

He's late.

And not just a little bit late, a whole freaking forty-five minutes.

"Do you think he forgot? I mean, could he have just forgotten?" I ask Trina on the phone in a complete and total panic attack. I stare at my outfit in the mirror and try buttoning and then unbuttoning the top two buttons on the purple blouse I borrowed from Piper.

"No!" she says, while reassuring me that Vance is just taking his time, trying to be cool and all. Or maybe he is having a bad-hair night.

"Right. Be serious," I say with a laugh. "I'm freaking out." This is true. I am. The last thing I want is for Vance to decide I'm not worth it. I mean, I'm allowed to question how I feel about him, but he's not allowed to question his choice in me.

She laughs. "Okay. You want serious? I am seriously in love with that guy who sat across from our table at lunch yesterday."

I crack up, remembering the cute senior we analyzed over our chili fries. "We don't even know his name!"

"It's Gentry," she says. "I asked Luke."

I smile. It's no longer Silas. "I have to go reapply my lip gloss," I say. "But are you sure it's okay he's so late? I mean, could he be having second thoughts about asking me out?"

"Only if it's chronic," she says. "Which means he could have issues."

I know better than to ask her what "issues" those might be, but before I can change the subject, I hear Piper calling me from downstairs.

"Oh crap!" I say to Trina. "He's here!" I grip my stomach and moan into the phone. "I feel like I'm gonna vomit."

"Do that breathing stuff. Quick!"

"Thanks. Bye!"

"Emerson!" Piper calls again. "Vance is here!"

Looking at myself one more time in the mirror, I pucker up my lips, grab my sweater, and walk downstairs slowly— you know, so he doesn't think I'm anxious or anything.

But the sight of him shocks me momentarily. Vance Butcher is here.

In.

My.

Kitchen.

💋

On the way into the restaurant Vance drops the bomb. "So I asked Frances and Thomas to have dinner with us. I hope you don't mind."

Huh? You hope I don't mind? What?!

"There they are!" I follow his gaze to the far corner, where I see Frances sitting at a table wearing the exact same purple top I have on! Not only is she on my first date with Vance, but of all the body-hugging atrocities she has in her closet, she chooses the shirt I'm wearing? You've got to be kidding me.

"I have to go to the bathroom," I say before we take one step farther, and then I do the unthinkable. I hole up in a stall and stuff my bra. Looking in the mirror, I think, *Not bad, Emerson. Fuller, but not ridiculous—just right.*

With renewed confidence, I exit the bathroom and strut to the table. That's right, a full-on strut. Frances looks up at me as I approach, and a self-important smile oozes across her face, making me even more self-conscious than I already was. Ugh.

Taking my seat, I lay the napkin in my lap and begin to look at the menu. However, not ten minutes pass before Frances has both guys in hysterics. I feel as small as my real breasts. I gotta give it to her, though. She's so funny and bubbly that I feel like I'm sitting across from a carbonated energy drink. I have no idea how to compete.

The night goes about like this:

"Have you seen *Dude, Where's My Car?*" Vance asks me.

"No." Sigh. I can't stand those old, goofball movies.

"You're kidding!" Frances practically shouts. "*Everyone* has seen that movie!"

"I laughed my ass off at that movie!" Thomas chimes in.

"I, I . . ." I start to say something, but Frances cuts me off with, "'I'm sensing something very Canadian about this place.'"

Huh? I look around, wondering what she's talking about. Vance starts laughing, and I realize she's imitating some dopey line from the movie.

"'Dude, it's a llama!'" he shoots back at her, and there begins a domino effect with Frances and the boys reciting line after line, reliving every stupid moment.

Left with no other option, I force a laugh that comes off way too high-pitched. *D'oh!* This whole date feels like something I'm watching from a distance. Like I have slowly floated above the table to avoid the pain of sitting here on what should have been my dreamy date with His Royal Hotness. I take a bite of my shrimp and grits to avoid crying while she goes in for the win.

"So, Vance, why isn't Coach playing Patrick at first base this year?"

Did she really just speak *baseball?* That's it. Game over. Vance lights up, and I bow my head in defeat. I know *nothing* about baseball. I try to remember what Luke said about game tactics the other day during our little poker match, but I can't. Not that I would be able to apply it anyway.

"I have to go to the bathroom," I announce to no one in particular.

Vance smiles and scoots his chair back slightly so I can stand up. I smile warmly at Frances and Thomas like the graceful girl I am and take a large sip of my Diet Coke before leaving.

"Again?" Frances asks loudly. "Are you having bowel issues?"

Huh? Diet Coke streams out of my nose at warp speed as I choke on her words.

"Awesome!" screams Thomas.

Grabbing my napkin, I try to wipe my nose while coughing on the carbonated gas that is currently burning my brain. This small effort sends my purse crashing down off my shoulder, knocking Vance's glass over, and finally, spilling Dr Pepper into his mashed potatoes.

Glorious.

"I'm so sorry!" I say, fumbling with the napkins.

"If she didn't have issues before, she will now!" Thomas says, busting a gut.

Tears are now streaming out of my eyes.

"I'm sorry, Emerson. I didn't mean to make you *cry*," Frances says.

"I'm not crying, dammit!" I tell her. "I just got Coke in my eyes." I pick up Vance's glass and apologize again before power walking it, Olympic-style, to the bathroom.

When I return to the table, the dinner is clearly over, and the boys are signing the check.

Thomas watches me approach and says, "Let's blow this joint! But not through Emerson's nose!"

All righty then. The Three Stooges crack up once more, and we head for the cars.

CHAPTER THIRTY-TWO

Wacky Watermelon

Wacky Watermelon is not a shade every girl can wear. Trust me. It's a tad neon, which makes most girls look clownish, but luckily not me. My French features balance the brightness just right—at least that's what Piper says. Be advised though, it's downright scary on a pale blonde, like Frances, which is why I offered her a free tube on the way out of the restaurant. Just sayin'.

"I don't know about dinner, but he sure seems into you here," Trina says after we're alone at her party. She's decorated the kitchen with streamers and pushed a table against the window, where several large bowls of pretzels, chips, and popcorn sit. Next to the snacks are various bottles of soda and a sampling of liquors. Mr. and Mrs. Strickland are clearly out of town. They'd never tolerate us mixing drinks at a party in their house.

"Maybe I overreacted," I say. "I'm well aware of the fact

that I can't read boys at all." *At least, not without kissing them.*

"Wanna play pool?" I turn around to see Vance, looking dashing as always. Trina and I exchange knowing smiles.

"Sure." I refrain from saying *Game on!* Fact: I have mad pool game.

Once in the basement, we walk past the couch where two of Piper's friends are making out. I have to physically restrain myself from gawking.

Vance continues over to the wall and pops out two cue sticks while I arrange the balls in the triangular rack, making sure to underplay my pool proficiency.

"Stripes or solids?" he asks me.

"Stripes." After shifting the balls, I remove the rack.

"You wanna break?" he asks, and I stare at his perfect teeth. "Em?" he asks again.

"Oh. No. You do it."

Leaning over the table, he drills the white ball into the mass of colored ones. A striped one falls into the pocket.

"Yay!" I say, then walk around to the other side and take aim at the green-striped one. I look up at him through the tops of my eyes before I hit and pocket it.

"You're pretty good at this," he says after knocking in a few more.

On my turn, I realize I have a hard shot. Leaning my side against the table, I put the cue behind my back and attempt to strike the ball that way. But I can tell it won't work. So I scan the table again. Shoot. I can't find a single way to approach the setup.

Vance watches me intensely from the other side of the table, and I catch myself looking back at the sofa couple. It's clear this would be the perfect place for a kiss, but I'm nervous. Part of me *wants* to kiss him and see inside his head;

but the other part of me knows that in order to have any kind of real relationship, I need to NOT see anything—to *resist* the images. And then there's the problem of Edwin and how I still can't stop thinking about him.

"Y'all have any beer?" Sofa Boy asks us.

Vance shakes his head no and walks around toward me.

In need of a beer, the adoring couple walks upstairs, leaving us alone. I hear the pinball machine beeping in the corner, bringing me back to that horrible day I kissed Silas.

"Let me help you," Vance says, now standing behind me. The mood in the room has changed, and I feel as if we're in some cheesy teen movie. He wraps his long, tan arms around my body and holds my pool cue *with* me, like a parent instructing a child. Suddenly, it really *is* kinda romantic. And I'm intimidated. With the decathletes, I've always been the one initiating a kiss; but this time I'm the *object* of desire.

Pulling back the cue, he directs me, and we hit the ball together. I feel light-headed and strange, unable to focus. *What am I doing? Do I really want this?* And then I'm frozen; my breathing slows. My brain is unable to process. My heart has stopped beating. I have no idea what I want anymore, or who I'm trying to please. Not to mention, how to get out of this little half-hug thing we've got going on.

He lets go of my cue, and I turn around to face him. "Your turn," I say.

He doesn't move. Instead he sets down his cue.

I know what's about to happen, and I kind of want it to; but I am out of sorts and can barely speak.

Our lips touch for like a second before his hands start to move under my shirt. Whoa, Nellie, he's fast! But I let him. The temptation to see inside his head is too great. Forget blocking his thoughts; I want to *know* them. I want him to think of me as sweetly as Edwin does. I want that feeling back.

He moans, and I shift slightly to the right, putting my hand behind my back onto the pool table. He kisses my neck, which feels good; but I need to feel his mouth to be able to see anything, so I hold his head gently and move it back up to my face while looking into his eyes. I want to know he likes me. I *need* to know he likes me.

Our lips touch, and like a spark ignites a flame, my mind lights up with the landscape of his memories.

He's standing in a field playing baseball with two other guys.

Yes, I can see Luke and Thomas. They're all laughing. No other girls. That's a good sign, I guess. So at least he's not always thinking about Frances.

Phew!

He continues fumbling with my shirt and moves his hands toward my bra. I know I shouldn't let him do this, but I am so glued to the movie in his head that I can't bring myself to snap back into reality.

Wait. There's Frances. At least the desire for her at some level. Damn. I can almost read their texts from earlier today, but they're too fuzzy. His memories taste dull, complicated by too many flavors. I can't get a strong sense of anything.

And then suddenly I'm choked by so many images of so many girls flooding my consciousness that I can barely breathe. And at the center of the vision is a conversation he had with some guys on the baseball team about how Frances apparently saw me kiss Fish in study hall. *Really? Where was she?* After asking around, Vance learned that I had kissed more than a few guys this semester. One of which was Grady that day in the gym. I knew I should have talked to him later about how I was kidding—how our kiss was a joke. Not that it would have helped. The vision reveals that right after Grady spoke to Vance, another boy called me a tease and dared Vance to "conquer me."

I'm a dare?

I pull back and gasp for air.

I feel sick, suddenly terrified that Edwin has heard about me, too.

But even worse . . . it's true.

My ear starts to buzz, so I grab it and press it against my head, trying to suppress the pain with my palm.

"What's this?!" Vance asks, pulling his hand out from under my shirt—with a long wad of toilet paper. I was trying so hard to read his mind that I forgot about my bathroom-boobs! His obnoxious laughter fills the air, and all I can think about is Edwin.

My eyes well up, and I snatch the paper away.

He leans back and looks up at me. "It's okay, Emerson. No big deal. I know you were just trying to impress me."

Impress him? I knew Vance was cocky, strutting around in his expensive clothes and always bragging about baseball, but what a tool! I was trying to show up Frances, not impress *him*; but now I see how stupid that was. I steady myself and nudge him away. I need to get out of here.

As I run from the room, he continues to talk, but I can't process what he's saying. It doesn't really matter anyway.

CHAPTER THIRTY-THREE

Rescue Me

For once I want to ignore the vision (and my toilet paper boobs) and pretend that I'm normal. I want to enjoy kissing one friggin' time. Will I ever be able to kiss someone and have it mean something?

Two things are for sure: 1. I don't know how I will ever be able to fall in love for real like Elizabeth Bennet and Darcy. And, 2. Frances and Vance are made for each other.

I grab my sunglasses from my purse on my way up the basement steps and put them on to disguise my red, watery eyes.

At the top of the steps, I see Frances talking to Luke.

"Hey, shades!" Luke laughs. "What's with the lenses?"

"My contact tore—can't see without 'em."

Frances giggles.

I give her a look that I hope conveys, *Who are you laughing at, you ridiculous cow?* But without the mean-girl eyes visible, it's probably not very effective.

"How's the big date going?" Luke asks. "Where is he?"

I point downstairs and scan the room for Trina.

Frances looks both pleased and confused by my answer. Her smile reveals a smudge of Wacky Watermelon across her front teeth, which pleases me immensely.

"Have you seen Piper?" I ask Luke.

"She was talking to Silas last time I saw her."

Not up for searching the party in this state, I head outside and dial her number.

"Hello?" a boy's voice answers.

"I'm sorry, I have the wrong number." I dial again.

"Hello?" the same male voice says.

"Is this Piper's phone?" I ask.

"Yeah. Who's this?"

"This is Emerson, Silas. Is my sister there?" I feel like an idiot having to ask for her on her own phone. Almost like I'm asking permission.

"She's busy. I'll tell her to call you."

"Busy? Is she still here? At the party?"

"Nah. We left a while ago. I had stuff to do."

"Well, she's my ride home." I am getting madder by the minute.

"Find another ride. I told you, she's busy."

Dick.

I walk back into the party and head straight for Luke. "Can you take me home?"

"Sure." His brow knits, and he reaches for my arm protectively. He's probably figured out that I am *not* happy. "Let's find Trina and get her to ride with us."

I'm not prepared to tramp around looking for Trina, so I answer, "I'll meet you at the car," then walk out the front door.

It feels good to be outside in the crisp spring air after my fiasco with Vance. Pausing in the stillness, I breathe in the night air and wait. But when they don't come out immediately, I climb up onto the roof of Luke's car and count the stars. A few minutes later, I tap my heels together three times wanting to go home and end this night. If only these shoes were ruby red and sparkly and could transport me somewhere else. *What if they forgot I'm out here?*

Sliding off the top of the car, I walk back toward the house. There's NO WAY I'm going back *in* there. So I duck behind a bush and peer through the window. *Where are they?* There are too many people inside to see anything.

Sitting on the curb, after sixteen more minutes, my anxiety level is at full tilt. It's time to break down and call Arch. Talk about a nightmare. She's going to ask me nine hundred questions about my date, but I have no other options. I just want to get out of here.

But before I dial, I get a new idea. And fueled by my complete and total desperation, I text Edwin instead. Watcha doin'?

Hey jazzy! I'm @ the bar *Aw.* I'm starting to like it when he calls me that. And I'd so much rather be at the bar tonight than standing outside, trying to hide from my date.

With theresa? Perhaps a stupid question, but I have to know. I just have to.

Huh? he texts back. *Come on, Edwin. Please don't lie to me. I've already heard.*

Your date? I can't believe I have to call him out like this.

Not my date. My cousin. She works with me sometimes. *Seriously?!* A massive smile breaks through my depressed face. I look at the phone. *Crap! What do I say now?*

Where r u? he asks.

Rescue me? I swear I had no control over my fingers

just now. They did that of their own accord. My heart starts palpitating.

Where r u? he texts again.

What do I say? On a date? At a party. Bt want 2 leave.

I sit there for a while, staring at my phone, rereading our texts and waiting for a reply that never comes.

Trina and Luke barrel out of the house a few minutes later, before I've caved into texting Arch.

"What happened?" Trina asks.

"Nothing," I say, which is partly true. Nothing I wanted to happen anyway.

This has got to be the worst night of my life.

CHAPTER THIRTY-FOUR

THE Kiss

Luke and Trina drop me off ten minutes later. As I walk into my house, I throw my purse on the sofa in the kitchen and check the clock. Almost fifteen minutes have passed since I texted Edwin—an eternity in cellular conversation. Maybe I could drive by Liquid to look for his car. But what would that do? Surely just make me feel worse. I have to face the fact that he is clearly not interested in me enough to "rescue me." *Oh, why did I ask him to?*

The TV lights are flickering under Arch's bedroom door, casting a blue glow on the hallway. So I walk down the hall to tell her I'm home.

"Where's Piper?" I ask from the doorway.

"Still out with Silas. How was your date?"

"Crummy," I tell her.

"I'm sorry, honey. Come here. You want to watch a movie with me?"

I feel like I should—she probably needs the company—but I'm too depressed to agree. "No thanks. I'm tired."

I head back down the hall and upstairs to my room. Looking in the mirror, I admire my supercute, wasted-on-a-dumb-date outfit and frown. After slipping it off, I take out my contacts and check my phone again. Nothing.

After wrapping a towel around my head, I wash my face and apply Arch's new miracle zit cream. Her laughter sneaks up the stairs, and I decide maybe her movie *would* make me feel better.

"Em!" she yells upstairs. "Come here!" It sounds like she's in the kitchen. *Fudge?*

I pull on my flannel pajama bottoms and head down the stairs. "Yeah?" As I round the corner into the kitchen, she says, "Look who's here?"

And sure enough, there's Edwin.

Holy cow! I smile awkwardly and unwrap the turban. "I didn't think you were coming." I glance down at my PJ's and remember my glasses and zit cream.

"My phone died. Sorry." A sheepish grin eases across his face.

Arch laughs and says, "Emmie, what are you doing coming down here looking like that?"

"I just said I didn't think Edwin was coming over," I mutter through clenched teeth.

"Do y'all have to study?" she asks in confusion.

"I, uh." I turn beet red. I don't want Arch to think *I* called *him,* because she would never approve. She's old-fashioned that way. Girls do *not* call boys.

Edwin speaks up. "I'm taking Emerson out. On a surprise date."

I can't contain my excitement, and I feel my cheeks press

up toward my eyes in a massive smile.

"Oh," Arch says, still confused. "Well, then shouldn't you be getting ready? Go on and clean up, and I'll hang out here with your boy."

My boy? Oh, kill me now.

"I thought you looked just fine in your PJ's," Edwin says on our way out the door. "You wanna go back to Liquid?"

"I would LOVE to go back to Liquid."

The two-story bar sits on the corner of the city square, crowded with people. But rather than park in front like the rest of the city, Edwin drives around back. This time we enter through a door in the rear of the building, which leads to Liquid's kitchen. The cooks all nod or say hi to us as we pass through, and Edwin grabs a basket of tortilla chips from a long counter. Then he pushes the revolving door into the bar. I follow him, and we walk upstairs to a table in the corner.

"Where are your parents?" I ask.

"Home."

"And they just let you hang out in a bar all night?"

"I'm working," he says.

"Working?!"

"Well, I *was* working, until you needed rescuing." He smirks, and I feel my cheeks bloom pink.

"Am I getting you in trouble? I mean, is your uncle mad that we're sitting here talking?"

"Nah." He pops a chip into his mouth. "He likes you."

"He doesn't even know me."

"He liked the idea of you needing rescuing, and he *does* know you. He waved at you from the bar that night."

"Some meeting. You told him I needed rescuing?" I gasp.

Edwin looks at me in this sexy way and clucks his teeth. "I did." Then, reaching across the table, he holds my hand. I swear, no boy has ever made me feel like this.

We sit there talking and laughing for so long that before I know it, the bartender yells, "Last call!"

Really?

"Come here," Edwin says.

I look at him curiously. "Where?"

He stands up. "Come on." He starts walking toward the steps, and I follow him downstairs and over to an empty stage, where only the ghosts of the band members linger. He jumps up, looks back at me, and extends his hand. So I reach up, and he pulls me onto the stage.

"What are we doing?" I ask.

He says nothing but leads me to the piano, where he sits down and pats the bench next to him.

I sit down slowly while he starts to play. Every once in a while he looks at me with an expression that I can't even begin to describe. It's quiet, serious, and sexy all at once. I watch his hands gracefully move across the black and white keys. His fingers are long, his hands strong and composed. I have never heard the song he's playing, but it's beautiful. "What song is that?" I ask.

He smiles but doesn't answer.

I want the world to disappear. This night to never end. The people around us to leave. And then he stops playing and looks me in the eyes.

Someone claps behind us, causing him to turn around and smile.

"Play something else," I tell him.

"Okay," he says. "This is something I'm working on."

He plays another song that seems to match that quiet,

sexy stare of his. It's stunning.

"I love this one," I say.

"I thought you might."

"Edwin?" the bartender interrupts.

We turn around.

"Can you lock up for me? It's midnight."

"Sure, Dave," Edwin replies. "Have a good night."

"You too, man."

"Oh my gosh. It's already twelve?" I stammer, getting up to leave.

Edwin puts his hand on my leg, pulling me back in place, and calmly says, "Wait."

I don't say anything as we watch Dave and the cook walk out the front door, locking it behind them.

Edwin looks at me. "I've wanted to do this all night." He leans over, and his lips gently touch mine. We kiss tenderly and slowly at first, and then I tilt my head and let the moment take over. He moves his hands from the keys and wraps them around my waist. It all feels as if it's in slow motion, and I realize that it is. Slow, sweet, and warm. I feel woozy. Or drained. For some reason, kissing Edwin drains me. In a good way, but still . . . it feels as if he's sucking something out of me when, in reality, it's I who have sucked something out of him.

My phone rings in my pocket and breaks the moment. "It's Arch," I whisper to him before I answer.

When I hang up, I look back into his eyes. "I have to go."

"I know."

I want him to kiss me again, but he stands up and offers me his hand. Fingers intertwined, we walk out the back door and lock up. It's not until the ride home that I realize that my ear didn't hurt quite as much during the kiss, despite the draining feeling. And the vision? It was weaker, too. I saw a little more than myself, but not much. The taste was as lovely and sweet as last time, though. Strawberries. Fresh, sweet strawberries. Pure bliss.

At my house he gets out and walks me to the door.

"I had fun!" I say cheerfully.

"Me too," he replies, stuffing his hands into his pockets.

I stand there, smiling and off-center. I have no idea if I make him as unbalanced as he makes me. He seems totally fine.

"Well, I guess I'll see you at school then," he says.

I look back and forth from his eyes to his lips. We are standing way too close to be having a casual conversation.

"Yeah," I whisper.

He backs up and smiles. Then he turns around and walks to his car with his hands still in his pockets.

I need oxygen.

CHAPTER THIRTY-FIVE

Spanish Flower

After my date with Edwin, I want to see Mama more than ever and tell her about it, if only through the act of seeing her in Arch's mind. Don't ask me why that would feel at all like telling her, because I can't explain it. It just would.

I walk into Arch's room after I get something to drink. She has a stack of papers on her lap and an old *Smallville* episode on TV. "What are you doing up?" I ask.

Setting aside the paperwork, she takes off her reading glasses. "Just accounting."

I press my lips together. "Is everything okay?" I don't know how dire our finances are, but I sure remember the sting of desperation I tasted in her thoughts that day.

"Of course it is, baby," she says. "It's not for you to worry about. We're gonna be just fine."

I ease myself down onto the edge of her bed.

"And if you keep your grades up," she begins, "I might be able to apply for a scholarship for you."

A knot forms deep in the pit of my stomach.

"Tell me about Edwin," she says. "Did y'all have fun?"

His name erases all concern, and I fall back on her bed, grinning and sighing.

"That good, huh?"

"Mmm-hmm." I roll over and look at her.

"Come sit up here." She pats the spot next to her, and I crawl in. "What perfume are you wearing?" she asks.

"Spanish Flower."

"It smells good." She makes a note about a client who might need a sample. Her job never ends.

Thirty minutes later, after I have told her every last detail (except about the kiss—parents can't handle that, in my opinion), she yawns. We decide we've stayed up way too late. Piper apparently called a while ago and said she's going to stay at her friend's house, so I stand up and head toward the kitchen to lock up.

"Wait!" Arch says. "Gimme a kiss good night."

I can hardly believe I forgot the one thing I was hoping for. The kiss that will reveal another glimpse of my mama. Tonight, of all nights, after my true love's kiss, seeing Mama again will be the cherry on top of my ice cream sundae.

Leaning over, I turn my cheek toward Arch to showcase my dimple.

She kisses it and I back up, slightly stunned. I saw almost nothing. No audio, no video, and a bland taste at best. *No vision at all?*

"Are you okay, Emmie?" she asks.

I furrow my brow and look around the room—for what, I don't know. "Just tired, I guess."

She hugs me again. "Well, I'm so excited about your date! And about all of your hard work at school!"

I turn to leave, still reeling when she says, "Can you turn off the TV for me?"

"Sure." I absentmindedly walk toward the TV when it hits me.

Hard.

I know why I can't see anything! It's the same thing that happened the first time I kissed Edwin, only the effect must be worse this time. It's the reason I feel so drained when I kiss him. And tired. It's what Lex Luthor is discussing with Superman right now on Arch's TV.

Edwin is sucking the energy out of me.

He is my kryptonite.

He dulls, if not *destroys,* my power!

"When were you gonna tell me?" Trina asks me the next morning after we look at the costumes Piper's been working on. "Even Luke knows that you like Edwin, and you've never mentioned it to me. I felt like an idiot when I called Arch to check on you, and she told me you were out with Band Man! I thought, or rather hoped, she was kidding. But Luke said you actually like him."

I sigh and then smile. I want to be upset during this conversation, but all I can think about is the kiss and how much I want to talk about it with my best friend. "I was coming over to tell you that day you got mad at me about Piper."

She shakes her head, trying to remember. "Wait. Back up. When did this all start?"

I pause, knowing that it started because I'd asked him to kiss me, but I can't tell Trina that. "It happened slowly. He just started talking to me."

"When? Where?"

"I don't know. Everywhere. The cafeteria. The music room. Spanish class."

She lies back on my bed and starts laughing. "I'm so sorry, but this is Band Man. It's kinda funny."

"I know!" I start laughing, too. "But, Trina, he's so different. He took me to a bar!"

"Band Man took you to a bar?!" She sits up, still laughing.

"Yes. He's like this closet rock star." I fill her in.

"So have you kissed him?" she asks when I'm finished.

I nod, trying not to get overly excited. "Last night, and once before. And let me just say. . . ." I can't come up with words, so I moan and smile instead.

"Holy mackerel. I want details. Go get some popcorn."

I rush out of my room, so massively relieved I can't stand it.

CHAPTER THIRTY-SIX

Work It, Girl

I can't believe March is halfway over, and within these few short months, my nearly three-year crush on Vance has officially come to an end.

Edwin stops me outside of second period Monday, and I'm both excited and terrified. Excited that I frickin' adore this guy but terrified to kiss him again. I don't want to kiss anyone *else*, but with Arch and the whole durn school watching the decathlon, I think I have to. And if Edwin reduces my power, I definitely can't be near *his* lips.

"How 'bout I come watch your dance practice today?"

"Really?" I ask, forgetting that I was *just* reminding myself that I can't lead him on. I finally know what I want, and it's so close—if I can get the decathlon behind me, then I can date him full out.

He nods, puts his hands on my waist, and tries to pull me close to him.

Whoa, Nellie! Chills shoot up from my toes. I would love to be all smashed up against him, but I can't. I just can't.

"Edwiinnnn." I duck my head and nudge him away. "I had so much fun this weekend, but I really have to concentrate on my grades now. My aunt is on my back about staying in Haygood, and with the decathlon approaching, I have to focus." I smile at him. "And you are quite the distraction."

"Then let me come see your kids dance, and I'll quit asking you out until after the decathlon."

YAY! Problem solved. "Okay, but the Spring Follies is coming soon, so it's serious."

"Gotcha." He smiles, and even the lockers glow in his warmth.

"Are you sure you want to watch us?" I ask Edwin after school. "I mean, it's not like a big deal or anything."

"It *is* a big deal, and I'm gonna love it."

"This is bizarre," I say, opening the door to my car. "I mean, I've never had a boy watch me dance before."

He smiles and walks around to the other side of the car, bringing his yummy smell with him. I swear, I would kiss him right here in the parking lot if I wasn't driving. Well, that, and, if he wasn't a danger to my gift. It must be the universe's sick joke that the one boy I love is the one boy I can't date.

Ten short minutes later we arrive at the Alvis Sisters School of Dance.

"So here we are." He reaches over and squeezes my knee, which causes me to flinch and giggle.

"Yep."

Once inside, I make Edwin hang out in the foyer while I change into my leotard and jazz shoes. Before I come out, I freshen up my smacker with the brand-new, not-yet-released

Work It, Girl gloss. Arch gave me a sample of it this morning. It's a metallic shade that I wouldn't usually sport, but what the heck; Edwin's watching me dance!

He whistles at me when I come out.

I shoot him a playful look of annoyance; but just between me and the dance barre, I love it.

"Follow me," I say as I escort him into Studio A, where eight little girls stop their chatter and stare at us. I should have known they would get all kooky when I brought a boy to class.

"Who are *you*?" Grace Myers asks him.

"I'm Emerson's boyfriend," he replies, much to their hysterical delight.

My eyes go bug-eyed at the mention of the word *boyfriend*. I look at him, curious and happy.

He smiles, and I swear the room sparkles.

"Okay, girls, quiet down," I say. "This is Edwin, and he is going to watch our dance. I know today is our dress rehearsal and we don't actually have our costumes yet, but just pretend. Piper is coming later to do our hair, so let's run through it a few times before she gets here. And"—I pause and look down at the attendance roster—"Ava is absent."

"Will we have our costumes for the real thing?" asks Kristin.

"Of course!" I tell her. "I can't wait for you to see them. They're these adorable flapper dresses. They're still drying, though. Piper glued some feathers on the edges of the sleeves, and the glue is still kinda sticky."

"Can Edwin stand in for Ava?"

He is beaming. "Are you kidding? I'd love to." He does a funny little twirl and curtsy, and we all die laughing.

"Thank you, Edwin," I say sarcastically while biting back a huge grin. "That was beautiful, but I'm afraid you don't know the dance." I push him toward the edge of the room where he has a good view. "You need to stand here."

Taking his place, he winks at the girls—a natural-born heartbreaker.

"Grace, can you start the music?"

Grace walks over and turns on the music: a song I chose off of the CD Edwin gave me. It's a strange feeling dancing in front of Edwin. He stays perfectly still and quiet. I can see him staring at me in the mirror as I lead the girls. When it's over, he claps and tells the girls it was "spectacular."

We let him sit in the corner for the rest of our run-through as our music master—he turns the music on and off as I instruct. He also claps and tells us how awesome we are at regular intervals. I should invite him to class more often.

Piper arrives with a half hour to spare. She has at least seven magazines in her arms. "I'm sorry I'm so late," she says, rushing into the room.

I reach out to get the magazines from her. "What happened?"

"Nothing," she says dismissively. "Can you guys sit down? I'll show you what I want to do with your hair." She looks up and sees Edwin.

"Oh." I look to Edwin and wave him over. He walks up slowly and extends his hand. "This is Edwin." And turning to Piper, "My sister, Piper."

"Nice to meet you," he says, and I wonder what he must be thinking. Surely he knows her. This *is* Piper Taylor, after all.

"You, too," she says, questioning me with her eyes. She recognizes him all right—thinks he's a monumental loser.

"Edwin is my . . ." I swallow. I'm going to have to tell her sooner or later.

He interrupts me. "A friend."

I'm almost sad for a second, wishing he had said *boyfriend* again. But I haven't totally embraced this whole Em-and-Ed thing yet—at least not publicly. Piper would freak.

"Let's do that hair!" I say.

The girls get loud and excited, and Edwin says, "I'll wait for you in the car."

Looking at my watch, I say, "All right, but it'll probably be twenty minutes."

"It's fine," he replies, headed for the door. "I have to study Spanish."

"What was that about?" Piper asks me after he leaves.

I shrug my shoulders. "I like him."

She narrows her eyes. "I hope you know what you're doing."

"That's funny," I say. "I was just thinking the same thing about you and Silas."

She laughs.

Clapping my hands, I feel stronger and more sure of myself than normal. "Okay, girls, gather 'round!"

"We'll discuss your choice in men later," Piper says under her breath.

"Whatever." I roll my eyes.

The girls move around us, and Piper lays out her magazines, then carefully fashions Bethie's hair to look like one of the photos.

"That's so cute!" I squeal.

Bethie picks up a large mirror. "I love it!" She spins her head around, admiring herself.

"Who's next?" Piper asks.

Six hands fly up in the air as the girls shout, "Me! Me! Me!" And slowly but surely, Piper fashions everyone's hair, finishing with mine and hers for fun.

"Piper's looks the best!" Kristin says, and I agree. Piper's long hair is pinned up perfectly. She looks incredible.

"Let's take it from the top!" I say with a giggle. "Get your feet ready!"

The girls line up excitedly, and Piper turns on the music.

"Stop touching your hair," I warn the girls. "You'll mess it up!"

They put their hands down, and we begin. But no sooner do we start than Silas sticks his head through the doorway. We have never had even one boy watch us before, and now we've had two in one day?

Piper stops the music, and I say "Hey, Silas" as he walks up.

"Emerson." He nods before directing his attention to my sister. "You ready, Pipes?"

"One more time?" she asks him as if he's her daddy and she needs his permission.

Leaning his head into his left hand, he rolls his eyes in boredom. "Okay. Last time, though." Then he turns around and walks back toward the exit.

"Don't you want to see the dance?" I ask, trying to lighten the mood and get him excited about what Piper and I have done. "I choreographed it, but Piper's doing our hair and makeup. She's made all of the costumes, too!"

He stops and comes back into the room. "Sure. Whatever. Break a leg." Walking over to the side of the room, he leans up against the wall.

I notice that the girls don't get all giggly and excited. "This is Piper's boyfriend, Silas," I tell them.

No reaction. Just stares.

Piper and Silas smile at each other, but the girls look apprehensive. Or maybe uncomfortable.

"Let's take it from the top. This time you girls need to do

it on your own for me, okay?" I signal Margaret to start the music. When it begins, I feel it erase all the tension in the room. At least for me. Sometimes the right song can change everything.

Before it ends, I glance over at Silas and see him playing on his cell phone. Nice.

After the music stops, Piper walks across the dance floor to him. "So? What'd you think?"

"It was good." Silas looks down at his cell phone again before saying, "Your hair looks . . . strange."

Her face blushes, and she begins smoothing down her hair. "I know. I know. I won't wear it like this again."

"No, it doesn't!" I say, directing my comment to the girls. I can see that his attitude is affecting more than just Piper.

Ignoring me, he shoves his phone into his pocket. "I'm going to wait in the car. Hurry up."

Piper starts walking toward the dressing room while Silas walks out the door.

I turn to the girls. "Thanks, guys. I'll see you next week. Great job!" They begin to talk to one another and change while I run to catch up with my sister. "Piper! Is he always that rude?"

"You don't know him, Emerson." She pushes open the door while pulling bobby pins out of her hair.

"But why do you even like him?"

She crouches down on the floor and gathers her magazines, then fishes through her bag for a brush.

"Piper," I say again, softer.

She glares at me and brushes out her hair so hard it must hurt. "I have never had anyone love me like he does! That's why, okay? He cares about me more than that dork Edwin cares about you! I can guarantee it!"

Did she really just go there?

"He sure has a crappy way of showing it!" I say, frantically putting my clothes back on. I slip on my shoes. Then, with my hand on the doorknob, I stop and look back at her. "I'll be glad when this dance is over! And for the record, Edwin could kick Silas's ass!" As soon as I say it, I feel stupid. We both know that Edwin could definitely *not* kick Silas's ass, unless maybe they're dueling with pianos.

I say goodbye to the girls on my way out, relieved that Ms. Alvis is still here to wait for their parents with them.

In the parking lot, I find Edwin in my car, peacefully reading. He looks up at me when I open the door and speaks before I can say anything. "Wow. You look really pretty." Reaching over, he lightly touches my hair.

"Thanks." And before I think better of it, I lean over and kiss him, feeling that warm wave of weakness wash over me.

"What was that for?" he asks.

"I dunno," I tell him. But I *do* know. He loves my hair, and I am falling in love with him.

CHAPTER THIRTY-SEVEN

Raven Red

Two weeks pass in a blur of studying, dancing, and avoiding alone time with Edwin, and before I know it, the day of the Follies has arrived.

I wake up looking like a raccoon.

The revelation that the one boy I adore is the one boy I can't kiss has caused me a serious lack of sleep. Arch's newest catalog lies open on my lap as I scan the pages searching for concealer. Thank goodness I have all the beautification tools I could ever need at home, but this seriously bites. What sixteen-year-old has dark circles under her eyes?

I find a few options, flag the pages, then pull the covers high over my head so I can sleep for as long as possible. How unfair that I have found my very first potential boyfriend, and I am allergic to him. Truly, I must have done something terrible in a former life, if there is such a thing. It seems that while Piper got Mama's infectious personality and rockin' bod, I got Mama's crazy. I can just hear people whispering to

Arch, "I'm so sorry Emerson went nuts. She seemed like such a normal girl. And she was so smart."

"Emerson?" Arch sticks her head in my room a few minutes later. "What are you doing? The Spring Follies is tonight. I would think you would be so excited you couldn't sleep."

I look over at her standing in the doorway, a smile plastered across her face. "Get outta bed, sleepyhead!" She walks to my windows and pulls back the curtain, sending too much light into my already-weak brain.

I groan. "Archhh . . . what time is it?"

"Ten o'clock," she says pertly while walking out of my room. I can smell her special perfume—the expensive one— and I can hear her heels clip-clopping down the stairs. She only wears heels on special days, and I suppose this qualifies as one: my big debut as a real choreographer, even though the dance is only three minutes long. But I have to say, I'm proud of it. Piper is, too. She made the girls these beautiful feather clips for their hair last night.

Tossing off my covers, I sit on the edge of my bed and run my tongue over my teeth, wishing I could still taste the strawberries from Edwin's kisses. But all I taste is morning breath.

Yuck.

I sling my backpack up onto my bed and read the decathlon manual Edwin gave me last week. It has got to be one of the most boring wastes of time ever. But I do it anyway. At the crack of noon, I finally walk downstairs, depressed. *Why does my soul mate have to ruin my gift? Why? Why!*

Soul mate, I think as I make myself a ginormous coffee. I would barely call him a friend in January; and now, a few months later, he's my soul mate? I sigh dramatically, wishing

I had never had to resort to this kissing-for-grades business. I had a particularly awkward almost-kiss with Juan yesterday, too. Ugh.

Piper walks in as I'm finishing my coffee, and I notice her eyes seem red, too—almost as if she's used Raven Red for concealer. She probably had a fight with the loser, Silas. Whatever the reason, I don't want to ask.

"I'm about to go to the Prescott Theater to make sure we have everything we need for tonight," I say. "Are the costumes ready?" She had two left that needed finishing as of last night.

She nods. "Yes. All done. They're in the back of my car."

"Great. You'll bring them to the Prescott?"

"Yep." She starts up the steps to her cave of seclusion before shouting behind her, "I'll be there an hour before it starts to do their hair and makeup."

"Thanks, Piper!" I yell up at her. "I'm really excited about what you've done!"

She waves her hand behind her.

Four hours and thirty-three minutes later, while pacing backstage at the theater, I look at my watch. Where is she? *Dang, Piper!* She said she'd be here. We have to go on in twelve minutes. I haven't seen or heard from her since she left for Silas's this afternoon, and the girls are getting anxious. Half of them are wearing practice leotards, and the rest have on their regular clothes.

"Where's Piper?" Jenny asks me.

"She'll be here any minute," I assure her. "Don't worry. But don't take off your clothes yet."

Jenny frowns. "I can't dance without the costume."

I start "The Trina," inhaling and exhaling at rapid intervals.

Thank goodness she pops her head backstage. "Ya ready?" she asks.

"Heck no!" I whisper with large, panicky eyes. "Piper hasn't shown up, and she has the costumes! And the makeup! And she was supposed to do their hair!"

"Have you called her?"

I give her my are-you-friggin'-kidding-me? face. "Of course I've called her!"

Piper's been acting like a flake and all, but she has a lot to lose, too. It doesn't make sense. She needs her college application to stand out, and this project is perfect.

Trina offers to do the girls' hair, and we laugh because there is so little time left that she would do about as well as Edwin. But at least she makes me laugh.

I peek out the side of the curtain and I can see Edwin, Arch, and the Wilsons sitting together. That works me up into even more of a lather. *Where is my stupid sister?*

After looking at my watch for the last time, I clap my hands. "Girls, line up."

They form a quick line, and I scan their outfits. "Bethie, give Anna your shirt."

She obeys.

"Margaret, take off your belt and give it to Ava."

She starts to unwind it. "But I need it," she whines.

"No you don't, Margaret. You look great! Now, roll up your pant legs. We are going to have to do this thing MacGyver-style."

She leans down, puzzled, and begins rolling up her pants. "Who's MacGyver?"

Reaching into my dance bag, I grab my tube of Sucker Punch lip gloss and hand it to Trina. "MacGyver was a supercool guy who always made do with what he had." (Arch has every episode of this wacky old show, and I've watched them a million times. Who knew you could make a bomb out of bubble gum?)

Trina takes the tube of lip gloss and stares at me.

"Use this to make their lips pink and glossy," I instruct her. "And put some on your fingertips and rub it into their cheeks like rouge."

"Rouge?"

"Blush," I tell her.

"Ten four," she says, then walks down the line applying lip gloss while I speak.

"Girls, it looks like we're going to have to dance without our costumes."

Bethie starts to cry.

"Buck up!" I tell her. "Y'all are incredible dancers. You have learned a very hard routine, and I want your parents to see it. We are simply going to be hip-hop jazz girls. I want your pant legs rolled up like Ava's. And I have a bunch of hair bands to put your hair up like this." I pull my hair into a knot on top of my head and secure it. "Take off anything you have on top except either your leotards, tank tops, or undershirts."

They quickly do as I say.

"And no jewelry. We have five minutes until you go on, and I, for one, am still very excited about this dance." I force a fake smile and thank Trina for helping.

"Now get on your shoes and let's rock this joint!"

CHAPTER THIRTY-EIGHT

Luscious-Length Mascara

Ms. Alvis peers around the corner. "Curtain time!" she says excitedly.

We walk onto the stage. I can just make out Arch, Edwin, and the Wilsons sitting in the crowd. Thankfully, that rouge idea popped into my brain, because the bright lights are blinding the dancers. Without the color on their cheeks, they probably would have been as pale and pasty as papier-mâché. I look at their sweet faces and give them my most confident smile and an enthusiastic thumbs-up. Inside, however, I am beyond pissed and embarrassed that everyone will see a ridiculous-looking group of insecure little girls.

Ms. Alvis hands me the microphone and rubs her hand across my shoulders in reassurance.

"Hello." My voice cracks, so I clear my throat. "Thank you for coming." Sweat is now dripping down my back from nervous excitement. I feel so responsible—not only to the girls, but to their parents who pay this studio. Parents who paid for costumes they are not going to see tonight. *Gulp.*

"I'm Emerson Taylor, and I've been given the opportunity to choreograph a dance based on the nineteen twenties. I hope you enjoy it."

I brace myself as Ms. Alvis starts the music, but nothing happens.

Ten seconds pass before I rush over to the side of the stage, fearing the worst. Sure enough, the stereo is broken. My face flushes red. What else can go wrong?

I look across the sea of people to Edwin and attempt "Help!" in facial Morse code. He reads my expression, stands up, and shimmies out of the row he's seated in.

"Can I help you?" he says, leaning over the stage and smiling at the girls.

"The stereo is broken." I am a visible wreck.

He nods to the right of the stage. "Isn't that a piano?"

I glance across the stage to a piano tucked behind a curtain. "Yes! Can you play our song?"

"Is the pope Catholic?" He jumps up onto the stage and walks reverently to the piano. Then he looks up at me for a signal to start.

I nod my head and cross my fingers, hoping this works.

In true Edwin form, he starts playing, the notes flying off the piano like birds fluttering. The whole room is embraced in a twenties' kind of jazz jam session; and, much to my surprise, the girls dance the whole three minutes without a hitch. It's brilliant!

I am so proud that I can't help feeling a momentary lapse of anger. I wish Piper could have seen how awesome it was.

After the girls walk off the stage, I rush over to Edwin and hug him so hard I probably hurt him. But I don't care. He literally saved my performance. Then we walk off the stage together to congratulate the girls.

Edwin turns to them and holds up his hand. "You rocked it, guys! Gimme five!"

They giggle and slap his hand.

"I am so proud of you," I tell them. "I know how hard it is to perform when you don't feel like you look good. But you showed me that true beauty and grace have nothing to do with costumes, hair, or makeup. You guys taught *me* something."

Ava runs forward and hugs me. "Aww," I say. "Come here, y'all."

The girls rush around me, and we all have a huge group hug.

"Where's Piper?" Edwin asks. "Is she okay?"

I moan. "I have no idea. I thought she'd be here by now."

"Well, I don't know how she could have possibly made it better, because it was the bomb! I loved it."

"Thanks to you," I say. "Without their costumes, they looked like a mess."

"No, they didn't," he says, holding my shoulders. "When you explained that this was part of a twenties' project, it just looked like they were ragtag Depression kids—all miss-matchy."

I groan in relief. "Only you would think of that, Edwin."

He gently touches the underside of my chin with the side of his finger. "Chin up, Jazzy."

I lose myself for a second in his eyes.

"The music was the best, though," he continues with a wink, then puts his arm around me again.

Ms. Alvis announces intermission, and Arch comes rushing backstage with the Wilsons, and yes, Piper, who I can tell is embarrassed. Her arms are loaded down with costumes.

"I'm so sorry, Emerson!" she says before anyone can congratulate us. "You said you were in the second act, and I

was stuck in traffic, and . . ." She pauses. "I never thought I'd
be so late."

"We *were* in the second act, but the girl doing the tap solo
in the first act is sick, so Ms. Alvis moved us up. It shouldn't
have mattered, though. You said you were going to be here an
hour before it started!"

Edwin takes the cue that this is a family matter, so he says,
"I'll call you later. But really, Em. It was awesome!"

"Thanks," I reply with a smile. "Later!"

He turns to leave, and Mr. and Mrs. Wilson embrace me,
ignoring all the tension. "That was top-notch, kiddo," Mr.
Wilson says.

"Thanks." I sigh. "If only you could have seen the costumes."

"Can't you put them on now?" Mrs. Wilson asks the girls.
"Come here, little angels. Let's see you in your *real* costumes."

The girls look to me for approval, and I know how much
they'd love to, so I nod in agreement; and they rush off to the
changing rooms, Piper following with costumes in hand.

"I need your dancers back out on the stage in a few
minutes," Ms. Alvis shouts from the door. "For the final bow."

"Yes, ma'am," I tell her. "They're just getting ready."

Arch puts her arm around me. "Emerson, it was adorable!
Costumes or not, I'm so proud of you."

"Thanks."

"Back to our seats!" Mr. Wilson says.

"Wait!" Bethie calls to Mrs. Wilson from the dressing
room. "Look at me!"

"You are as pretty as a picture, young lady!" Mrs. Wilson
hugs the little girl, then follows her husband out the door.

"Go get the rest of the girls," I tell Bethie. "It's almost time
for your final bow."

When I get home, Piper is sitting on the sofa in the keeping room. "I just don't get it," I say, exasperated. "I've been working on this for more than two months. You know how much I needed your help."

She hangs her head in shame and pleads, "Really, I'm so sorry."

Arch is right behind me. "Piper, I'm disappointed in you. Where on earth were you? And why didn't you call?"

"I was at Silas's and . . ."

"Stop right there, young lady," Arch says. "You are spending way too much time with that boy. And now your college application is a two-second bow instead of a whole dance."

"I know. But I'm not lying. There really was a lot of traffic."

"That's no excuse." Arch puts her purse down on the kitchen counter. "Piper." She pauses in frustration. "I just don't know what to do with you anymore."

"I know what to do," I say. "You can ground her!"

"Oh, she's grounded all right."

Piper wipes her eyes while I grit my teeth in fury. "Hmph. If I get a bad grade because the girls looked a mess, I don't know what I'll do. I could have ordered costumes with the money we used for the material!"

"And I'll tell you something else, Miss Piper," Arch says. "You will write every one of those girls' parents and apologize. They spent good money on those costumes. In fact, you need to pay them back."

"Yeah," I chime in, reveling in her punishment.

"Yes, ma'am," she replies to Arch. "May I go to my room now?"

Arch nods.

Piper leaves the room, and I moan to Arch some more

before she cuts me off. "Emerson, stop. I'm just as mad at her as you are, but you have to accept her apology and move on."

"Huh?!"

She walks to the counter and picks up a small box full of Luscious-Length mascaras before settling down on the sofa to work. "If there's one thing I've learned from makeup, it's that it reminds me of just what it says: whether you are sixteen or sixty, it's never too late to *make up* for lost time." She draws quote marks in the air when she uses the words *make up*. "It's never too late to change your pattern of behavior. To start fresh." She looks at me. "When I make up my face, I also make up my mind to start the day fresh. To remake myself."

I scowl at her dumb advice, still mad at Piper. But I'm *really* mad at Silas. I hate him. He's the reason she was late, and we both know it. Why does Arch always have to be so positive? She acts like it's so easy to change. I doubt Piper will stop being a flake (and I doubt I can just apply my makeup tomorrow and decide to make myself new).

"I have to study," I say, needing out of this Room of Positivity. Ick.

CHAPTER THIRTY-NINE

Iced Tea

"Gather 'round, ye fellow athletes," Grady says the next day at school.

This cracks me up on several levels. One, his tendency to speak in his own Old English hybrid. And two, how he refers to us as "athletes," which we definitely are not.

Edwin winks at me, and I feel the warm breeze that always blows around him swallow me whole.

We're sitting at a long table in the library, planning Project Dork Domination. Just kidding—it's the decathlon. That was rude. I like these guys.

Malcolm, Sawyer, Grady, and Oliver join us a few minutes later; and I notice Grady's face is still in dire need of Acne Blaster, and Sawyer could use some lip repair.

"Where's Mallory?" I ask.

Sawyer shrugs his shoulders. "I saw her with Luke after last period."

I smile, knowing that Luke has finally found his girl.

"No matter," says Don. "Let's get down to business."

Grady rubs his hands together excitedly.

"So," begins Don, "we need a math expert."

Several heads nod in agreement. Edwin explained to me last night (when I talked to him on the phone for two hours!) that in the past it worked best if each team member specialized in a certain subject as they approached the day of the decathlon.

"Emerson?" Don asks. "Can you take it?"

I cough and laugh at the same time. *What a joke.* "Math? Are you kidding? Why can't Sawyer or Malcolm do it?"

"They're handling science. It's the largest subject, and we always put two people in charge of it. But Malcolm will be the math backup as always."

"Maybe English?" Edwin suggests.

Fish glares at us in complete astonishment. "Y'all know full well that I am our resident English genius."

Edwin and I make eye contact, then burst into a fit of unprofessional chuckles for no reason at all.

"What's wrong?" asks Fish. "Did I miss something?"

"No. No." I laugh. He doesn't even know we were kidding.

I put my brain back on. "Okay. Okay. But math?"

"Your last few tests were as good as Malcolm's in that class," says Oliver.

"Yeah," agrees Grady. "And you aced the pop quiz."

They're right. I guess I am improving. I didn't need a kiss to pass that quiz, after all. But still . . . I'm no mathematician— more like a mathemagician. "I don't know," I say before clenching my jaw. The reality of what they're asking me to do hits me hard. I seriously can't kiss Edwin anymore—at least not until after the decathlon. If I do, I'll let them *all* down, Edwin included. And I'm gonna have to break my promise to myself not to kiss the other guys.

Cue depressing music.

They talk about other subjects for a while and decide I should also be the chemistry backup. I try my best to pay attention, but my brain keeps jumping from how I'm going to have to avoid Edwin Alone Time to the vast amount of skin care these boys need. Not to mention the vast amount of studying I will have to do to master not one but two subjects.

I walk out into the hall after our meeting and see Silas up ahead holding a small trash can next to his chest. *What is he up to now?* I slow down and watch him. The janitor, Mr. Thibodaux, approaches him and calmly asks for it back. Silas smiles his predatory smile before turning it upside down and dumping its contents at Mr. Thibodaux's feet. Then he laughs and walks the other way.

Who does that?

Rushing ahead, I lean down to help Mr. Thibodaux pick up the trash.

"Thank you!" he says. "You're Edwin's friend, aren't ya?"

I nod.

"He's a good boy, that Edwin. Always helping other people."

I nod again and put the last piece of trash into his big, black trash bag.

"Helping others," he says. "Now, that's the key to a happy life."

That afternoon when I pass Oliver in the hall, it dawns on me that I've never kissed him. I set up that Spanish tutoring session with him but ended up kissing Edwin instead. My brain takes a short vacation from thinking about Oliver to reliving my first kiss with Edwin. Ahhh . . .

But before Oliver can make it to class, I stop and ask him

about helping me prepare for the next Spanish test. It kills me to have to do this.

He tilts his head down to look at his watch; and I stare at him, assessing the situation, wondering if I can actually go through with kissing him. "I'm meeting Edwin in the band room now."

Guilt courses through my veins like adrenaline, and I suddenly hate myself—which leads me to think about Frances, of all things. And how fake she is. She and Vance. And yet here I am, just like them. I spend my days pretending to be smart, not to mention all but denying to the world my true feelings for Edwin.

"Okay," I tell Oliver. "Let's talk later."

Up ahead I see a large, gold sun on a poster advertising the spring formal. After reading the deets about the solar system theme, I notice Mrs. Parker struggling to carry some boxes into her classroom. Right then and there I remember what Mr. Thibodaux said.

"Can I help you?" I ask her.

She smiles, and as I lean down to pick up the other side of her box, I can smell her perfume—a quiet, flowery musk. I'm struck by the fact that she has a whole 'nother life outside of first period.

"Thanks, Emerson," she says.

"Sure." My eyes rest on her hands holding the other side of the box, and I can see that her nail polish is all chipped. "What color is that?" I ask, motioning to her nails.

She curls her fingers in with embarrassment. "Iced Tea."

"Really?" I ask. "They don't make that one anymore."

She nods. "How'd you know?"

"My aunt sells Stellar Cosmetics."

"I need to do my nails," she acknowledges.

"Well, I can bring you another bottle," I tell her casually. "I mean, I'm sure we have a few more of those at home."

"Seriously?" she asks, and for a second I'm reminded of how magical makeup is. So I decide to track down others in need of my *particular* kind of help. Mr. Thibodaux was right. I do feel a bit better.

I find Malcolm and Grady after second period and hand them a catalog and point out their necessary products. "I'll bring you samples tomorrow," I tell each of them. Malcolm laughs at me but takes the catalog. And after he leaves, Grady leans over and kisses me, as if kissing me is totally normal now.

Bam! Math floods into my brain in a zipadee-doo-dah flash. It's so fast, it scorches my tongue, tasting like the sweet sugar crackle on the top of a crème brûlée. I pull away and spin my head around in a rush, panicked that someone has seen me. Someone being Edwin. Thank goodness, the hall is empty.

"Grady!"

"Yesssss?" he smiles smugly and leans up against the wall like some kind of mustached playboy.

"I'm sorry. I never meant to lead you on. I . . ."

"I know," he says, straightening up. "I just wanted you to know that I was thankful!"

Awk-ward . . .

He self-consciously ducks his head. "I didn't know what to do about it. The acne, I mean. It's gotten worse this year."

I shake my head. "No worries. So I'll see you later?" I'm embarrassed, but I have just accidentally gotten a free pass to skip the homework this week, and I can't help but be relieved. "The products I circled should fix it right up," I say, zipping up my backpack. "I have to get to class."

"Thanks, Emerson."

"You're welcome," I reply, then turn to walk to chemistry. But I feel as though my do-gooding was just voided somehow.

CHAPTER FORTY

Beauty Bomb

After school I head next door to Luke's to chill for a while and see if he's studied for the history test. Nothing cures I-didn't-see-it-coming kiss guilt like *real*, hard-core concentration on my schoolwork.

The Baldwins' house is just like ours on the outside—a classic brick bungalow—but inside it's quite different. Luke's great-grandparents owned a string of antique stores in the Northeast, so his house is full of old furniture. When you walk in the back door (which is the only door for besties like me), you can immediately smell the antiques. A musty concoction of old wood and wax. Trina thinks it's depressing, but I love it. It's homey. And when Mrs. Baldwin is cooking, there's no other place I'd rather be.

"Luke!" I yell before taking the stairs two at a time. "What's up?"

"Me," he says from his chair in front of his computer. As I enter his room, I can see a dozen playing cards displayed on the screen. "I'm up thirty-eight to seventeen. You?"

"Have you done the history homework yet?"

"Hold on," he says, pushing a button. "Take that!" The screen congratulates him on winning the game, and he swivels around in his chair. "Yep. Finished it a while ago." He has on a new vintage shirt with HANNIBAL written on the pocket.

"Hannibal?" I ask in shock, remembering that awful movie *The Silence of the Lambs*. Luke made me watch it with him and Trina last Halloween and I've never recovered.

He nods. "Cool, huh?"

I scrunch up my mouth. "Creeepppy. You've crossed the line with this one."

He looks down at his shirt and laughs. "I couldn't help it. When I saw it, I thought of you."

"Ew!" I punch him playfully before sitting down on the edge of his bed. "I'm gonna pretend it's about Hannibal crossing the Alps then. Take that, sucka!" I say.

"Since when did you get to be so smart?" He sucks on the air and quotes *The Silence of the Lambs*. "'I ate his liver with some fava beans and a nice chianti.'"

"Stop! Gross!" Opening my book in my lap, I ask, "So can you help me with history?"

"Sure, but it's easy."

I turn to the chapter in question while he stands up and moves another chair next to his desk. "Come sit over here. I have to start another hand."

I do as he says, and he sweetly tries to explain a decade's worth of information to me in between a few rounds of poker. "Have you thought about the spring formal yet?" he asks.

I shrug.

"McNeely hasn't asked you?"

I shake my head.

"He will."

"What makes you so sure? I haven't been all that available lately." I want him to gush to me about how much Edwin probably adores me and how we look so cute together and how he isn't as nerdy as everyone thinks he is.

"I'll bet you that hair crap you wanted at the mall the other day he will."

A bet—now *this* is more like Luke, and it makes me feel good. "I'll take that hair crap and raise you a vintage shirt," I joke.

"Good one, Ace! I've taught you well."

Two hours later, ten dollars poorer, and with the scent of Mrs. Baldwin's rosemary-infused pork tenderloin wafting up their staircase, I leave, feeling hungry, happy, and overflowing with knowledge. And it didn't cost me a single kiss.

Before I go to bed, I head into Arch's room to borrow some eye cream. *Sometimes you have to lose your mind before you can come to your senses* is written in Arch's bubbly cursive across the top of her mirror. After picking up the cream, I read it again, wondering why she wrote it. It's not as if she never writes on her mirror—she is definitely a mirror writer—but usually it's a Bible verse. Something like *Be still and know that I am God.* I see that one so much I've memorized it: Psalm 46:10.

Arch walks in a minute later. "Whatcha doin'?" She's holding a large laundry basket of clothes, and I can tell she's been crying.

"You okay?" I ask.

"It's nothing." She smacks the big wad of gum she's chewing, which is clearly her poker tell. Luke was right about that tell stuff.

"Is that my Beauty Bomb?" she asks.

I look down at the cream in my hand. "Oh yeah. Can I borrow it?"

"Sure, baby." She lifts a sweater out of the basket and begins to fold it.

"What does that quote on your mirror mean?" I ask her.

She smiles and wipes the skin underneath her eyes. "I like it," she says. "I heard it at a makeup party last week. One of those rich women in Steeplechase said it." She hands me another sweater, and I begin to fold it.

"You think it's true?" I ask.

After popping a large bubble, she says, "I do. Sometimes you have to get to that place of hopelessness before things start looking up. Sometimes . . ."

I think about the place of hopelessness I've been in and how alone it can make me feel. I wonder if I should press Arch to talk about what's upsetting her. But before I make a decision, she speaks. "There was a time early in my career when I was so focused on achieving great things that I lost sight of who I was. I was concentrating so hard on the goal that I forgot to appreciate the climb."

"But," I say, "isn't that what you're always telling us? To have goals. To work toward perfect grades by studying hard and all?"

"Well, sure." She starts on a pair of jeans. "But not to the degree that you lose yourself."

I reach in and get out a shirt. "How do you know if you lose yourself?" I ask, desperately wanting the answer.

"I guess when you start sacrificing what you believe in for what you want."

I slowly fold one arm over the back and then each side. *Is that what I've been doing?*

"I have to go study." I sigh.

"Wait. How's the decathlon coming?"

"It's great," I lie.

"I'm proud of you, Em. You have a lot on your plate, and you're managing beautifully."

"I guess so."

She pats me on the back. "And if you feel crazy, don't worry. You're right where you're meant to be at sixteen."

"Thanks," I say sarcastically. "That's great news."

I leave the room feeling completely tangled, which reminds me of the poem I started writing in class a couple of weeks ago. So sitting at my desk, I pull out the depressing poem and read it again. I still have to turn in one more, so I might as well finish it.

Maybe Arch's mirror message is right, and my tangled mess *is* the path to sanity—or at least the path to a good grade.

CHAPTER FORTY-ONE

Reality Red

I'm not really that stupid.

I know it's a catch twenty-two.

Edwin is both the problem standing between me and performing well in the decathlon and the solution to finally ridding myself of the kissing curse. I'm thinking about this very nightmare a week later when Arch walks into her bathroom and interrupts my shadow fest in her drawer. I'm looking for the perfect shade of "peacock" eye shadow. Some might think peacock is a freakish shade to wear on an uneventful Tuesday, but I'm not like most people when it comes to color. And for the record, peacock shadow on brown eyes is perfectly non-startling. Now, against blue eyes, I might be concerned.

Pushing several shadow squares aside, I dig down under what seems like ten lipsticks before I find it. Ahhh, the perfect peacock: not too blue and not too green.

I run my brush across it, admiring how funktabulous it will look with the smoky-gray T-shirt I borrowed from Piper this morning, and try to push my dilemma to the back of my mind.

"Any decathlon news?" Arch asks.

"No news," I say. "We've just been studying." I turn Arch's makeup mirror to face myself and curl my lashes, hoping she'll leave.

"Have they assigned you a subject yet?" she continues.

"Math and chemistry," I say, casually applying some navy mascara in a focused effort meant to convince her I can't talk now.

"No surprise." She turns on the water and wets her toothbrush.

"But I also have to write a poem for English, finish up my history paper, and do a bunch of other stuff, too." I feel like I need to prepare her for the fact that I might not do well.

"Look up," she says, grabbing my face in her hands. "You've got a mess-up." She wets her thumb and rubs it underneath my eye, removing the spot. "There ya go."

"Thanks."

We leave the bathroom and walk into the kitchen together, where she puts a few plates from last night into the dishwasher. "You and Piper need to start helping me with the house more. It will be summer in less than two months—my busiest time of year—and I don't have time to keep up with all the cooking and the cleaning."

"Yes, ma'am," I reply while packing my lunch.

"I mean, look at my nails!" She rinses her hands, and I can see that they're in dire need of a manicure, which is *so* not Arch. After drying them off, she shakes her head again, then reaches into her purse on the counter and pulls out a small Stellar makeup bag. It's metallic blue—a free gift from the Winter Blush Blitz. I wanted one so badly, but she ran out.

I lean in close to her so I can peer inside. As she unzips the little bag, I imagine fireworks flying up and popping around my face. But out comes Reality Red nail polish instead.

"Did you always know you wanted to sell makeup?" I ask her.

"No." She pulls the tiny brush out of the red liquid and begins to touch up her nails. "But I never felt beautiful before I discovered it."

"But you tell me and Piper that we don't need makeup to be beautiful."

"You don't," she says. "That's not the kind of beautiful I mean."

"I don't get it."

"Makeup saved my life and taught me what real beauty is. And oddly enough, real beauty doesn't come in a tube. Although I wish it did! Can you imagine?" She giggles. "We'd be zillionaires!"

I grin.

Looking into my eyes, she says, "I didn't have a happy childhood, Emerson. My father abused your mother and me."

I look at her, stunned. I've never heard this before.

Her eyes begin to look watery. "Our mother was afraid to leave him. When I was your age, I got very depressed and had to go to a hospital."

"For crazy people?" I ask.

She smiles and pulls a small silver compact out of the bag and opens it to reveal a mirror. "Gosh darnit. Look at this. You're making my mascara run." She wipes the corner of her eye with a tissue and continues talking. "I suppose. But it saved my life. It saved all of our lives. My depression was the event that woke up my mother and caused her to take us and run." She dumps her purse contents out on the counter. "Where's my gum?"

I pick up her gum from the center of the pile and hand it to her.

"Thanks." She unwraps a piece and puts it into her mouth, then exhales in gum-induced calm and chews. "But it was too late for Marie. She'd already started dating your father."

"Oh," I say.

She shakes her head, dispersing thoughts of my mama, and stares off into the side yard. "At the hospital, the first thing they did for the depressed patients like me was put makeup on us. It made us feel alive. It helped us look past our circumstances for a minute and see the beauty that lies within. As patients, it was kind of like we viewed ourselves as black-and-white shells—mannequins—blank and dead. With the makeup on, we felt and saw our own innate beauty. I can't explain it, but it gave me and the women the little pick-me-up we needed to just get out of bed."

I nod, fascinated by her story.

"Every day I would look forward to seeing the girl who did my makeup. She was a Stellar rep, too. After she did my face, I would take a walk outside. And every day I would walk farther, until I was out of bed more than I was in it."

"Makeup did all that?"

"It did," she says. "As I became more confident in my exterior, I realized that my insides were just as beautiful. I learned that they'd always been beautiful—I just couldn't see it before." She picks up a Stellar box and points to the snow crystal on the packaging. "You know what this represents, don't you?"

I shake my head.

"It's one of the six types of snow crystals. And just like every snowflake is beautiful yet different, so is every woman."

"Is that why you volunteer at the hospital?"

"Yes."

"Do you put makeup on those ladies like that lady did for you?"

"I do."

"That's so cool, Arch." I've never admired someone so much in my life. "Can I help sometime?"

She reaches over and hugs me. "Sure, baby. I would love that. And you'd be great at it."

"Oh!" I add. "I need some samples of Acne Blaster and lip repair."

"For whom?"

"Just some zitty boys at school."

She smiles. "Take as many as you need from the hall closet. And Acne Blaster is on special this month, so take a few catalogs, too."

CHAPTER FORTY-TWO

Numbered Cologne

The history test I studied for with Luke?

I bombed it.

No question.

I had no idea there'd be so many fill-in-the-blanks. Luke and I didn't prepare for that at all. Guess I should've studied a bit more this week, too.

After packing away my books, I stand up to leave class.

"Emerson?" Mrs. Parker says.

I turn back and motion to Edwin that I'll see him later. I'm secretly hoping he'll ask me to the formal today.

Walking to the teacher's desk, I mentally prepare myself for a lecture. "Yes?"

Mrs. Parker narrows her eyes in concern. "Emerson, I've been looking over your answers because of your involvement in the decathlon team, and I'm very troubled."

Bam. There it is. "Yes, ma'am. I thought we would have choices for the blanks."

"Look," she says. "I know how much you want to be on the decathlon team this year. But you got a C on this test. I admit, you just missed a B–, but even that wouldn't have been up to decathlon standards." She hands me my paper.

"I studied," I mumble. "I promise."

"You need to study harder then. This isn't what I've been used to seeing from you this term."

I nod and put the paper in my backpack as my phone vibrates in my pocket.

"I'm on the faculty advisory board for the academic decathlon, so I know you have a math test this week. Make sure you get an A."

"Yes, ma'am," I say. Then I walk out into the hall and look at my phone. It's a text from Arch.

Good luck on your test!

Too late.

After arranging my books on the long wooden table in the library, I hunch over them to make a plan. It seems the math test is critical. I'm so tired of all this. Acid climbs up the back of my throat, and I wonder if I'm going to cry or explode in anger. I know I've gotten myself into this mess, but now I want out.

One more week, I tell myself. One more week until the decathlon. Surely I can make it just one more week and then everything will be fine.

One. More. Week.

Taking out my pencil, I begin to tackle my geometry homework, which is due next period. I can do most of the problems by myself. But at the end of the chapter, they get harder, and the examples in the front of the book aren't helping. Frustration sets in, and I chew on the end of my pencil before someone slaps a book down in front of me.

"Hey, Em!" Malcolm says. "You ready for the test?"

I shake my head and stare at the page again.

"You want some help?" He stands and walks around to sit next to me. I can smell the faint aroma of numbers enticing me like good cologne.

Reaching over, he tilts my book to face him, then points to the section that's troubling me. "It's this, huh?"

I start to get a hot and desperate feeling. I need that math grade.

"Well," he starts, "you have to understand this, or next year will be a nightmare." He leans over until he's within inches of my head. Kissing him would be so easy.

"Great," I say with my best sarcasm. "How do you know about next year already?"

"I've studied ahead."

Of course. I feel myself getting jittery. Reaching up, I press my ear to my head with the palm of my hand. I can almost feel it beginning to throb. Malcolm copies the equation on my paper, and before I know what the heck I'm doing, I've lifted his head and kissed him. Right there in the middle of the library!

He smiles, and his pupils multiply in size.

What have I done? I feel the formulas lock into place in my head and my ear tingle in pain, but it's not the same. I don't want it. I grab my head with both hands, trying to reject the knowledge.

A tear falls, and I wipe it quickly before checking for witnesses. And that's when I see him watching me through the window.

Edwin.

My mouth opens to scream his name, but Malcolm leans in fast and kisses me again, his lips landing on the side of my mouth. I yank my head back and press my hand to his chest to push him away. "Malcolm!"

"What's wrong?" Malcolm asks, and with good reason. I *did* just kiss him first.

I lean around his head to find Edwin again, but he's gone.

CHAPTER FORTY-THREE

Glamour Gloss

Things go from bad to barfy in last period. I have just spent the previous two periods trying to find an opportunity to speak to Edwin, but, of course, he's avoiding me. And now, when I'm exhausted and completely panicked, Malcolm comes over to sit by me. I ignore him. But at the end of class, during quiet reading, he passes me a note. It's a poem. A love poem.

Oh boy. Suddenly I feel as if I am watching myself from above. It's *The Emerson Show*, and I don't like what I see. Is this really my life?

I'm the one who needs a makeover.

I look at the poem and recognize it immediately as one of Grady's favorites. Just reading the words again brings back the taste of my kiss with him: lonely, sweet, and desperate, like a cold plum with a hard stone center. It's the way I've imagined all these boys: lonely, desperate, so eager to please. But it's not them who feel that way, I'm realizing . . . it's me. *I* feel that way. Ever since my mother left.

Lonely.

Desperate.

Trying to please everyone.

I stare at the words, not knowing what to say. So I just look at him quickly and smile. Like, *That's nice, thank you, I'll be going now.*

He writes another note and slides it over.

Dear Emerson, would you like to go to the spring formal with me?

And for the first time in nearly three months, I choose total honesty. "Malcolm," I say. "I'm sorry."

He leans across the space between our chairs. "For what?"

"I'm sorry for the way I've treated you. You've been a good friend to me, and I've let you believe that maybe there's a chance for more."

He looks down at the poem.

"I just don't have feelings for you. Like *that*."

"I don't understand," he says.

"It's complicated," I reply. "I'm sorry. I can't explain it."

He tilts his head and looks at me. "Complicated? That's an understatement. You just kissed me!"

My face gets hot, and I look around the room. Several people are staring at me now, including Fish. My shoulders slump forward. Frances snickers behind me. This is my filthy reality. I feel like scum. But scum with wings—lighter and finally on the right path.

After school, I text Grady. I have to quit the decathlon team.

Why? he asks, but I don't respond. I feel so bad, I don't know what to say. And then I see Edwin up ahead, in the distance, leaning against my car. Faded blue jeans, shaggy hair, and leather jacket.

I push my backpack farther up my shoulder and walk ahead.

"Hey." He pushes his bangs back and crosses his arms across his chest.

"Edwin," I say, tears filling my eyes. "It's not what you think!"

"That's not what Malcolm said. He told me that you've kissed several of my friends."

"It's wasn't like that," I begin.

Edwin continues. "You know, Emerson . . . come to think of it, his story sounded almost exactly like what happened to me that day I took Oliver's place and tutored you in Spanish."

I feel my face turning red.

"Would you have kissed Oliver if he had shown up?" he asks.

"No!" I say loudly, but I would have, and I hate it.

"What's your deal?" he asks. "I mean, who *are* you?"

I look pleadingly into his velvet eyes. "I'm not that girl anymore! I'm only interested in you."

"*Anymore?* As in, since you got caught today?" He kicks some gravel and starts to walk away. "You're not who I thought you were, Emerson."

I stand there, numb. Unable to even argue with him.

CHAPTER FORTY-FOUR

Cracked

"Heavens to Betsy!" Arch exclaims. "You look awful."

She's right. For the first time in my teenage life, I have denied myself makeup, and it feels good. Feels right. Feels like my outside finally matches my inside: *ugly*. I used to wonder if Hester Prynne hated her scarlet A, but now I almost think it was a relief.

I smile at Arch before the tears start falling down my face. She leans in. "What's wrong, honey?"

I'm going to tell her, I decide. I don't care anymore. I am too tired of hiding who I am. "I quit the decathlon team. I don't deserve it. And I cheated on those tests, Arch, because I wanted to stay at Haygood so badly."

Her face falls. "Emerson. *Why?* You're so smart. You didn't need to cheat. You just needed to apply yourself."

"I didn't set out to do it," I say. "Not at first. It was an accident. Sort of . . ."

Arch sits down on the sofa in the kitchen and pats the

cushion by her side. For some reason, her calm demeanor isn't as reassuring as I would have hoped. I want anger. I want frustration. I want what I deserve.

"What do you mean, it was an accident?" she asks. Less than two seconds ago I was planning on telling her everything, but now my tongue is sticking as if I've got a mouthful of peanut butter. What if she doesn't believe me? What if it scares her? *What if it makes her not want me anymore?*

"Emerson?" she repeats. "What did you do?"

I can feel the tears slipping silently down my face. "It was the kissing," I say. "Mama wasn't crazy. I can do it, too." I bury my head in her chest and wrap my arms around her, not wanting to see her face react, and not wanting her to let go either. I'm scared she'll leave me like Edwin did. Like Mama did. But then, just when I think I can't take it any longer, she puts my face in her hands and looks me in the eyes. "Listen to me, Emerson. Please explain what you said about the kissing and your mother. I don't understand."

I take a deep breath, and before I know it, I tell her everything. About how I can see Mama when Arch kisses me. How I kissed test answers out of all of those boys. How I can taste and experience their emotions at the same time. What it was like when I first kissed Edwin. How he diminished my powers.

I let it all out.

Except one thing: the kiss with Silas. I'm not sure what to do about that yet.

Arch is crying now, too. But instead of lecturing me, she kisses my dimple. Probably not thinking about what that kiss might reveal. But it *does* reveal something. Something she'd never say out loud.

I see my mother. And Arch's one thought: *I didn't believe her.*

"I am so sorry, Emerson," Arch cries. "So very sorry."

"I know," I reassure her as she succumbs to the tears.

She wipes her face with the palm of her hand. "Does Edwin know?"

"He saw me kiss one of the boys."

She sighs. "Oh, Emerson."

Not the response I was looking for. I start to cry again, too. "Do you think he'll ever forgive me?"

"I don't know. But if you love him, you should tell him what you told me. Let him know the *real* you."

"The real me is pretty hard to believe," I say.

"I know. But being real is the only way to really love. I'm not saying it's not scary, because it is. It's terrifying. It's why I'm still single." A sad little smile appears on her face.

Piper and I have discussed Arch's lack of a consistent love life over the years, but we never figured out why she didn't get married. Being "too scared" never crossed our minds.

"But what if he doesn't believe me?" I ask her.

"Well, there's only one way to find out. But I suspect he will. It's clear you and Edwin have something special. Why else wouldn't you be able to read his mind? There has to be something to that. And if he can't see it, then screw him!"

I laugh and hug her again.

"Thank you, Arch," I say. "Thank you so much. Thank you for believing me."

"I've always believed you, sweetie. I love you. But I'm going to have to think through what to do about this kissing business. How are you ever going to have a normal life?"

"I don't know," I say. "I wish I knew why I have this gift.

And why Mama had it. But I think finding *real* love might be the thing that takes it away. That's one thing Mama never had."

She pushes my hair behind my ears. "Does Piper know?"

I shake my head. "I'm not ready to tell her yet."

"That's okay," she says. "We can talk about it as often you like, but maybe keeping it a secret from most people is a good idea." She sits up and smoothes her skirt. "This not-wearing-makeup business has got to stop, though. It doesn't achieve anything. I think you'll feel better with a little color on your face. Trust me on this one."

CHAPTER FORTY-FIVE

Golden Raisin

Saturday is as gloomy and depressing outside as it is inside. After working at my desk for a few hours, I go help Piper drape fabric on Penelope. Piper's back to her obsession of designing and has been sketching ideas nonstop for some sundresses she hopes to make this summer. Of course this isn't completely by accident; she has been grounded from spending time with Silas outside of school, and we're one of the few families home for Easter break. Still . . . Piper seems to be more like her old self, and it's nice.

On Easter Sunday I change my clothes after church and come downstairs to the sound of Arch humming cheerfully in the kitchen. She is merrily mashing potatoes with her new hand mixer, Speedy.

"Hey, baby. I need you to take over here. Speedy has worn me smack out." She grins and hands me the mixer. "My arms aren't what they used to be."

"That's what you get when you cheap-out and buy the clunkiest mixer around." I look into the bowl. "Whoa. And this is a *ton* of potatoes. No wonder Speedy is struggling."

"You're not kidding." She walks to the sofa, lies down, and massages her biceps. "Audrey asked me to make extras this year. They're taking a meal to the homeless shelter after dinner."

The Wilsons have invited us over for their annual Easter dinner, and it's the only thing I've looked forward to all week.

"What else do we have to make?" I ask her.

"A pecan pie and that Spinach Madeleine we all love."

"Mmmm," I say. "Can I make the spinach?"

"Yes, you can." She smiles. "I'll just lie right here and direct you."

Piper walks into the room dressed as if she's stepping out of one of her magazines. She's wearing black leggings with a long, jade-colored sweater and her new, peep-toe pumps in electric blue. It's a mismatched masterpiece that only Piper could pull off. Last year she started wearing bold-striped tights with all of her skirts—looked stupid if you ask me—but before long, every other girl in school had a pair. That's the one thing about setting trends that Piper hates: she always has to keep thinking *ahead* or she'll look like everyone else.

"Pretty," Arch says. "But those aren't what I'd call comfortable clothes."

Piper shrugs. "I thought you might let me see Silas for a couple of hours since it *is* Easter and all." She sticks a finger into the potatoes and licks it. "Needs salt."

Arch presses her lips together. "I think that might work. Did you finish your application essay?"

"Yes, ma'am."

"All righty then. Be home by five!"

"See ya," I say while turning off the beater. I wait to remove the blades until she's out the door so I can have them all to myself, sampling the warm whipped potatoes.

"Bring me one," Arch says sleepily.

I walk a blade over to her, and she tastes it. "Yep. Needs more salt."

I nod.

"And sour cream. There's a container in the fridge."

I add the salt, then whip a large container of sour cream into the potatoes, making them perfect while Arch rests.

Seeing Piper pull out of the driveway, dressed to go see Silas, fills me with a jumble of emotions more complicated than the spinach dish I'm about to attempt. I've heard several rumors about his cheating ways, but with no evidence, I can't dare bring it up.

Arch falls asleep a few minutes later, and I continue cooking. She's as organized as Piper, so all of the necessary ingredients for the spinach dish are sitting next to the recipe. After putting the cheesy concoction into a casserole dish and topping it with bread crumbs, I go back upstairs to shower and get ready.

On my way into the bathroom, I check my phone for something, anything.

A text from Trina flashes. Guess who found a new hottie at church? Hallelujah!

💋

"Get yourselves in here!" Mrs. Wilson says when she answers the door. She's still dressed in her church clothes and has on a yellow apron with a bunny rabbit in tennis attire. She is also wearing an older shade of Golden Raisin. Not a good color on her, honestly, but we won't tell her so. I make a mental note to bring her something more suitable soon.

"I like your apron," I say.

She strikes a pose before taking the pie from me. "I just picked it up at Gigi's Gifts. Say that again in front of Mr. Wilson. He hates it."

Piper laughs. "Doesn't he know that bunnies in tennis gear are all the rage?"

"Exactly," says Mrs. Wilson, bubbling over with holiday cheer. "That's what *I* told him, but he's an old doodley-doo."

I chuckle.

"It smells wonderful," Arch says.

"Why, thank you. We can't wait to dig in. I've had to pacify Mr. Wilson with butterscotch candy for the last hour. He gets grumpy if his blood sugar drops."

"Are they here yet?" I hear his deep voice call from his recliner in the den.

"Yes, they are, buttercup! Get up out of that chair and turn off the TV."

I peer around the corner to see him making his way out of his leather perch. He's wearing a pastel-yellow jacket with khaki pants and the most hideous shoes I have ever seen. For him to disapprove of his wife's silly apron is hysterical. "Hi, there, princess. Happy Easter!"

"Ditto!"

I turn back to Mrs. Wilson and Arch, who are setting our casseroles on the stovetop. There are sweet potatoes, roasted vegetables, ham, green beans, and a salad.

"Did you make those good rolls?" Piper asks Mrs. Wilson.

"Of course I did, Piperoni." She grins. "I know what my girls like."

Mr. Wilson is already seated at the table, fork in hand, so I walk over and sit next to him. "What's new?"

"I hear you're going to compete in the King Cotton Decathlon," he says, beaming.

I look at my plate. "I'm not in it anymore."

"I was in it, you know. Back in the day." He sits up straighter and pushes out his chest. I notice that his lavender tie has hundreds of tiny Easter eggs stitched on it. Hilarious.

"Really?" I ask.

"Sure enough. Three years in a row." He holds up three fingers. "I kicked butt!"

"Watch your language, honey!" Mrs. Wilson shouts from the kitchen.

His eyes widen, and he quiets his voice. "Ooops. Why aren't you in it anymore?"

I sigh. "It's a long story, but I'm not sure I'd do very well."

He takes my hand. "For the record, I think you'd be spectacular."

Arch walks in, sets down some glasses, and takes a seat. Piper and Mrs. Wilson follow, carrying steaming dishes.

"Dee-lish!" Mr. Wilson reaches over to serve himself some mashed potatoes before Mrs. Wilson slaps his hand playfully. "Not so fast, honey! We haven't said grace."

He pulls his hand back and smiles up at her. "You're right, darlin'. Where are my manners?"

Audrey bites back a smile, and we all close our eyes while she thanks the Lord for our food.

And Jesus's resurrection.

And the decathlon.

And Piper's costumes.

And the weather.

And her new Stellar foundation.

And her friends.

And her bridge group.

Until Mr. Wilson starts coughing and she finally says, "Amen."

One hour later, so full I feel sick, Mrs. Wilson says, "Gift time! Now, go into my bedroom and get those three gifts on my dresser. This holiday wouldn't be the same without presents."

"Oh, Audrey, you shouldn't have," Arch says.

"Nonsense," she replies. "I never get to dote on my girls anymore."

Piper and I run to Wilsons' bedroom, which is the definition of froufrou. Floral wallpaper, floral rugs, floral bedding. Flowers, flowers, everywhere! And it smells like flowers, too. I honestly don't know how Mr. Wilson sleeps in here.

"Got 'em," Piper says, picking up the gifts. They are unusually small, mine being the smallest. And they're wrapped in—you guessed it—pink floral paper. I smell mine, thinking for a moment that it might smell like roses, but it doesn't. Just paper.

Mrs. Wilson smiles when we return. "All righty, girls. Let her rip!"

Piper tears hers open first and holds up two gift cards, one of which is for the most expensive clothing store in town. She gasps. "Oh my gosh! I love this store!"

"You're gonna need some new duds if you want to stand out at that fashion school," says Audrey.

Piper gets out of her chair and rushes over to hug the Wilsons.

"That's awesome!" I say. And before she can open her second one, I'm frantically tearing open mine. Just like Piper's, there are two small gift cards, the first of which is to the bookstore.

Wah wah . . .

"We thought you could use some extra books, as studious as you've gotten these days," Mr. W says. "There's a great book of trivia I wanted to get you to prepare for those crazy decathlon questions, but Audrey said you should get to pick." He winks at me sympathetically since I'm not even doing it anymore.

"I love it," I lie. The *last* thing I want is more books. Piper has now opened her bookstore card and is excitedly telling Mrs. Wilson about the pattern-making book on sale. As I open the second gift card, I cross my fingers, praying for clothing and not office supplies.

Phew! It is! Hugging ensues.

Arch is next. She was given an envelope and not a wrapped box. She slowly opens it while explaining to Mrs. Wilson the amazing properties of Stellar's new anti-aging serum. When she opens the greeting card, a small piece of white paper falls out.

"What is it?" Piper asks.

Mrs. Wilson puts her arm around Arch, who has picked up the little piece of paper and is staring at it, unable to speak. She looks across the table at Mr. Wilson, who appears to be getting emotional, too. *What's going on?*

"What is it?" I ask out loud.

Arch clears her throat. "It's a receipt." Her voice cracks.

"What's wrong?" asks Piper. "A receipt for what?"

"The Wilsons have paid the balance on both of your tuitions for the year."

CHAPTER FORTY-SIX

Twinkle Toes

I cannot believe this.

I have spent the entire semester kissing a bunch of Ivys, which has led to the loss of my boyfriend, and it was all for nothing?! I get to stay at Haygood anyway? And here I am, thinking Edwin's ability to steal my power is as cruel a joke as it can get? That's *nothing* compared to finding out that all of this kissing wasn't even necessary. Not that I'm not grateful for such a generous gift. I am. I *really* am. It will help us tremendously. But I still can't believe that I've ruined my relationship with Edwin by kissing other guys. What was I thinking? And now, I might be letting him down even more by not participating in the decathlon. *I* won't lose anything by staying at home and watching TV, but *they* might be disqualified if they can't find a replacement.

I suck.

And I totally don't deserve this generous gift.

"Hello, milady," Fish says when he answers my call later.

I can't help but chuckle. It feels good to be talking to an Ivy without a kissing agenda for once in my life. "Grady," I begin. "I just want you to know that I'm sorry I let you guys down and quit the team."

"That's okay. Campbell agreed to do it this morning. And you can still be an alternate, ya know. In case he gets sick or something. I mean, if you want."

"Really?"

"Sure. You just have to tell the principal."

"Consider it done," I say.

"By George! That's a fabulous change in plans!"

Arch is always telling us we can do anything day by day, so I write a big 24 on my hand and hang up, reminding myself that I can change my ways twenty-four hours at a time. Then I pull the thick, yellow chemistry book out of my backpack and open it. I need to stay on top of my regular homework.

The next morning I wake up with my chemistry book still open across my chest and a 24 smeared across my cheek. Strangely, I'm feeling pretty good. Not about Edwin. I tried to call him twice last night but he didn't answer. I was scared to talk to him anyway. What would I have said?

I'm feeling okay about school for the first time in a long while. It's like the way I felt after the girls performed my dance. I finally know what it is. Simple satisfaction from hard work. It's what has always been lacking in my grades. I haven't felt proud of them because I haven't worked very hard for them. Or . . . I've stolen them.

After washing my hands and face, I get dressed and apply my newest gloss, Twinkle Toes. It's a supersparkly peach color. It makes me feel only slightly better. Lip gloss can do a lot of things, but it can't cure a broken heart or mend a crummy reputation.

The first four periods drag on endlessly, and Edwin avoids me like the plague. I find Trina in study hall. "T?" I ask. "Can you talk?" I know she's heard the rumors, and it's time to face her.

She walks with me over to the corner and we sit down. "Did you really kiss Malcolm Reynolds?" she asks.

"Yes." I get a sick feeling as I recall what happened.

"Wait!" she says. "It's true?! That's so nasty."

I sigh. "It's my fault. I led him on."

"What?" she asks. "Why would you do that?"

I take a breath. "I can't explain it. I needed his help in math, and it just happened."

"Unbelievable." She leans back on her hands and shakes her head in confusion. "Then Frances wasn't lying about you kissing Ivys?" she asks.

"What?"

"Frances said you made out with Grady in study hall a couple of months ago."

My face turns red again before I nod. "It was so *not* a make out, and I don't *like* these guys or anything!" I assure her.

Trina tilts her head and gives me her serious eyes. "Emerson, I don't get it. I really don't. Why on earth would you kiss *any* of these boys?"

I put my head in my hands. "You'd never believe me if I told you."

"Try me."

I shake my head. "I can't."

She starts to stand up. "Well, I can't help you with Edwin unless you trust me enough to tell me what's going on. I'm your best friend."

I start to tell her, but I know I'd have to kiss her and then tell her what's in *her* mind to make her believe me. And although that wouldn't be a big deal, I know that no matter how much she'll want to keep it a secret, she won't be able to. Keeping secrets—especially big ones—has never been Trina's strong suit. And let's face it: my secret's just too juicy.

"I wanted to do our plan, ya know—the one about having a study partner fall in love with me?—and things just got out of hand."

Her jaw drops, and a deep crease forms in the center of her eyebrows. "I *knew* that plan was genius!" she shouts, pride shooting from her face like sun rays. "But you were supposed to ask *Vance* to help you—not those nerds!"

Relief fills me, and I decide to admit a little bit more. "I needed practice before I approached His Royal Hotness."

"Let me get this straight. You kissed a bunch of Ivys for *practice*"—she pauses and has to bite back disbelief—"and then yesterday one of them tried to kiss you, and the new Ivy love-of-your-life saw it?"

It sounds so bizarre hearing it like that. "Yes." I purse my lips. "But Edwin is different. I reeaallllly like him, Trina. I didn't see it coming, but I guess it *was* due to your plan. I asked him to help me with Spanish, and I fell for him. But I'm not sure if he can forgive me now."

"Hmmm . . . ," she says, and I can tell she's referencing one of the hundreds of articles she has no doubt read on the subject of finding true love, broken hearts, or something similar. "I don't know, Emerson. I. Don't. Know."

I press my lips together. "Yeah me neither. If you come up with a brilliant solution, let me know."

"You'll figure it out," she tells me. And then she says what I *really* need to hear. "You're stronger than you think."

I smile. "Did you read that line somewhere?"

"No," she says with a smile. "It was in a song. But it's true." She puts her fist up toward me like we used to do during our superhero phase in third grade. "Go forth in power, sister."

I push mine into hers and grin through my heartache. "Power."

And with that, I power myself right to the principal's office to sign myself up as an alternate for the decathlon.

CHAPTER FORTY-SEVEN

Twisted Sister

The front door opens and Arch stumbles in, dropping her gigantic blue bag on the floor. "Whew! What a night. I ran out of Twisted Sister before nine o'clock! Can you believe that? That one lip gloss paid for our dinner tonight."

"Shoot. I wanted one of those," I say. Twisted Sister is Stellar's newest gloss. It has two thick bands of red and yellow gloss that wind around each other in a clear, hourglass-shaped tube. When applied, it looks orange. But not circus orange, more like golden-amber orange. It's hard to explain, but I'm not surprised she sold out. It's one gorgeous color—even on a redhead.

"I'll make sure to order some more next week," she reassures me. "Can you girls help me get my table and displays out of the car?"

Piper and I nod and walk outside to Arch's car.

"Help me with this," Piper says, picking up a folding table. She was so much fun over spring break, but now that we're back in school, she's withdrawing again.

I grab the other side and carry it into the garage. "Is everything okay with Silas?"

"Yes," she says. But I can tell she's lying.

Arch comes out and gets a few bags from the car. "You guys wanna see the new catalogs?"

That's a duh. I *always* want to see the new catalogs. But I stop myself. I have a few more chapters to study before bed. "Can I take one with me to bed?" I ask.

Arch reaches into her bag and hands me a catalog. "Sure."

We all head back inside. "Arch?" I ask. "Can we talk?"

She puts her arm around me. "Follow me into my room. I have to put these orders into the computer."

I follow her down the hall and into her bedroom.

"What's up?" she asks.

"I don't know if you've figured this out yet, but after I quit kissing . . ." Just saying it makes me feel gross. "Well, my grades fell slightly." I pause, my legs getting shaky. It hits me how much I love her and how much I want to please her.

She puts down her bags and papers on her desk while I stare at my feet, waiting for her reply.

"I figured," she says, sitting down. "And it's okay. After what you've been through, it's understandable."

"I also quit the decathlon. I knew I didn't deserve to be up there."

She faces me and smiles. "Emmie Girl, I have never been so proud of you in my entire life."

"But I feel like I've let you down," I say.

She rubs my back.

"And by quitting, I let the boys down, too. . . . So, I agreed to be an alternate."

"You haven't let anyone down. We all make mistakes, and I'm glad you're facing yours."

Just then Piper yells from the other room. "Emerson! Someone's at the door for you!"

I hug Arch, then run to the front door, desperately hoping it's Edwin. But it's not. It's the boy who replaced me on the decathlon team: Campbell Adams. He's holding some books.

"Hey, Campbell," I say, inviting him inside.

"I can't stay, but I wanted to come talk to you. About the decathlon."

"Okay," I say, confused.

"I can't be in it."

"Why not?" I ask. "Grady said you agreed to do it."

He blushes and looks down at his feet. "I didn't really agree to it. I told him I had to call my parents first because, well . . . I'm moving, and I wasn't sure exactly when."

"Really?" I ask.

"I haven't told anyone, but my father was laid off six months ago. Things have been pretty hard at home, and then last week Dad got a new job in Evergreen—effective immediately. But I wasn't sure what immediately really meant for me."

"Wow. Are you okay about it?" I ask.

He smiles. "I'm pretty pumped, actually. And get this. Since I've already met the criteria for participating, the decathlon board is allowing me to compete on *Evergreen's* team. Against you guys!"

"No way!" I chuckle. "Get out! That's hysterical!"

He hands me a notebook. "I heard you were the alternate."

Uh-oh.

He continues. "It feels like I'm cheating by playing for the other team and all, so I've decided to give you my notes. You know—so we'll be on equal footing. I've memorized and studied every critical chemistry fact and recorded the most important ones here." He hands me a notebook.

I look down at it. Kissing him goodbye right here and now would be so much easier than studying, and no one would ever know.

The problem is . . .

That's not the girl I am now.

I thank him, wish him well, and shut the door—fast.

CHAPTER FORTY-EIGHT

Infinity

The night of the decathlon I pace the house feeling squeamish for what seems like hours. Mr. Wilson is so excited that he's decided to go with us. Kill me now.

"Emerson? Are you ready?" Arch shouts from downstairs. When I walked back into her room the other night and announced I was going to be a *participant*, her excitement was back in full swing.

"I guess so," I say while checking myself in the mirror one more time. I got a new dress with my gift card: black linen with a dark-green sash. Arch also bought me some black tights with a beautiful vine design down the sides and a fabulous pair of heels—higher even than Piper's *highest* pair, making her insanely jealous.

I walk down the steps and into the kitchen, where Arch is clip-clopping around with a glass of wine in her hand. She has on her heels, too, and head-to-toe Stellar blue.

"You need to eat something," she says. "Are you nervous?"

I glare at her. "If you call feeling like I'm gonna pass out nervous."

She hugs me, smelling strongly of pride with a quiet bottom note of apprehension—a strange combination that reminds me of magnolia flowers sprinkled with cinnamon. I rub my nose, fearing I might sneeze.

"Now you listen to me," she says, getting in my face. "You are capable of grand things, my Emmie Girl. That dance you choreographed was just a warm-up for the things you will achieve in this life; and I, for one, am beyond proud of you."

Piper's on the couch, dressed up and eating cereal. "What about me?" she asks, to which Arch rolls her eyes before hugging her, too.

"Of course I'm proud of you, Pipes. Everything you've made on Penelope has knocked my socks off. And just like I told Emerson, I can't wait to see what God has planned for you in this life. It has been a privilege being your . . ." She pauses. "Your parent."

Piper turns to me. "You'll do fine. Just don't answer anything wrong."

Right.

The King Cotton Decathlon is held annually at the Franklin Center downtown. It's the largest venue in town. Tons of people come from all over to watch this thing, which is beyond me. Judging by the traffic, you'd think it was a rock concert.

Once inside the building, I'm given a pass and directed to the Haygood Academy prep room, where my teammates are waiting. After smoothing down my dress, I lick my lips. Arch let me wear her newest gloss, called Infinity. I'm hoping it adds something pretty to my look, because Edwin will see me in T minus three seconds and counting.

"Right this way," the administrator says.

T minus two.

I follow his lead and see Mrs. Parker up ahead entering the room. She's one of the decathlon advisers. "Hello, Emerson," she says. "Ya ready?"

I swallow and nod. It's now or never.

T minus one.

She pushes open the door, and I walk inside. Across the room, Don, Grady, and Oliver greet me warmly. But Malcolm and Edwin are what I would describe as "cordial." Similar to the way I act toward Arch's clients, or maybe the dentist. The boys are dressed in suits with red-and-blue striped ties.

I put on a practiced smile and take a seat on the long, black leather sofa next to Fish.

"I'm so psyched! I can't wait to get out there!" he says, pointing to the door.

"I feel like I might puke," I mutter.

Grady laughs. "Emerson's nervous, y'all."

Mallory arrives and sits next to me. "You look gorgeous!"

I smile, feeling a whisper of compliment-induced confidence.

"Is Luke here yet?" she asks excitedly.

"I think so." I'm relieved to be discussing something other than academics.

"Is everyone ready?" Mrs. Parker asks us, sticking her head back through the doorway a few minutes later. Her hair is all poufed and strange-looking, but I notice her nails have been freshened up with that new bottle of Iced Tea I gave her.

"Bring it," says Grady.

She laughs. "Atta boy, Grady!"

I steal a glance at Edwin, and he meets my gaze with a look I can't quite place. Is he still angry? Hurt? What?

Mallory grabs my hand, pulling me out of our mini stare-off. "Come on!"

Standing up, I start to laugh nervously.

Grady notices my panic and whispers, "You'll do fine, Emerson. Once you get out there, it's just like karaoke."

"Karaoke?" I ask.

"It's scary until you get the mic in your hand. But once you're on, you're on *fire*. Fire, I tell you!"

I shake my head, doubting I'll feel the power of the mic so easily.

As we walk across the stage, the crowd goes wild. A voice on a loudspeaker says, "Haygood Academy is here to defend its title!"

Microscopic condensation forms under my arms. If I don't calm down I'll have armpit circles like a mechanic by the end of the hour. I move my elbows out slightly from my sides to encourage a breeze, but it's hopeless.

Grady walks proudly over to a row of seven podiums, and I follow. Each podium has our school crest on the front. There's no telling how much all of this costs. It's incredible. It looks like a real game show. I touch the wooden stands with my finger as we pass. There are flashing lights, big screens on which the questions are displayed, and giant red buzzer buttons on each podium. I don't know what I expected, but it's exactly like on TV. I can't believe I've never cared to see this.

Thankful to have something to lean on, I grip the sides of my podium and lean into it for support. There's no telling what will happen tonight, and I don't want to faint. My podium is between Edwin's and Malcolm's, who are both oddly solemn. I want to smile at Edwin, to let him know I still care about him. And then I wish he'd reach over and pat my back or pinch my knee . . . or kiss me.

"Good luck!" I tell him, hoping he smiles.

He does.

But I'm not sure it means anything.

The announcer brings out the Evergreen team next. Once again the crowd goes nuts, and the kids from Evergreen walk to their side of the stage. They're all dressed in green coats and yellow ties: their school colors. Campbell gives us the peace sign when he walks in, and I see Oliver give him a thumbs-up.

I push my button while the crowd is still cheering for the other team, just to make sure it works—not that I plan on using it or anything. But a loud siren silences the room.

"Whoa there!" the announcer says, laughing in my direction as my podium lights up. "It seems Miss Emerson Taylor is ready to get this party started."

I turn green, gripping the sides of the podium and waiting for my heart to fail. "No. No. I, uh . . . I was just testing my buzzer."

"I think we have a live one, everyone!" he says jokingly to the audience. "This should be a big night!"

I inhale and exhale, thinking I might be having a stroke. *Can sixteen-year-olds have strokes?*

The crowd laughs, and I frantically look for Arch but can't find her. Then the announcer quiets the crowd to explain the game and rules. I am way too busy trying not to collapse to even listen.

"And now we shall begin!" he says loudly. "Get your buzzers ready."

I raise my hand (which is shaking) above the buzzer in an attempt to appear focused. It's go time.

CHAPTER FORTY-NINE

Congo Red

Edwin answers the first question correctly, and I have to stifle a squeal. I look over at him wide-eyed, and he grins. He's smiling at me! All hope is not lost. *This might be kinda fun?*

But eleven questions later it dawns on me that I am completely focused on him and not on the game. That's not fair to my teammates. So during the break I go to the bathroom and make a new plan. The questions have been so ridiculously hard that I haven't tried to answer a single one. Can you imagine how embarrassing it would be to answer one *wrong*? Oliver missed one a few questions ago and he punched the podium.

I'm emotional enough without five hundred people staring at me expectantly. I'm not sure I have the courage to even try.

But when we return to our podiums, I decide to just try and see what happens.

"We're ready to start the second half, folks!" the announcer says to the crowd. "This has been one close contest!"

I swallow, thrilled that it's almost over.

He jumps right into the second half with a question. "What is the printing process by which ink is forced into recessed lines?" he asks slowly.

A guy on the other team hits his buzzer and says, "Lithography?"

"Wrong!" The announcer turns and directs his attention to us. "It's up to you, Haygood. What is the process by which ink is forced into recessed lines?"

Is it intaglio? I look over at my team, hoping someone answers.

Grady pushes his button. "Intaglio?"

"Yes! Great job, Haygood!"

Dangit! I knew that one!

"Next question," the announcer says. "And it's a chemistry one."

I panic, keeping my eyes in front of me. I can feel my teammates boring holes in my head with their eyes. They expect me to know this.

"What chemical is responsible for the burning sensation we get from chili peppers?"

I feel my chest *burning* from an anxiety-producing chemical I know is norepinephrine. *Why can't they ask me that?* I look across at Campbell, who is staring at me with his hand raised over his buzzer. We lock eyes, and without knowing how, I feel like he is waiting for me to answer first and win the question. The only problem is that I don't know the answer! I close my eyes in defeat, and he hits his buzzer.

"Capsaicin!" he says.

"That is correct."

I sigh and look at my teammates. They give me faint smiles. Maybe they're not mad at me after all. I decide to keep trying.

But by the end of the hour, there still hasn't been one

question I can answer. To tell you the truth, it's starting to give me a headache—such focused concentration and all.

Grady has noticed, too. He leaned over a few minutes ago and whispered "I'm sorry. You'll get one. Don't give up!" I nodded at him like the wimp I am.

We take one last quick break and then the competition continues for the final round. It's neck and neck. The opposing team has 34, and we have 33, making this the first time in four years that Haygood Academy has even had to struggle.

Edwin, boy of my dreams, answers two more questions, and I feel myself beaming with pride and, yes, hopelessness. If only I could go back in time and redo everything. I look out at Arch. She's chewing gum, which she considers to be particularly tacky in public, so I know she's nervous for me.

"And now for our final question," the announcer begins. "For the first time in King Cotton history, we have a tie!"

The crowd gets loud.

"The winner of this question wins all!"

I stand up straight, shaking off my sadness, and prepare to get my ninja eyes on. I glance to my right at Malcolm and to my left at Edwin. Their hands are raised, so I raise mine, too.

The announcer continues, slowly and purposefully. "Which pH indicator changes from blue-violet to red in the pH range of three to five?"

A loud buzzer sounds, and the announcer laughs. "Emerson Taylor! Well now, Miss Taylor. It's about time you got to answer one."

The audience joins in his laughter.

Huh? I think out of sheer nervousness, my hand must have come down on the buzzer. *Oh, sweet child o' mine, I'm going to have to answer this.* I grip the podium again for fear I may fall.

I inhale deeply before the announcer says, "Let me repeat the final question."

The audience gets quiet, and I hear a few screams. "Go, Emerson!" Mr. Wilson roars. Trina shouts a "Woo hoo!"

The announcer speaks again. "Which pH indicator changes from blue-violet to red in the pH range of three to five?"

pH indicators? I have no clue. I look at Edwin, who is expressionless. In that moment everything slows way down, like in movies when people talk and it sounds like, "Whaaaaattt issssss tthheeee aaaannnnnnssswwweeeerrrrrrrrr?"

I blink in slow motion and look out again at Arch, who is beaming and whispering to Mr. Wilson. Poor things. They are so proud.

Biting my bottom lip, I remember pH indicators are colors. But not the kinds of colors you read on the sides of crayons, like sunshine yellow or grass green. pH indicators have names like paints—names like bromophenol blue and methyl orange. But those aren't right. He just said it's a red. *Oh my gosh, who am I kidding? I don't know this.*

I look back out at Arch, who is flashing shiny Congo Red lips; and before I can stop my mouth from speaking, I've said it. "Congo red."

My own voice knocks me out of my trance, and I know even before he says it that I got it. *I KNOW THIS!*

"Congo red!" the announcer's voice booms. "She has answered Congo red!"

I look over at Edwin with big, petrified eyes—but he is smiling at me.

Big.

"That's correct!" the announcer says. "Congo Red is correct! Haygood Academy wins!"

I bring my hands up to my face in shock. That lipstick is named for the indicator. It's the truest red Stellar makes, the one tube that was named by their chemist. Of course it would be named for a pH color. Holy smokes. We won.

I grip the podium and laugh as Grady hugs me fiercely from behind. "You did it, Emerson! You did it!" he shouts.

Confetti falls from the ceiling, and the crowd goes wild. My teammates crash into a group hug, and I think my back is going to break. But I feel happy—oh so happy. Even Campbell rushes over and joins the big hug.

After the hug breaks up, Edwin looks at me and smiles. Then walks off the stage.

And I am alone.

CHAPTER FIFTY

Kiss of Air

"How on earth did you know that?" Piper asks in the car on the way home, laughing.

"It's Arch's lipstick. Can you believe it? It was an accident. At least I think it was. I just looked out at Arch and spoke the name of her lipstick. Crazy."

Arch and Mrs. Wilson laugh.

"In. Sane," says Piper. "Was it fun? You think you'll do it again next year?"

I pause, knowing that I won't, that I need to ditch this gift and get on with my life. But it's bittersweet at the same time. "I doubt it."

"I bet you do!" says Mr. Wilson proudly. "I can coach you!"

"Edwin sure did well," Arch says.

"Yeah," I say. "He did." I stare out the window at the bare, leafless trees and feel a familiar, lonely chill settle into my heart.

I exhale onto the car window and draw a heart in the fog. I go over that last day with Mama for the thousandth time in my head, trying to understand why I have this gift. I know that day by heart, even though I have never seen it again—because it's not in Arch's memory.

As the heart and fog fade from the window, I remember Mama's red eyes looking into mine when she blew me that last kiss.

My breath catches. . . .

The last thing she did was blow me a kiss.

That's it! That last blown kiss from Mama! *That's* how I got this gift! I can't explain how I know this to be true, but I do. I *know.* She blew it to me, and now I need to *blow* it away. I sit up, tempted to just blow it right out the window, into the dead, cracking branches; but Arch's words stop me. "You are so gifted, Emerson," she says from the front seat.

"That she is," echoes Mr. Wilson. "That she is."

Gifted. The word stabs me. And suddenly I know in my heart that I haven't yet done whatever it is I am meant to do with this gift. I lean my head against the glass. Maybe I can *use* my gift to benefit someone else. It's high time this "gift" stopped being a curse.

"I'm hungry!" says Mr. Wilson. "Let's celebrate!"

Arch takes a right, and we head toward our favorite restaurant, the one we only go to for very special occasions: Mandrelli's. As we pull into the parking lot, it hits me. I *can* help someone. And I know just who that person is.

Luke catches me after history, and we walk together to assembly. Edwin and his adorable self is strolling up ahead, forcing me to inhale deeply, then shake it off.

"You okay?" Luke asks.

I haven't seen him much in the last few weeks. Been too busy studying.

"I heard about Malcolm," he says. "Vance told me you kissed him a couple of weeks ago?"

"Don't ask," I say.

"Okay, but I thought it was McNeely you were interested in this whole time."

"It is," I say. "Let's go. I'll tell you about it later."

We walk on toward the auditorium.

"Hey, man!" Trina says from behind us, and I'm thankful for the friend sandwich I find myself in. "Em, can you help me with the next Spanish test? You're rocking that class!"

"Sure."

Sawyer and Grady pass us going the other way. Sawyer smiles at Trina, and she actually smiles back. Ever since Malcolm announced our little "relationship" to the general public, people have been nicer to those guys. It's helped that Luke has started dating Mallory, too. I swear, peer pressure is a strange thing.

"Grady!" I say as he passes. "I'm bringing chips and cheese dip to lunch Friday!"

He spins around and moonwalks backward. "Cool!"

I don't know why none of us ever gave the Ivys a chance. They're totally where it's at.

Principal Overton walks across the stage and stands at the podium, facing us. "Good morning, students."

The room quiets down.

"Today I want to congratulate those who made this semester's honor roll."

I cross my fingers underneath my chair. With my test scores this past month, I just might have made it.

"Several of these talented kids competed in the King Cotton Decathlon, which we won!"

I look around the room for Edwin as the room erupts in cheers.

"When I call your name, please come up here to receive your certificate."

"Did you make it?" Luke whispers.

I shrug my shoulders.

The principal starts announcing names. A few names in, I hear it:

"Edwin McNeely."

My heart stops. I knew he'd make it, but hearing his name hurts just the same. I can see people clapping, including myself, but I hear nothing. The room goes silent as Edwin stands up and walks onto the stage. His hair is hanging in his eyes, making it hard to really see his expression. He receives his certificate and goes to stand next to Grady. I think I see him look at me, but I'm not sure. Principal Overton reads a few more names before saying, "Please give another round of applause to this year's honor roll recipients!"

Luke tosses me a sympathetic smile as I uncross my fingers and play with my hair. I really wanted to make this, for Arch.

"We have one more thing," Principal O says while fumbling with some paper. "Your English teachers submitted their favorite papers this semester, and one was chosen for publication in our local magazine, *Haygood Living*!"

Clapping ensues.

"What's *this* about?" asks Trina.

"I have no idea."

"The winning paper . . . is a poem by Emerson Taylor."
What?!

Luke punches my leg and laughs.

Oh my gosh. Principal Overton is going to READ MY POEM TO THE ENTIRE SCHOOL!! *Gulp. Please no. Please no.* I wrote that durn thing during a particularly honest night of depression. It's not meant for human ears! My jaw drops, and I slink down in my chair, aware of everyone's eyes resting solely on *moi*.

"'Tangles,'" Principal Overton begins.

Tangled childhood
Tangled gift
Tangled understanding
And feelings left to shift

Tangled pressures
Tangled grades
Tangled ways to remedy
The messes that I've made

Tangled hopes
Tangled dreams
Tangled tasteless love life
Simply used to scheme

Tangled gain
Tangled needs
Tangled wins and losses
Have led me to concede

Tangling and untangling
The whos and whats and whys
Have muddled all perceptions
And left me in disguise

No amount of tangling
Has led to love that lasts
Except the one that mattered
When seen without my mask

Untangled lies
Untangled pride
Untangled pain that will subside
When left with truth so pure and free
Inside, the gift that's real
is *me*.

CHAPTER FIFTY-ONE

Mint Mouth

The room goes silent, and I fear I may cry. The attention is intense, and I'm desperate for something to happen. *Anything.*

And then something does.

One clap.

Then two.

Three loud claps come from the stage.

From Edwin.

I meet his familiar eyes, and my whole body feels light again.

"Get up there, Ace! You apparently belong onstage." Luke smiles, and he and Trina clap wildly.

As I approach the stage, I'm vaguely aware of all my friends clapping. But I can only feel Edwin's eyes on me. The only eyes that really matter. Nearing the steps on the left side of the stage, I spot Arch standing in the doorway, beaming. She must have been notified in advance.

Principal Overton waves me over to shake his hand. "It is

with great pleasure that I award you this certificate for your poem. Good work, writer!"

"Thank you," I say in disbelief.

Writer, huh? The one thing I'd never been able to wrangle any help with.

After the assembly, I walk toward the class that started it all: geometry.

As I turn the corner, I see Edwin standing alone, outside the classroom, in the empty hall, waiting for me. He isn't smiling, and since I can't read his thoughts, I have no idea what's going on in that hot little head of his.

"Hi," I say as I get closer. Looking down, I'm faced with the moment I've practiced over and over again for the last month. But now that I have my opportunity, I have no idea what to say to him.

"Nice poem," he says. "What was it about anyway?"

"About the mess I've made of things. I've been a fake." I feel ridiculous trying to explain my poem to him, and how sorry I am, even though I really want him to understand.

He tilts his head, silently asking for more with his eyes.

"Edwin, it's true that I kissed those boys. But . . ."

He sighs as if I've punched him.

"But for the wrong reasons!" I reach out to take his hand. "It was stupid, I regret it, and I'm sorry. After you, I . . ." I look up into his eyes, searching for some emotion—some evidence that he still likes me. But I can't sense anything.

"Why?" he asks, knitting his brow.

"I thought I needed them. I thought they would help me get good grades. I thought if I pretended to be interested in them, they'd be more interested in helping me." I feel myself starting to cry. "I was wrong and ended up losing the only boy

I've ever really cared about." I look down at my shoes again.

He shuffles from side to side. "You know they would have helped you study even if you didn't kiss them."

If he only knew.

I can't look at him anymore. "I know you're right. It was a selfish thing to do." And I'm so embarrassed that I turn around and rush down the hall the other way.

"Wait!" he shouts, but I keep going.

CHAPTER FIFTY-TWO

The Butterfly Compact

This week will never end. Everyone is aflutter with plans for the formal, and I can't bear to be around Edwin, so I force myself to dodge him constantly. I've even skipped our classes together a few times. By Friday afternoon I'm zapped. He's texted me, but I'm not sure I'm brave enough to tell him about my gift, or about the depths I went to with Operation Liplock. And without the truth, what do we really have?

After dinner I go into the bathroom to watch Piper get ready for the dance.

"What are you gonna do tonight?" she asks me. She's brushing her hair in the mirror.

I shrug my shoulders and dig around in her makeup.

"You should come anyway," she suggests. "You know he wants to see you."

I scan her vast collection of glosses, wondering which one to wear. "As if."

She brushes her hair. "Well, if it makes you feel any better, I heard he didn't ask anyone else."

"Really?" I feel myself perk up a bit.

"Really. I don't understand why you care about him so much; but, yes, I asked around, and according to my sources, he's not taking anyone."

I smile. Maybe there's still a chance. And maybe, once I ditch this curse, I can finally move forward.

Piper looks in the mirror one final time. "How do I look?"

I freeze, knowing tonight is the night. "Spectacular," I tell her.

She's wearing a dress she bought with the Wilsons' gift certificate. It's a deep-purple strapless number that goes all the way to the floor. Piper said most of the girls will wear perky, short minidresses in bright colors, so she's going in the opposite direction (as usual). Her long hair is pulled up in a surprisingly messy twist, a nice contrast to the very form-fitting, simple lines of the dress. And her earrings? They're long, black, vintage teardrops Mrs. Wilson lent her. Absolutely gorgeous and one of a kind.

"Thanks," she says. "If you change your mind, you can wear my green dress."

"Seriously?" The green one is the dress I *thought* she'd wear. It's one she designed *herself* as part of her portfolio. The assignment was to make a dress suitable for the Oscars. I have tried it on for her several times, acting like Penelope in motion. "Thanks, anyway," I say, "but I refuse to go without a date."

Arch walks in. "Oh, my, Piper. You. Look. Beautiful." She hands Piper a small compact in the shape of a butterfly. "I thought you might like this. It's new."

"Thanks!" Piper takes the compact from her and opens

its wings to reveal a dazzling palate of lipsticks with two tiny brushes.

"You can mix them to make your own unique shade," Arch says.

I pout. "I want one."

"I knew you would," Arch says, handing me another one.

After licking my lips, I dip the brush into a creamy shade of pink with just a touch of brown. It's earthy, beautiful, and perfect for what I'm about to do.

Piper applies the lipstick as her cell vibrates. Then she picks her phone up off the counter and looks down at the screen. "He's here!"

What a loser. Texting her instead of knocking on the door like a proper date!

"Tell him to come inside," Arch says.

"Okay," Piper says, already typing. "I'll get the door."

They walk out of the room, and I inhale deeply before heading downstairs after them. The next time I look in the mirror, everything will be different.

Silas and Piper are posing for pictures with Arch when I walk into the kitchen. "Posing" is an understatement. Silas is behaving as if this is a photo shoot for *GQ* magazine, curling his mouth into a sort of snarl. I imagine he thinks he looks wicked cool. He smiles when he sees me, and then it's time for them to go. I follow them out the door and watch them walk down the steps when all of a sudden Silas looks back at me and winks. "Have a good time at *home*, Emerson"—emphasis on *home*.

Now I know for sure that I've made the right choice. "Piper?" I say nervously.

She turns back and looks at me. Silas is already in the car.

I close my eyes, and the adrenaline settles into a strange sort of peace.

"What?" she says impatiently. "I have to go!"

With two fingers crossed by my side, I extend my other hand, palm up in front of me, lean down, and blow her a kiss. . . .

She tilts her head, confused for a minute; but for the first time since Mama left ten years ago, she instinctively reaches out and pretends to catch it, then touches it to her chest.

Just like I did.

Falling to my knees, I feel the source of my power leave me.

Piper and Arch rush over.

"Emerson! Are you okay?" Arch says.

I prop myself up. "Yeah. Yeah, I'm fine. Just lost my balance."

Piper rolls her eyes. "That was weird, sis. You scared me." She turns to leave, and I grab her wrist.

"It'll be okay," I tell her.

"Good, because I can't leave you home if you're all wonky." She laughs and runs to the car.

I feel a little sad for her. Tonight she gets to see Silas's true character for herself.

That whole night I'm unable to sit still. Finally, I walk down the hall to where Arch has settled in to watch a movie.

"Hey, baby!" she says. "Wanna watch with me?"

I look at her relaxing, her makeup done to perfection like always, and suddenly I'm filled with so much love and admiration for this woman who has given me everything.

"Arch?" I ask. "You think it would be strange if I called you *Mom*?"

She looks up, and I can see tears in her eyes. Without

words, she extends her arms, and I walk over and embrace her. Then she kisses my dimple for the umpteenth time.

I feel myself tense up, waiting for the earache, or the vision; but nothing happens. I have truly lost my gift. I pull back and smile at her, my eyes now filled with tears, too.

"Are you sure?" she asks, and I nod.

I don't know why I've waited so long. She's the best mom a girl could ever have.

CHAPTER FIFTY-THREE

Sheer Crystal

After taking out my contacts, I go to plug my phone into the charger. That's when I notice I have a text. **Ya busy?** is staring at me from Edwin's number. I blink, shut the phone, and reopen it, thinking surely I must be going crazy. But there it is, as clear as my Sheer Crystal gloss: **Ya busy?**

Nah. I text back.

rescue me? *Seriously?*

Uh . . . **Sure!**

I'll come get u. Ready?

For the dance?

of course!

"Arch!" I shout, running down the stairs. "Edwin's coming! Edwin's coming!"

She sits up in bed, smiling. "Tonight's the night."

I shake my head, grinning. "In more ways than one."

"Call me when he gets here," she adds. "I need to take pictures!"

After bursting back up the steps, I step into Piper's green dress. I can't believe she's actually letting me wear it!

Edwin shows up exactly thirty minutes later, and I yell at Arch that he's here. She comes out of her room, armed with her camera; and I wave at Edwin from the porch, asking him to come in.

"You look amazing," Arch says when she sees me. "Utterly glamorous." Then she smiles at Edwin, who is looking luscious in a black tuxedo. "Come here, handsome. I wanna take your picture."

He grins, leaving me breathless. I have never seen a boy look so fine in all my life. Standing next to me, he wraps his arm around my waist while Arch clicks away. "Okay, guys," she says, finally satisfied with her photos. "Be good."

"We will, Mom." I emphasize the word *Mom*, and we giggle.

Edwin walks me to his car.

"Edwin," I say as soon as we get close.

"Mmm-hmm?" He stops and faces me.

"You look," I begin, but he reaches out and puts his finger up to my lips, silencing me.

"I've wanted to talk to you all week," he says. "But more than that, I've wanted to do this." He tilts his head, and I feel his warm lips touch mine in a way I have never felt before. It strikes me that I have never been kissed without worrying about seeing anything or feeling pain. And although I can't taste his memories, I can still taste his emotions: dense and rich like gingerbread. It's the sweetest gift I could ever wish for—*forgiveness.*

I pull back and smile at him. He wraps his arms around me and kisses me again for what must be seven whole seconds—a total record breaker.

"Before we go," I say, "there's something I have to tell you."

He steps back a little and looks at me intently.

"I think you might need to sit down for this. It's a long story."

Taking my hand, he leads me to his car.

Before I know it, an hour has passed, and I have told him everything. He's barely said a word except to ask me again and again how my gift worked. Here I was, thinking he wouldn't believe me; and all he wants is the scientific explanation behind the theory of mind reading. I barely understand a few of his questions.

"So you're not mad?" I ask when I'm done.

"Mad? No, not really. Not anymore. I mean, I understand why you did it. I might have done the same thing. But I'm embarrassed. I *hate* the thought that so many of my friends have kissed you." He makes his hand into a fist, and for a minute I think he might punch something. In that moment I know it's true, what Mr. Wilson said. There *are* boys out there who want just what I want: true love. And Edwin is one of these boys. He wants me to himself.

Oh my gosh, he wants me. He wants *me*!

"But look," he says. "You're not the only one with baggage. Everyone has junk they have to deal with. I just wish you had told me earlier that you needed help with school. I could have helped you study, you know." He runs his hand through his hair. "I'm smarter than all those guys. *Combined*."

Oh heaven, he's cute when he's cocky!

"Edwin, I wouldn't have told you my grades sucked. It's humiliating."

He puts his hand on my thigh. "Well, from here on out, I intend to help you if you need it. But if we're telling our deep, dark, dirty secrets, I think you should know I have also been cheating."

"Really?"

"Yes, so before you decide if you're going to stick with *me*, I better come clean, too."

"What have *you* been cheating on?"

"Swords and Soldiers." He says this with a completely straight face. As if playing Swords and Soldiers in the tenth grade is normal.

I punch him in the arm. "That is so not the same and you know it!"

He laughs. "Yes, it is. I am a serious cheater."

"Right. I can't believe you still play that dorky game."

He puts his arm around me and pulls me close, laughing. "Dorky, huh?"

"Um, yeah. Major dorkdom as in King Dork of the Universe."

"Actually, my cheating did make me king. Sergeant General King. It's the highest position you can have, but I intend to relinquish it tomorrow."

"Lawsy." I roll my eyes, unable to even comment. But that's just as well, because he kisses me.

At the dance, massive strobes weave streams of light into the sky like laser beams, and a large cardboard black hovercraft is perched to the side of the front door. Two men in black suits with earpieces in direct us onto a strange bumpy carpet.

"Top secret," I say with a giggle.

Turning the next corner, glitter falls on us like snow. There are tremendous gold mountains on either side of us, and bizarre-looking vegetation covers the door to the gym.

"This is incredible!" Edwin says while I twirl around in the glitter.

"It really does feel like we're on another planet!"

"I know," he replies. "I had to help the band set up this afternoon and saw the machines blowing it. They've even built a UFO around back."

I wave my hands up in the sparkling air. "No way!"

"Way!" he chuckles, grabbing my hand.

"So you know the band?" I ask.

He nods and wraps his arm around me as we walk into the gym. "They play at Liquid a lot."

More sparkles deck the inside of the gym, and there are orchid flowers everywhere.

"You wanna dance?" I ask him. The music is booming, and I can see Luke and Mallory bustin' a move on the dance floor.

"Sure," Edwin says. "Let's get a drink first."

I nod, scanning the room for Piper and Silas. They're talking calmly in the back. *She obviously hasn't kissed him yet.*

"This way," Edwin says, walking over to the refreshments table. Mrs. Parker is standing nearby, heavily flirting with the gym teacher.

"Hey, you guys," Mrs. Parker says. She is wearing a bright-orange sequined dress. Next to her, the PE teacher we fondly call Mr. Macho says something in her ear, making her giggle. No matter what, it's flat-out creepy to see your teachers dressed up and acting flirty.

Edwin pours us some punch. Then he nods his head at the lead singer onstage. "Uh-oh."

"What?" I ask.

"I think . . ."

The lead singer interrupts the song he's playing to shout, "Get up here, Ed-man!"

Good golly, Miss Molly! Edwin is about to perform.

"Do you mind?" he asks me. "If I don't go up there, he'll never leave me alone. He's a good friend."

"Do I *mind*?" I ask. "Are you crazy? Go show these people how it's done!"

And before he's even two feet from me, I know that this night will change my life forever. Not only because I am here with the love of my life who has forgiven me, but because everyone in this room is about to see what a badass rock star he is.

With a monstrous smile on my face, I step back and lean against the wall in preparation for my hot Ivy boyfriend's transformation from zero to hero.

CHAPTER FIFTY-FOUR

Hot Sauce

Three fabulous hours later we sit across from each other at The Waffle House.

"Pass me the hot sauce, hottie," he says.

I pass him the bottle and watch him douse his hash browns. "Ew. You ruined them."

After stabbing an orange mass of potatoes, he hands me his fork. "Try it. You'll like it."

"All right." I sigh. "But I'll have you know that when I was probably ten, Luke made me eat some kind of pepper his dad grew in their garden, and I swear, I almost died."

He cracks up. "Well then, it's a good thing I know mouth-to-mouth."

Now I'm laughing. "In that case . . ." I reach for the fork, exhale, and put the fiery potatoes into my mouth, chewing rapidly.

"Water!" I cough. "Water!"

He slides out of the side of his booth and approaches the

counter. "Can I get a milk for my date?" He motions to me. "And fast?"

She smiles and tosses him a carton.

Sliding in next to me, he cracks it open. "Drink this, drama queen. Water will make it worse."

My eyes are watering and we can't stop laughing, so I drink the milk and then he kisses me.

The fact that I can enjoy something as normal and easy as kissing is almost too good to be true. And yet it is.

"What time is it?" Edwin asks.

I look across the room to the clock on the wall. "Twelve seventeen."

"Good. We still have forty-five minutes until your curfew."

I pick up a piece of bacon and bite it. "Who were those Martian people? That was so awesome."

"I know! I swear it was Mr. Cox."

"Did you see Mrs. Parker get abducted by that cage machine?" I ask.

Edwin laughs. "Yes, but did you notice it was Mr. Macho who was driving it? I think he likes her."

On the way home Edwin reminds me that tonight actually *is* some kind of magical night. Apparently, you can see Mars without a telescope—which is where they got the dance's theme from.

We get out at my house and walk around the side. "For the best view."

"See it?" He puts his arm around me and pulls me toward him while pointing with his other hand up into the sky.

I strain to make out whatever it is he sees, but all I see are a gazillion stars, which are kind of incredible anyway. "I just see stars," I tell him.

"Notice that really bright one?"

"Mmm-hmm."

"That's it." He whispers, as if we are doing something extremely reverent, and I suppose we are.

Just then a car door slams, and Piper and Silas start yelling in the driveway.

"Should we go help her?" he whispers. "I can't stand that guy."

I shake my head. "Nope. She's going to be just fine."

CHAPTER FIFTY-FIVE

Sweethearts

Sunday night I open my geometry book and sit down at my desk. I read through my assignment and take some notes. Then I reread them, highlighting all of the information that's important with my new yellow highlighter. I've replaced my Sharpie with a package of rainbow highlighters, which I've heard can help even the most distracted types.

Arch peeks in. "I was wondering if you'd help me with something."

"I have to study," I tell her.

"Can't it wait?"

I look at her with my jaw dropped.

She laughs. "I know, I know. I don't usually insist you *quit* studying. But some things are more important than grades."

"This is *so* not you, *Mom*." I exaggerate the word *Mom* and drag it out for effect, making us laugh again.

"Come here," she says, taking my hand and leading me downstairs and into her room.

On her bed are three blue UPS boxes. Probably some new lip gloss she wants to show me.

"Emerson," she says. "You've made quite an impression on your friends at school, and I've had numerous orders from those catalogs you took a few weeks ago."

I'm pleased.

"You have an eye for makeup. So if it's okay with you, I've signed you up as a Stellar rep." She points to the boxes. "Here are your new catalogs and everything you need to start. I thought maybe you could sell to your friends."

"Seriously?!"

"Yep. You'll be fabulous, and you can make some extra money, too."

"Wow." I smile. "Like, I'd have a job?"

She nods.

"But what about my grades?"

"I actually think this will help you be more organized. You can start on a small scale and see how it goes."

I reach into one of the boxes and take out a stack of papers. "Order forms?"

"Mmm-hmm." She pats me on the back. "Put these in your purse. You never know when you might spot a potential customer."

I hug her. "Thanks!" And I know exactly who my first client will be.

💋

I can smell her a mile away. There she sits, gabbing away with some girls outside the library.

"Frances?" I say.

She looks up at me, beaming her Wacky Watermelon lips all over the place.

"I started selling Stellar last night, and I think I might have a better color for you." I point to her lips.

"But I love this color!" she says, puckering. She really looks grotesque.

I take a small, glittered bag out of my backpack.

"Glitter!" She reaches for it.

"I've put in some samples of the colors I think would look really good on you," I tell her.

She snatches the bag from me and peeks inside. "Cool! I've always loved your makeup."

I reach back into my backpack. "And here's a catalog, if you want to order any of it."

"I'd like a catalog." Another girl holds out a hand.

"Me, too!" says another.

I feel myself getting excited as I pass out a few more. "I could do a party for y'all, if you want."

"Oooh, party," says a third. "We can do it at my house!"

I point to the bag. "I gave you a free lip gloss, Frances. I think it will really flatter your skin tone. Why don't you try it on?"

She takes a tissue and rubs off her Wacky Watermelon. Then she applies Sweethearts, which looks much better, if I do say so myself. It's a more mellow shade of pink and complements her olive skin.

"That color rocks!" says one of the girls. "Can I order it, too?"

"Sure," I say. "Whenever you want. Just call me. My number's on the back." I flip over the catalog to show the girls.

"Thanks, Emerson," Frances says, giving me what's perhaps her first genuine smile.

I can't have Frances walking around in a clownish gloss and telling people I gave it to her. I'm a Stellar rep! I need my girls looking goooood.

Edwin meets me at my locker, and we walk off toward the parking lot after school. I notice Grady and Malcolm staring daggers at us as we pass.

"What's wrong with them?" I ask. "You didn't tell them about me and the kissing, did you?"

"No." He puts his arm around me. "Relax. They're just furious about the S and S game."

"I thought you were going to give up your position as king?" I say.

He smiles. "I did. But I never said I wasn't gonna win."

"Edwin . . ." I start to laugh. "What'd you do?"

He stands up a wee bit taller and pushes out his chest. "I did what any Peon Peasant would do to get inside the castle and rule the land. I made you queen . . . and then I married you."

I crack up. He is completely adorable. Swords and all.

Acknowledgments

The fact that I am actually writing this page is surreal. And hard. People say all the time that one doesn't write a book alone, and I have found this to be true. It's kind of like being the CEO of a large corporation, without whose staff support the company would never succeed. In my case, the people who helped me are many, so I'll stick with the corporation model to thank them.

First there's the Boss Man. This is the guy who pulls the strings—the mastermind behind the book—the one who calls the shots, inspires me, teaches me, and comforts me. This job is lovingly and faithfully filled by none other than Jesus Christ. Thank God He works at Corporation KISS! I could have never done it without Him.

Next there's the CFO. He pays the bills, manages the money, and barely winces when I announce the need to go to a conference in LA, Atlanta, New York, Nashville, or Birmingham. This job is forever assigned to my über-supportive husband, Lindsey. Occasionally my father has also made appearances in this department. In fact, it was his gift of my faithful laptop that led to this novel being written in the first place. Lindsey and Dad are my two leading men, and I love them.

The largest and most crucial department at Corp. KISS is the Encouragement Division. This division has offices all over the world and is headed locally by Sarah Frances Hardy, who has been by my side from day one. For the last nine years, we have studied together, traveled together, laughed and cried together; and I wouldn't want it any other way. However, encouragement from beyond Oxford is reserved for the one to whom this book is dedicated: my mother. I simply could not have written it without her. She is not only my biggest cheerleader, but she should have been an editor, because she is my toughest and most loving critic. She has spent almost as much time editing this book as I have spent writing it. Mom, you are quite literally "the wind beneath my wings."

Behind Sarah Frances and my parents comes a long list of people, but mostly this large branch of encouragement is overseen by Shelli Wells, Robin Mellom, Jessica DeHart, David Romanelli, Trissi Lemons, Laura Barber, Catherine Dahlman, Jeff and Berry Johnson, my extended family, and *all* of the wonderful women at Christ Presbyterian Church in Oxford, Mississippi.

I'd also like to thank John O'Haver, who advised me in matters of chemistry. What a load off my mind to have access to such a wise chemical engineer. Thank you, John!

And then there is my agent, Cheryl Pientka.

Where do I even begin to talk about Cheryl? I can't quite find the words to convey the gratitude I have for her. Like my mother, she believed in me and this book when it was merely an idea. She never ceases to encourage me, help me, advise me, love me. Cheryl, I adore you—plain and simple. God gave me the perfect agent.

A couple of years into the process, Dan Romanelli joined our team in a flurry of excitement, and he has been by far my most energetic marketer. When the value of this corporation was flagging, Dan, along with his wife, Luana, swept in to recover my lost spirits and helped me soar. It also helps that Dan just happens to personally know pretty much everyone in the United States. Dan, you are truly the man, and I have loved every minute of working with you!

In addition to the above, there were also several critical readers who helped shape this book for submission. They include Debbie Epes, Julie Cantrell, Bess Currence, Elana Johnson, Lisa and Laura Roecker, Sami Thomason, Luana Romanelli, Sarah Frances Hardy, Robin Mellom, Betsy Garrard, Betsy Simpson, and Graeme Stone. They helped me polish and perfect my book and, together with my mother, were largely responsible for correcting any and all errors— that is, before I met Marilyn. . . .

Marilyn Brigham is my editor at Amazon Publishing, and her involvement was not only unexpected but a massive blessing for which I will be forever grateful. I'm not sure if all editors work like she does, but I doubt it. What she has done to make this book suitable for the world goes far beyond what I had assumed an editor would tackle. Throughout this entire process, I continued to be shocked and amazed by her foresight and direction. She is absolutely brilliant, and I feel honored to have been able to work with her. I'd also like to thank the whole team at Amazon Publishing, with a special nod to Tim Ditlow, who not only acquired my book but has remained such a support to me. Honestly, I couldn't have asked for a more helpful and enthusiastic publishing house.

And now for my daughters, who occupy the heart of this corporation. Girls, I want to thank you for putting up with my need to do this—my insatiable desire to mold words and disappear into my laptop at times. I love you more than you will ever know. You are my greatest achievement on Earth and far more precious than any book.